MOUNTAIN RAGE

MOUNTAIN TIMES BOOK 3

JOHN LEGG

**WOLFPACK
PUBLISHING**
— EST 2013 —

Mountain Rage
(Mountain Times Book 3)
John Legg

Paperback Edition
© Copyright 2018 John Legg

Wolfpack Publishing
6032 Wheat Penny Avenue
Las Vegas, NV 89122

Library of Congress Control Number: 2018951419

Paperback ISBN: 978-1-64119-361-0
EBook ISBN: 978-1-64119-272-9

MOUNTAIN RAGE

JACOB MEISNER ENTERED the room cautiously. He was always uncomfortable in such a place. Not that the sitting room of Fort Union's chief, Kenneth McKenzie, was all *that* fine. It was just that he felt quite out of place amid the relative finery — the various plush peltries hanging from the walls along with the pieces of art from fancy eastern shops; the good, highly polished furniture; the crystal and silver cups, and serving bowls; the good china; and more, McKenzie himself, with his finely-tailored clothes and regal bearing.

McKenzie was coming toward him now, a smile plastered on his cleanly shaven face, his hand outstretched. He wore, as he had every time Meisner had seen him, a tailored, cutaway coat, waist-length in front, sweeping tails behind. The jacket was of good wool, deep blue in color, and was settled neatly over a frilly-fronted, high-necked white silk shirt. A narrow black tie was knotted precisely at the throat. Trousers of a lighter wool matched the color of the jacket and were tucked into highly polished black boots.

Meisner wiped his stubby hand on his crusty buck-skin pants and then shook McKenzie's hand. He cursed inwardly at the unwanted discomfort he felt standing here in his odious leather pants; torn, faded osnaburg shirt; and moccasins. As usual, he needed a shave and his person was dirty, coated with grease, old blood and sweat.

The factor known by one and all as the "King of the Missouri" did not flinch when he shook Meisner's filthy hand, though he did wonder again at the differences between himself and the trapper and trader who stood before him.

Where McKenzie was fairly tall and entirely elegant, Meisner was short and blocky. Where McKenzie spoke genteelly, Meisner had a gravelly knot of a voice. McKenzie's social actions were smooth and well-mannered, Meisner's were jerky and unrefined. They were a remarkable contrast of humanity.

"Come, sit," McKenzie said jovially. He knew Meisner's discomfit. Normally, he would not give a buffalo fart about it but — since Meisner was here on business, business that could boost the American Fur Company's profits handsomely — McKenzie could very well be pleasant to this putrefying dung heap of a human being.

Meisner swept across the room silently on his moccasins. He moved easily for such a stubby man but wherever he went, he left behind a lingering stench. McKenzie tried not to notice that as Meisner plopped smoothly into a plump chair that sat in front of McKenzie's large, polished desk.

McKenzie, to Meisner's surprise, did not sit behind the desk. Rather, he took a seat that matched Meisner's. Only a small, low table separated the two men. McKenzie smiled, determined that there would be no formality here. Not now. He did wave a hand, though at an Indian woman standing silently against one wall.

The servant — Meisner figured her to be a Hidatsa — hurried forward. She stopped at a sideboard and picked up a decanter and two glasses. At the table between the two men, she put the glasses down and then filled them from the decanter.

McKenzie picked up his glass and held it out, waiting for Meisner. The trapper hurried to do the same. The glasses clinked. Meisner then chucked his whole glass of whiskey down at once while McKenzie sipped, a smile of annoyed bemusement on his lips.

"Are you hungry, Mister Meisner?" McKenzie asked after Meisner's glass was replenished.

"Ya, I could do vit a bite," Meisner said in the thick German accent he retained despite many years in Canada and with the Blackfoot. Like all men who lived in the wilds of the Americas, Meisner ate as much as he could when it was available. One never knew where the next meal was coming from so he was not about to turn down this one. Still, he did not want to seem to eager with McKenzie.

Again McKenzie waved his hand. Within a few minutes, the Indian woman and three others had loaded a larger table with food. When they were done, McKenzie rose and indicated the big table with his hand. "Shall we dine, then, Mr. Meisner?"

"Ya," Meisner said, the delicious aroma of the foods sparking some excitement in his voice. He pushed himself up, again cursing his awkwardness in McKenzie's presence.

The two men went to the long table and sat across from each other. McKenzie neatly tucked a white cloth napkin into the high, tight collar of his shirt.

Meisner ignored his own napkin. Instead, he looked hungrily for a moment at the dishes piled with fat, fresh buffalo meat, newly churned butter, biscuits, even milk for the coffee, wondering where to start. Then he dug into the food, shoveling it onto his plate and then into his mouth, forgetting for the moment where he was.

McKenzie ate more sedately, almost prissily. Still, it was not long before both men were done. McKenzie offered a long, thin cigar to Meisner who shook his head. McKenzie shrugged and lit the cigar from a candle on the table. He puffed quietly.

"Is okay to smoke a pipe?" Meisner asked.

"Yes."

Meisner pulled out a twist of black tobacco and then a clay pipe with a small bowl and long stem. He cut a piece of the tobacco, slid his knife away and then half-crushed, half-stuffed the tobacco into the pipe. He too used a candle to light it.

McKenzie tried to hide his wince as the clouds of bilious smoke spiraled up from Meisner's pipe. The German almost looked at peace as he sucked at the pipe, his face quickly obscured by smoke.

A black male servant cleared away the plates and such while the Indian woman poured coffee for the men. She put the pot back on the table and then began helping her companion.

"Satisfied, Mr. Meisner?" McKenzie asked.

"Ya."

"You have enough coffee? And sugar for it?"

"Ya. Enough of all." Meisner's bulbous head bobbed up and down a few times.

"Good." McKenzie drew in some smoke from the cigar. "Now, what have you to tell me?"

"Is not goot." Meisner scowled. "Carney and the others ... Got-damn, they failed." He sounded far more angry that apologetic.

McKenzie looked for all the world as if he were fine though he boiled inside. "What happened?"

"That got-damned Squire again. I svear, he is like a magician. Son of a bitch! First he is one place, then - poof! - he is in another. From what the Blackfoot tell me, they just about had dose bastards overrun when vot should hoppen but a got-damn couple hundred Shoshones and Nez Perce — friends of that giant son of a bitch — showed up."

"And drove off your friends?" McKenzie guessed.

"Ya." Meisner ran a grungy, callused hand across the lower half of his face. He smiled grimly. "But vorse, Squire chased Able Carney and the others."

"I expect that he caught them," McKenzie said dryly. He had never met Nathaniel Squire but Meisner had spoken of the mountain man the previous year. It was not the first time he had heard of the giant the Indians and French-Canadians called *L'on Farouche*. He knew it would not be the last either.

"Ya." Meisner leaned forward, elbows on the table. He slurped some coffee before setting the fine china cup down again on the saucer. The cup looked vastly incongruous in his hand. "One of the Blackfoot saw part of it; others saw der results. It vas ... gruesome. Looked like der Blackfoot had done it themselves."

McKenzie nodded. "He's a tough character, is he, this Squire?"

"Ya."

McKenzie nodded again. He sat quietly, wondering where all this would eventually lead. He watched as Meisner sloppily poured himself more coffee, spooned several doses of sugar into it and then noisily drank some. Finally McKenzie asked, "So, what do you propose now? This man Squire has ruined our plans twice. We can't have that, you know."

"Ya, I know." Meisner looked around for some place to empty his nose. He saw nowhere so settled for wiping the drip on his sleeve. He did not see McKenzie's look of disgust. "I vill take care of it," Meisner said flatly, suddenly seeming to cast off the black mood that had settled on him.

"How?"

"I vill think of sometink. But mein Blackfoot and me will make sure that that got-damn *L'on Farouche* is made gone beaver. I'll see to it personally. I think there's a many of der Blackfoot have a few scores to settle with that son of a bitch. Ya."

"That's what you said in the spring — just before you sent Carney and all those Blackfoot down there to Horse Creek."

"Ya, I did dat," Meisner admitted more than a little uncomfortably. "But then the Blackfoot had bad medicine after Squire overran Elk Horn's village last winter. Damn."

"You believe in that foolishness?"

"Vot?"

"About Indian medicine."

Meisner's great, rounded shoulders shrugged. "Sometimes I do. Other times, I'm not so sure." He was uncertain but there were too many times when he had seen those super-stitions work for him to make light of them. "Anyvay, once Squire has been rubbed out, I'll see to vorking out finding new people to build us a fort up there among der Blackfoot." He sighed, the sound like rocks falling on a sheet of tin.

"When?"

"Spring," Meisner said after a moment's hesitation. "Vinter is almost here and we can do nothing in that cold. Not something major." He paused, thinking. "If ve vait, ve can make foolproof plans."

"They better be foolproof this time. The Blackfoot will turn against the company after a few more failures like this past couple of adventures." There was a hint of warning in McKenzie's voice.

"Ya." Meisner knew it without having to be told. Besides, he had his own reasons now for making sure the next plan worked to perfection.

The silence grew uncomfortable for a while. "Is it true there was a white woman with Squire's men?" McKenzie asked suddenly. He had heard the rumors from some usually reliable people but he could not really believe that a white woman would be roaming around out here.

Meisner knew there was no use in lying. "Ya," he offered with another nod of the big, round head. "She vas dere, all right. She played like a boy, I hear. But she was found out by ... the two men ve had the deal vit."

"And where is she now?" McKenzie was intrigued with the whole thing.

"Traveling vit them still, I suppose." Meisner wanted nothing to do with any white woman who would disguise herself as a man and run through the mountains playing trapper.

McKenzie nodded. He was still intrigued but the thoughts were going nowhere. Besides, there were more important things for him to consider right now. "Will you be able to find them in the spring?"

"Ya," Meisner said without hesitation. "Mein Blackfoot friends vill find them no matter vhere they hide."

"Is there anything you need?"

"My usual supplies." He paused. "Und some extra presents for the Blackfoot."

McKenzie nodded. He rose, walked to his desk and took out a sheet of paper. He dipped his pen in the inkwell. Moments later, his pen was scratching across the paper. He blotted the paper, then folded it, carried it back to the table and held it out.

Meisner took the paper as McKenzie said, "Give that to Mitchell, up at Fort McKenzie. Or to Cumberland if Mitchell isn't around. You can get your supplies — and the presents, but not too many — there so you don't have to haul them all the way up there."

"Is goot," Meisner said, slipping the note into the bag hanging about waist level by a strap around his neck. He slobbered up the last of the coffee. As he stood, his eyes drifted longingly to the sideboard where the whiskey resided.

McKenzie saw it but did not betray the annoyance he felt. "Would you like a last drink before leaving, Mr. Meisner?" he asked.

"Ya." The big head bounced, graying black hair flapping about.

Moments later, Meisner had polished off a decent-size glass of fine brandy. He headed for the door and grabbed his rifle where it leaned against the wall, a knit wool cap resting over the muzzle. He slapped the cap on and left without looking back.

McKenzie finally allowed his revulsion to surface. He looked at the Indian woman. "Get rid of all the dishes, cups and whatever else that man touched," he ordered.

CHAPTER 1

August 1833

Nathaniel Squire rolled out of his robes and stood, trying to ignore the pounding in his head and the sourness that wrenched his innards into knots. He shuffled over to the fire.

Star Path watched him with a mixture of sympathy and disgust. She had seen what the white man's firewater did to the men of her village and though it didn't affect Squire quite as much as it did them, it made him sick afterward when he had too much liquor and that bothered her. Especially when it drove him into a bout of melancholy. That didn't happen too often but, when it did, he was another man entirely.

Squire squatted, then sat at the fire. Star Path handed him a tin mug full of hot, black, heavily-sugared coffee. "Are you hungry?" she asked.

Squire looked at her and smiled, belying the hangover that was pulsing through his veins. "I'll just be havin' coffee for now, woman," he responded in a growl that could not disguise the feelings he had for her.

Star Path nodded and turned back to her work; she was making herself a new dress of buckskin. She was beginning to show signs of her pregnancy and wanted a new, larger dress to accommodate the belly that would be growing soon.

Squire watched her as she worked. Real fondness was stamped on his big, furred face. She was a good woman and he loved her in his own way. That surprised some people he encountered since they seemed such an unusual couple. He still wondered himself on occasion just why he was so drawn to her.

Star Path was a short, rather dumpy woman with ample amounts of flesh. Some wrinkles were beginning to appear in her wide, moon face and strands of gray were scattered through her otherwise glossy black hair. Squire liked her broad bottom, thick, firm thighs, and heavy breasts. Her smooth, coppery skin excited him as did the laughing, dark eyes.

Squire pulled his eyes away from the woman as a sharp pain stabbed deep behind his right eye. "*Merde*," he muttered, mostly under his breath. At almost thirty-six, he was, he figured, too old for such a spree as this one had been. *But*, he thought, grinning in thinking about it, *it had been one hell of a summer*.

Nathaniel Squire had signed on almost a year ago to lead a brigade of inexperienced men west in search of beaver for Colonel Leander Melton. Along the way, they had encountered a lifetime of difficulties, including war with the Blackfoot when those Indians had kidnapped one of the brigade members — a teenage white woman who had disguised herself as a young man to join the group — and had two others plot with the Indians against the brigade.

Squire, with Abner Train — the young woman's paramour who had discovered her secret and fallen in love with her — and the tough, cocky young man known only as Li'l Jim, had gone after her. They had rescued her but only after taking on a whole village of enraged Blackfoot warriors at a great cost. One of Squire's mentors, the old man LeGrand, had gone under.

Squire had thought by the time they had gotten to rendezvous - almost three months ago now - that their troubles were over. He had planned that they would have a small spree there — only he, old friend Slocum Peters, whom they had run into up in the mountains, and their stock handler, Homer Bellows, had seen a rendezvous. Squire figured it would be an eye-opening experience for the young trappers, kind of a graduation ceremony for them. They had experienced about everything else Mother Nature, the land and the Indians could throw at a man.

Then some old enemies of Squire's had shown up in the company of a couple hundred Blackfoot warriors out to raise hair on Squire and his men. They had taken off, hoping to outrun the Blackfoot, but to no avail. And the brigade was forced to make a stand. They had about resigned themselves to going under, each and every one of them, when a couple of other old friends of Squire's had arrived with more than two hundred Shoshone and Nez Perce warriors.

After Squire had taken time to dispatch the enemies who had sought him out, he had led the brigade triumphantly back to St. Louis. There the beaver plews the men had taken were piled up and sold, making

Melton — and, more importantly, his backers — a substantial profit. With the exception of the men who had been killed along the way, which was to be expected of such enterprises, the expedition had been a rousing success.

Melton had paid the men what he still owed them — plus a small bonus for their loyalty — and then everyone had gone off to celebrate. That had been more than a week and a half ago.

Squire had celebrated harder than anyone, as was usual for him. More than once he had not even made it back to the lodge set up half a mile outside the city. Star Path did not like such things but there was nothing she could do about it here.

Squire finished off his coffee and set the cup down. He rose to his full six-foot-eight and stretched. He was imposing, with his height and the two hundred eighty pounds - none of it flab - he carried on his frame. His fierce glares, the long, tawny beard that reached his chest, and the massive, callused, powerful hands made most men think twice before coming against him. His clothing added to the effect: heavily fringed buckskin pants; either a long buckskin war shirt or a "settlement" shirt of some cloth; thick, buffalo hide moccasins; a felt hat with wide brim in town or a bobcat fur cap with tail out in the wilds; and a necklace of the claws of one big beast of a grizzly bear.

His reputation, though, probably created the most fear in other men. He was known as *L'on Farouche* — the wild man. It was a well-deserved nickname most had found and almost anyone who knew of it gave Nathaniel Squire a wide berth.

"I be hungry now, woman," Squire said gruffly. "I'll be back directly." He stepped outside to relieve himself.

Star Path pushed herself awkwardly up, already trying to protect the growing baby inside her by subtly changing her movements. She used a buffalo horn spoon to scoop some stew into a wood bowl. She set that aside and refilled Squire's coffee cup. Instead of dosing the coffee with sugar, though, she found a small bottle of whiskey Squire had stashed in his packs. She poured a generous dollop of the liquid into the mug and set it next to the bowl of food.

Squire returned a few moments later. He sat, picked up the bowl, and spooned in several mouthfuls. All the while, he hoped it would stay in his stomach. Then he reached for the mug. He took a healthy swallow, eyes opening wide in surprised pleasure when the whiskey bit into his throat. He drained the cup and then polished off the stew. He held the cup out for more coffee and whiskey. He nodded his thanks when Star Path refilled it.

"Ye be takin' too good care of this ol' chil', woman," he said with a grin. "I ain't so sure I be deservin' such treatment."

"I expect you ain't," Star Path said. Her English had improved considerably in the past year though it was still heavily accented. She released an exaggerated sigh. "But what can I do?" She hid the immense pleasure that his words had given her with her words and expressionless face.

"What you could do," Squire said with a chuckle, "is haul your ass over here and be carin' for me proper."

Star Path smiled. There was no coyness about her. She was a lusty woman, one who enjoyed the pleasures of a man — particularly this one — and not one to hide such feelings. Without hesitation, she skinned off her dress, leggings and moccasins and moved toward the buffalo robe bed.

Squire watched for a moment. His hangover was forgotten in his sudden jolt of lust, aided by the dose of whiskey that had settled his stomach and head. He enjoyed watching Star Path, clothed or naked, though he figured the latter a heap more fun. For some reason, the sight of her fleshy rump always excited him just a little extra. He could not explain it, nor understand it, and he tried to do neither. He simply enjoyed it.

Star Path knew that about him and she moved more slowly than was necessary to allow him plenty of time to enjoy the scenery. She was not ashamed of herself; indeed, she was outright proud that she caused such feelings in her man. She stopped and turned, then sank down onto her knees on the bed.

Squire polished off the whiskey-coffee and set the cup down. He was feeling considerably better already. He rose and peeled off the dirty blue calico shirt and dropped it. A moment later he had kicked off his moccasins and shucked his pants. It was obvious he was ready for her.

Star Path watched, nodding in anticipation, as Squire marched proudly toward her. She grasped him lightly in her hand and sort of pulled him along as she lay back on the robes. She guided him skillfully, directly into her. She, too, was ready.

Minutes later, both were shouting with delight as their bodies reached a crescendo within moments of each other.

Later, when they were lying comfortably entwined, Squire said, "I reckon it be near time for us to leave."

Star Path nodded, her greased hair rubbing on his massive, scarred chest. "Soon?" she asked.

"Next couple days, I reckon. Soon's I be gettin' e'ery-thing we need."

"Can the others get ready so fast?" Star Path asked, surprised. While her people could pack up and move a whole camp in a matter of hours, it seemed impossible for a large group of whites to get ready to move at anything more than a snail's pace.

"Don't matter none." He had been thinking of this all summer and had suddenly made his decision. "I ain't aimin' to be takin' no one with us this time."

"None of them?" Star Path pushed up and away from him so she could really look at his face.

"Nay." His great chest rose with a breath and then sank as the air flowed out. "I think there be too goddamn much trouble with that many folks around. I ..."

"But not all're trouble. What abut A'ner and Little Flower and ...?"

It was Squire's turn to interrupt. "They all be good folk but I reckon I be needin' some time alone. Just you'n me. Don't that suit ye?"

"I don't know," Star Path said truthfully. "Normally I'd say yes to such doin's. But ..." She paused. She had never been this indecisive and it was worrisome to her. She normally would want to travel to the mountains and winter up alone with Squire. But she had come to admire and like several of the people who had been with Colonel Melton's brigade. She would hate to not have their company anymore.

Before Star Path could get started again, Squire had eased her gently aside and stood. He strolled to his clothes and began dressing. He felt odd about it, too. Those people had been with him for a year but, in some ways, it was as if he knew them his whole life. They had come a long way in that year, proving themselves time and again.

"Mayhap we can be takin' one or two of 'em along." He grinned a little, teeth white amid the mass of tawny beard and mustache. He slid the metal clip of his pistols onto the broad leather, brass-tack-studded belt. A long tomahawk went through the belt at the small of his back. He picked up his hat and slapped it on. "Ye best see that e'erything's in order for us to be movin'," he said just before slipping out the flap of the tipi.

It was a sweltering hot day, the air thick with humidity. Squire took a look around. It was a pleasant enough spot in a glade just off the banks of the Missouri River. There was plenty of grass for their horses and mules; trees grew in scattered spots, heavier nearer the riverbank. Wildflowers grew in colorful profusion though they were beginning to fade.

Squire's lodge could be considered the center of their camp. To his right was the Colonel's tipi. His Shoshone "wife," Rising Sun, stayed there. Melton showed up when he could. Mostly, though, he stayed in town to take care of business affairs and to spend time with his wife who had arrived from Boston. Next to Melton's lodge was the one shared by Homer Bellows and his Sioux wife, Silver Necklace. Bellows had owned the livery where Squire and Melton had gotten all their horses and some of the mules for the trip west the past year. Squire had been impressed with the lean, lanky Bellows and so had hired him on to handle all the brigade's horses. Bellows had bought Silver Necklace from her grandfather, the civil chief of the Lakota band from which Star Path came.

On Squire's immediate left was the lodge of Train and Hannah. Whenever she went into town, which was more often than Train would have liked, she once again disguised herself as a male. It was easier that way. No one would deny her entrance to the saloons or try to keep her from some frivolity. She and Train had both learned, though, to keep their consumption of spirituous liquors to a minimum. Nothing was better for loosening the tongue and causing a heap of trouble than someone who had had more than his — or her — share of alcohol.

Next to Train and Hannah's lodge was Li'l Jim's. He was a hellion, that one, who had won not one but two Shoshone women in shooting matches at the rendezvous. He had been trying to get rid of at least one of them ever since, to no avail.

Squire turned to his left, walking toward Hannah and Train's lodge. His hangover was just about gone and, now that he had made his decision to leave, he was in good spirits.

CHAPTER 2

"LEVÉ, LECHÉ LEGO," Squire called. "Wake up, turn out."

A small, feminine head poked out of the tipi. "Hi, Nathaniel," Hannah said brightly. Her light green eyes sparkled with joy; her face glowed with a just-made-love-to look. She showed no signs of the horrendous ordeal she had suffered during the winter.

"Mornin', lass," Squire said with a grin. Hannah Carpenter was one of Squire's favorite people in the world. She was the daughter he would have picked if the Great Spirit ever allowed such a thing.

"What doin's you got planned for us today?"

"Ye'll be findin' that out soon's ye and that lazy ol' lad ye been consortin' with get your asses out of the robes. I aim to be meetin' with the Colonel right off. Down at the Water Rat."

Hannah squinted at the giant. Not sure she liked what she saw in his faded blue eyes, she stepped out of the tipi. She was short and slim though with a well-rounded figure. It was apparent that she was naked under the four-point blanket she had pulled tightly around her, covering all of her except her fair face, slim, milky white shoulders, and her small, bare feet. Her fairly long, almost golden, hair was mussed.

"Something wrong, Nathaniel?" she asked, her thin lips pursed a little in worry.

"Nay, lass," Squire said with a grin. "Just need to have a council with e'erybody."

"Christ, Nathaniel," Abner Train said, stepping out of the lodge, "you tryin' to steal my woman?" He was smiling as he said it.

"And if I be, goddammit?" Squire responded with a mock scowl at the young man.

"I'd have to thump ya good," Train said boldly. He thrust out his broad, bare chest. He was wearing buckskin pants though he was barefoot. His thatch of light-colored hair was even more of a wild tangle than it usually was.

Hannah giggled and Squire laughed. Train was a big young man, having grown some over the past year. But at about six-foot-five and two hundred thirty-five pounds or so, he could not stack up against Nathaniel Squire. He was not as fierce as Squire, either, though he had shown his mettle in more tight places than most men faced in a lifetime. He was big, strong, and courageous and had a steely determination. He was young, though, barely nine-teen, and had some maturing to do. He also thought the world of Squire.

The giant mountain man would not let it become too evident but he felt the same way about the young man. "Ye'd be needin' the whole goddamn brigade to take this ol' niggur, lad."

All three knew he was not lying just as all three knew that Train had no intention of even attempting it. Not that the youth was afraid of Squire. Well, he was, but that would not stop him from going against Squire, or anyone else for that matter, if he thought it necessary. It was just that they were joshing each other and all knew it.

"Pshaw, Nathaniel," Hannah snorted.

"Just do what I tell ye, girl," Squire snapped. He was never quite sure how to react around Hannah. On one hand, he saw her as a daughter and so had a father's protectiveness toward her. On the other hand, she was quite attractive and as lusty as any Indian woman. She was straightforward and honest, and had been through hell. But she still retained a coy coquettishness that she seemed unaware of, one that many men mistakenly took for interest in them.

He moved off to the next lodge and gave the same wake-up call. When he got no response, he did so again. Then a third time.

Finally a muffled, tired voice issued from inside the buffalo-skin walls, "Go away, Nathaniel, dammit."

"Haul ass, lad. We be havin' business."

"Damn, leave me alone, for chrissakes." It sounded almost like a groan.

"Just be doin' what I tell ye, lad."

Suddenly a deep, gruff voice issued from the last lodge on that side. "Christ, can't you two shut the hell up? There's folks tryin' to sleep over here, dammit all."

Squire grinned. "Council down at the Water Rat, Slocum. So best be movin'. *Vite.*"

Squire spun and strode off. He grinned as he passed Train and Hannah's lodge and heard contented murmuring from within. He considered for a moment slipping inside and scaring the hell out of them just for fun, but then he decided he had things to do.

He called for entrance at Bellows's. A reedy voice

responded, "Well, come on in, goddammit. Yep. Whatever goddamn no good son of a bitch is out there, you can
come on in. Yep."

Squire chuckled and ducked inside. He found
Bellows sitting by the fire, sipping coffee. Squire sat across
from him. Silver Necklace handed him a bowl of food and
set a cup of coffee down next to him. Squire did not
bother to look at the woman. He knew what she looked
like. Besides, he was being a little perverse.

Bellows was not all that handsome a man. He was in
his mid-to-late thirties, medium height, thin as a rail, with
a very prominent Adam's apple and thin, bloodless lips.
Faded blue eyes peered out from deep sockets surrounded
by a forest of crinkles over a long, hooked nose.

Because of all that, Bellows was inordinately proud of
having acquired Silver Necklace. She was only about
sixteen. She was not the handsomest woman on earth but
she was lithe and comely, with soft skin and fine features.
Bellows liked others to take notice of her, seeing it as a
way for him to show off. To be irritating, Squire at times
would not acknowledge her, just to annoy Bellows.

"I aim to be leavin' out afore long, Homer," Squire
said.

"How soon?" Bellows asked, squinting through the
light smoke of the fire.

"Couple days maybe."

"We ain't got time to get all them goddamn boys
together, get supplies, load 'em and all that other shit we
got to do. Nope. Not in two days. Not even a week." As
always, his large Adam's apple bobbled wildly when he
spoke. "Nope. Can't do it. Not with that worthless
bunch."

"I be knowin' that," Squire said quietly but apologetically. His face was expressionless.

Bellows sat silently for a few moments, seemingly frozen. His face betrayed none of the emotions that boiled through him. Finally he nodded. "I see. So it's gonna be that way, is it?"

"Aye."

"Ye takin' anybody at all?"

"Ain't figurin' on it. 'Cept Star Path, of course."

"What's she got to say about all this?"

Squire shrugged. He put aside his now-empty bowl and picked up the coffee. "She ain't happy o'er it." He half-smiled. "Seems she's become some fond of a few of ye folks though, for the life of me, I can't be figurin' out why."

"Prob'ly 'cause we're a welcome relief from the likes of you," Bellows said with a sickly smile. He admired Squire and had been certain they would be together again for a new season. Now those hopes were suddenly dashed. It was a little difficult to accept, as cold as it was. Still, he didn't think it right that a man should wear his feelings on his sleeve so he tried to hide his disappointment.

"Shit," Squire snorted. "I think she just wants ye Pawnee-humpin' sons of bitches around for somethin' to laugh at when times be gettin' hard." He was already beginning to regret his decision to head west alone. He had come to like most of Melton's men, some more than others, of course. Like Bellows, and Hannah and Train and Li'l Jim. And, yes, the Colonel, too. It was not often he felt that way about people, which was just as well considering how many men went under in his profession.

"I expect it's more like she wants us along to keep you

from gettin' your overstuffed ass kilt by some Blackfoot boy lookin' to count his first coup," Bellows countered.

"Hell, it's just that I don't want ye along since I can't stand the smell of someone's been rollin' in horseshit all his life."

"Horseshit's bettern'n buffler shit."

"Hell, I'd rather *eat* buff'lo shit than roll in horseshit." Squire grinned widely.

"I reckon ya would at that." Bellows could not stop himself; he began to chuckle. Squire joined him. "You best get on your way then," Bellows said after a few moments.

"Aye. But I plan to be havin' a council with the others, includin' the Colonel, down at the Water Rat."

"They don't know this?"

"Nay, lad." He stood. "Ye comin'?"

Bellows nodded, his skinny head flapping up and down. "I'll be along. Yep, goddammit."

"Best bring Cletus, too," Squire said just before he swept out of the lodge and headed toward the next tipi. Marcel Ledoux was standing outside stretching, enjoying the hot, humid morning with its taste of dew still lingering in the air.

Squire explained his plan, then asked Ledoux to tell Pierre Dumoulin who had the last lodge on that side.

"*Oui, mon ami.*" Ledoux headed toward Dumoulin's tipi while Squire moved toward his own.

His horse — *Noir Astre* — was saddled and picketed outside. The massive black stallion nickered softly when Squire came up and patted the long, glossy mane. "Pretty soon we'll be out on the peraira again, ol' hoss," he said as he pulled the reins free. With an easy leap, he was in the saddle and moving slowly toward St. Louis.

He stopped at the hotel where Melton and his wife, newly arrived from Boston, were staying and left word at the desk for him, then strolled outside. He mounted *Noir Astre* and rode down toward the seedy part of the city along the waterfront. He left the horse at a livery nearby and then walked the short distance, rifle in hand, to the dim, foul-looking Water Rat saloon.

Inside, he leaned his rifle against the wall in a corner and then gathered several tables together in a small group. He set out two jugs of whiskey and nine cups. He spoke to the bartender a few moments. The man nodded, then called for a youth who helped out at the saloon and issued him some orders.

Minutes later, Slocum Peters arrived, followed almost immediately by Train, Hannah and Li'l Jim. They also made their greetings and took seats.

Li'l Jim poured himself a drink, tapped Peters's cup, and tasted the liquor. Then he noisily proclaimed, "I see ya bought the best, Nathaniel. Yes, sir, this here's excellent — excellent buffler piss."

The three others laughed as Ledoux and Dumoulin showed up and settled in with full cups before them. The talk buzzed around the table though Squire sat quietly in the corner, listening and sipping whiskey. Bellows suddenly hustled in, followed by his assistant, young Cletus Ransom. They sat and joined the conversation though Bellows was rather quiet for a man who was normally garrulous. They all waited for Melton.

The Colonel finally arrived, making less-than-heartfelt apologies for his tardiness. Melton was a big man though no match for Squire, running more to chubbiness than to muscle. Still, he had gone the whole route with the brigade the past year and had passed every test. And he looked to be in fine shape considering the abuses he had faced at the hands of the Blackfeet when he had been their prisoner. Squire liked him.

Melton sat and, with a shrug, poured himself a cupful of whiskey. He held it up. "To your health, men." He gulped deeply. "Now, Nathaniel, what have you to say?" He sat back, content with life these days. That contentedness fled in a hurry.

"Well, lads," Squire said, "it's been some shinin' times I've had with all of ye. Damn right it has. But I figure to be takin' my leave of ye now."

There was a burst of shocked protest from everyone but Bellows. Squire let it run on a little before he finally said, "Christ, lads, it ain't that big a thing, ye know."

"I don't like it the least goddamn little bit, you overgrown son of a bitch," Li'l Jim snapped. He was a small, cocky man with a streak of wild abandon in him that often brought him trouble. This time, though, he knew exactly what he was doing.

"Don't make me no nevermind what ye like, lad," Squire offered, not offended.

"Well, I don't like it neither," Hannah said, pushing up and leaning forward, her hands flat on the table. "I think you're a chicken-consortin' son of a donkey for tryin' such doin's."

CHAPTER 3

No ONE at the table was shocked, though any outsider would have been. No one with any sense would talk to Nathaniel Squire like that and expect to live. No one, that is, except Hannah Carpenter. She was the only one who could give Squire any guff and get away with it.

"Best watch what ye be sayin', girl," Squire muttered.

"Or what?" Hannah was furious. "You gonna come at me with your 'hawk? You aim to take my hair?" She paused a moment, trying to let the fury inside her subside a little.

"Dammit, Hannah," Squire started lamely. "Ye got no call ..."

"I got all kinds of call, damn you. Even though all of ya suffered at the hands of the damned Blackfeet, I suffered more'n *any* of you. I earned my right to say anything to ya I want. Includin' callin' ya what I did. Dammit, we need ya along."

"No, ye don't. Ye'll make out just fine. Ye — all of ye — have growed considerable in a year. Ain't a fur company in the Stony Mountains wouldn't take anyone of ye on. Ye be real mountaineers now. Aye, that ye be."

"But the Colonel needs ya, Nathaniel," Train said, trying to sound reasonable.

"He ain't goin'," Squire said, shocking them all anew. "Are ye, Colonel?"

Everyone's eyes turned to Melton who coughed a bit, self-conscious at the attention — and the reason for it.

"Well?" Li'l Jim demanded.

"I have been considering the idea of not going west this season," Melton admitted in embarrassment. "I am not used to such rigors and I'm afraid I am rather weakened by my experiences among the Blackfeet. And with my wife having arrived from Boston ..." He tapered off, his discomfiture growing.

"When the hell was you gonna tells us, hoss?" Peters asked, voice angry.

"Well, I . . . I . . ."

"Did you know about this, Nathaniel?" Bellows asked. His voice had a note of tension in it, as if he were about to explode in anger.

"Nay, lad. I thought it might be so but I didn't know for certain."

"So now what the hell do we do?" Peters asked in annoyance and disgust.

"Please, everyone, let me explain," Melton interjected.

"Ze 'ell wit' you, Monsieur Fancy Pants," Ledoux snapped. "You 'ave nothing to say about zis no more."

"But I do," Melton insisted, a bit of command seeping back into his voice. "I had not decided on this until the day before yesterday. But what I had decided and was going to tell you in the next day or two, after I had started making arrangements, was that I was going to send you out as a brigade again, with Nathaniel leading. Everything would be the same except I would remain here. Nathaniel's announcement came as much a shock to me as it did to you."

There was silence for some time as everyone thought that over. "Well, Nathaniel," Hannah finally said, "I suppose this'll change your mind."

"Nay, lass. But there be no reason why ye can't go as a group without the Colonel or me."

"How will they make do out in the mountains?" Melton asked, worried. He had come to rely on Squire tremendously and was at a loss now, having planned to have Squire lead the expedition.

"Slocum be a fine mountaineer. I reckon he be havin' the sand to make ye a good leader. There be Abner and Hannah and Li'l Jim, all of 'em seemin' eager to be headin' out again. Ledoux and Dumoulin are good men and I be thinkin' they'd be happy to throw in with ye. And there be Homer and Cletus. Plus ye got some of the lads was with us this time, ones ye can be puttin' your trust in."

"So you're just gonna go off all on your lonesome?" Hannah demanded.

"Star Path will be along." Squire almost grinned.

"That ain't what I mean and you damn well know it."

"I do. But other than my woman, I'll be by my lonesome, aye."

"Then you're plumb crazier'n anyone I ever met," Hannah continued, fire still blazing in her eyes and voice. "You got the entire Blackfoot Nation hungerin' to take your hair and you're going out there alone. Damn fool if I ever met one."

"Callin' him a damn fool don't nearly come to truly

tellin' how foolish he is," Li'l Jim threw in. "Wasn't for me shootin' that redskin son of a bitch, your carcass'd be out there feedin' coyotes and your hair'd be flyin' high from Elk Horn's lodgepole. So now we ain't good enough to go with you?"

"Now I ain't ary said such a thing. I just want to be shed of a brigade of so many people."

"So you're gonna forsake us all because there's too many of us?" Hannah asked, her anger not notched down at all.

Squire's anger was starting to rise, too. While Hannah Carpenter was special to him and he would let her get away with saying just about anything to him, he was getting tired of being harangued. He was not used to such doings and it did not sit well with him. "I be havin' enough of your nonsense, girl," he growled halfheartedly. "And all the rest of ye. My mind be set and that be all there be to it. Be leavin' off scoldin' me. I'm goin' off on my own – me and Star Path - and that be all there is to it."

Hannah looked as if she were ready to cry but she'd be damned if she would in front of the others. "You ain't heard the last of me yet, you overgrown, buffalo-headed lummox. Like Li'l Jim said, he saved your bacon sure enough. And we've all been through some mighty tryin' times. The Colonel there was almost skinned alive, all the others were treated poorly – more than poorly — by the damned Blackfeet. Even Star Path was taken and sorely abused." She paused, thinking hard. There had to be a way, she figured, to get Squire to change his mind.

"That's enough, Hannah," Train said. "He's made up his mind. Reckon we ought to give the man his due. He ..."

"A real man don't forsake his friends. A real man

sticks with his friends, friends he's suffered with, who suffered for him."

"Enough, Hannah," Train snapped, more harshly than he wanted. He glanced at Squire, whose eyes were burning with fury at having his manhood impugned. Were Hannah a man, she would be dead now at his hand. But being who she was, he could not hurt her no matter what she said. But the rage boiled inside him. Train knew that Squire was near to exploding and if someone other than Hannah said anything, there was a strong likelihood that there would be death here this morning.

"He's of his own mind, Hannah," Train said more quietly. "He's saved everyone of us more times than we can count. The man has earned the right to do as he pleases. And if headin' to the mountains alone is what he's hankerin' for, we got no right to deny him that."

The others were silent for a bit before Melton spoke up quietly. He too had seen Squire's anger and was surprised but thankful that Train had managed to calm things somewhat. "Mr. Squire," he said more formally than usual, "you were of great service to us this last year. Led us all through the wilderness, bringing most of us all back alive. But we had counted on you during our time here in St. Louis to lead us again. It is getting late in the summer and had we known that your plans did not include us, we would have had time to prepare and likely would have been on the trail by now. Without your strong guiding hand, we will be hard pressed to get our supplies, other equipage, horses and mules together and get on the trail before it's too late. If these men even agree to go without you as leader."

The anger in Squire subsided a little but he shrugged. He was not about to apologize. Doing such a thing was not his way. "They'll make out," he allowed. "Long as Homer be along, you'll be fine in gatherin' whate'er ye need and getting to the huntin' grounds in time for the fall hunt. But ye best not be delayin'."

Melton nodded. He was sad but now more worried. He had counted on Squire not only to lead the group but to help, as he had the year before, in getting the many things done that needed doing: Hiring more men; getting supplies not only to sustain the men but for trade with the Indians; buying traps and guns and munitions; and bring in horses and mules for the journey, making sure they were properly shod. And in addition to taking time, it would also take money. While the previous season had been a success, it had not been quite as successful as his backers had hoped and all summer long they had been niggardly with money.

"Then so be it," Melton said quietly. He started to rise but stopped when Hannah again voiced her objections, though this time a meager bit less furiously. "What does Star Path think of this, Nathaniel?"

"She be thinkin' the same," Squire said, his rage lessening even more.

"That so?" Hannah asked with something of a smirk on her small, pretty face. "How's about I mosey on over to your lodge and just ask her? I wager my best pair of moccasins that I'd get a different answer."

"Hell, Hannah," Li'l Jim threw in with a snigger, "ain't nobody here wants your mocs. I'm the only one might be small enough to wear 'em and I ain't about to put my feet in things worn by you."

A small chuckle ran around the room for a moment by all but Hannah.

The young woman's jaw tightened. "That'll be

enough out of you, you pipsqueak," she snapped. "Ain't nobody here interested in your opinion in such matters." She turned back to Squire. "So you still say she'd say the same thing if her friend Little Flower asked her?"

Squire surged up from his chair and slammed his massive, meaty hands flat on the table with a resounding smack. "Now all of ye best be listenin' to me. I've made up my mind and I be leavin' here in the next day or so with just Star Path in my company. You others are free to do as you choose. Be the Colonel's men like you was before, which I say be the best thing, or hire yourselves out to someone else ..."

"Ain't likely," Peters muttered, "with near anybody else long gone."

"... Or stay here. Don't matter much to me whate'er ye be doin'. But ye ain't comin' with me." With that he stomped out, leaving a confused, worried, even scared group in his wake. Hannah, Bellows and the others sat there dumbfounded, shocked not only at Squire's decision but the way he had announced it. And they all felt abandoned, as if their father had just walked out of the house, leaving the children to fend for themselves.

Squire pushed his way into another saloon and gulped down two large glasses of whiskey. He was about to have another but thought better of it. He headed back toward his lodge, a swirl of feelings inside him. He was angry at himself at how he had treated his friends; he was angry at the way Hannah had sassed him in front of the others; he felt guilty about what he was planning though he was certain it was right for him.

He was still in high dudgeon when he shoved into his tipi. "I need food, woman," he commanded.

Silently, Star Path handed Squire a bowl of buffalo

stew. As he took his first bite, Star Path said, "You be a damn fool."

Squire's second spoonful of stew stopped hallway to his mouth. "What did ye say to me, woman?" he asked rather harshly.

"You hear me. You damn fool."

Squire set down his bowl and spoon. "Now you be listenin' here, woman, I don't have to be takin' no guff from ye."

"So the others say the same, eh? I be thinkin' so. Yes, I be thinkin' that."

"Mayhap they did but it be none of your concern. I might listen to some of them sassin' me but I don't be havin' to take it from ye."

"No?" Star Path said angrily. "You go to saloon today, you come back to find your things outside the lodge again. We be no more. This time final."

"Ye wouldn't be doin' such a thing," Squire said, but he was not certain. He suddenly grew a little smug. "Hell, if you be doin' so, what'll happen to ye?"

"I go with Colonel and Little Flower and the others. They bring me back to my people. I no see you again."

"The Colonel ain't goin' anywhere."

Star Path was a little shocked. "Then Little Flower and A'ner take me."

"What the hell do ye want, Star Path?" he asked in exasperation.

"Go with others."

"No."

"Then take some with us."

"That what ye be wantin'?" When she nodded, he asked, "Why?"

"They be good people. Plumb good. Help protect you and me."

"I don't need no protectin'. As long as I'm around, neither do you."

"Maybe. But plenty of Blackfeet be wantin' the hair of *L'on Farouche*." She smiled a little. "And maybe Little Flower, she help me when time comes for our son to be born."

Squire stared up at her for some moments. He wasn't sure what he felt for her was love but it was damn close, at least. He sighed. "Damn, woman, you are a perplexin' female." Then he smiled. "If it be so important to you, I reckon I can be takin' a few of 'em with us. Now let me finish fillin' my meatbag."

Half an hour later, he wandered back to the saloon. The group was still there, apparently making their plans for a new hunt. Without preliminary, he pointed at Abner, Hannah, and Li'l Jim. "Ye three be at my lodge, daybreak day after tomorrow. Be ready to move and move fast."

He glared when the three began to hoot and holler. Then he walked out.

CHAPTER 4

"The Colonel's maddern'n a hornet, Nathaniel," Train said. He grinned but it faded fast. He liked Colonel Melton a lot, owed him a lot, and felt bad for the man right now. But he owed more to Nathaniel Squire and it was with him that he threw in.

"Reckon he be, lad. How's he handlin' it?"

"Like always, with determination and impatience. He was already out yesterday mornin' first thing, far's I know, arrangin' supplies and such. Hired a few men. Had Homer out buyin' horses and mules."

Squire nodded. He was certain that Melton had things under control. "Ye three be set? Traps? Rifles? Powder and lead? Horses? Mules? Supplies?"

The young mountaineers nodded to each. "You can see that for your ownself," Li'l Jim snapped.

Squire grinned. "I see ye got your two women along, too," he said.

Li'l Jim scowled.

"He still can't find nobody foolish enough to take one of them off his hands," Hannah threw in cheerfully, drawing another scowl which she answered with a merry grin.

"Then it's time we be movin', lads." He winked at Hannah. His lodge was down, things packed on a travois. His giant horse, *Noir Astre,* was saddled and waiting. "Up you go, Missus," he said, tossing Star Path up onto her pony.

They rode out of the city, half a dozen mules following, roped together, and Li'l Jim and Hannah herding the same number of extra horses. They headed west on a trail worn deep by the mountain men and the traders and the supply trains; ground torn asunder by thousands and thousands of hooves, feet, and even wagon wheels.

They did not go far that first day, being out of the routine of traveling after the summer's spree, but the pace was picked up the next day. As they always did on the trek out from St. Louis, the days eventually grew tiresome. The path from St. Louis was well traveled and they could move fast, yet still encountering plenty of men coming and going to the mountains or heading for Taos and Santa Fe down in the Mexican country. For the journey this close to the city and its related activity, Hannah kept to her male dress just to avoid encountering any annoyance from passers-by.

Once they passed the Kansas River, heading for the Little Blue, they entered the edge of buffalo country. An eagerness spread among them all as they encountered the first of the giants herds.

"You aimin' to run them buffs tomorrow, Nathaniel?" Train asked around the campfire that night.

"Supposin' I was to say no?"

"Then me'n the others'll be doin' it on our own while you plod along on your ol', slow fat ass," Li'l Jim piped up.

"Old and slow I be, eh lad?"

"Either that or your stones've gone and dried up, you ol' buzzard."

"We'll just be seein' about that, lad. Aye, we will."

"So you'll be ridin' with us then?" the young man asked.

"Ye must've lost your reason, boy, to even ask such a damn fool question. *Sacre bleu*, it's been a time since we run buffler." His eyes gleamed with the thought of it.

In the morning, Squire raised the others. As they scrambled to fill their tin cups with coffee, the giant mountain man announced, "There be a fair size herd not more'n two mile away. We'll ride till we spot 'em, then be settin' up camp near as we can."

"We stayin' there?" Hannah asked.

"Aye. Might's well start makin' meat whenever we can be doin' so. Now be fillin' your meatbags. *Vite!* We be havin' things to do this day."

Within two hours they had their simple camp set up along a small, slow-moving stream in a little grove of cottonwoods: A small tent for Hannah and Train and one for Li'l Jim and his two wives; Squire and Star Path slept out in the open unless the weather was bad, heedless of what anyone thought or saw.

"Will Star Path be all right here alone?" Hannah asked, more than a little concerned at them leaving the Sioux woman alone while they were out hunting.

"She'll be fine, girl. I ain't seen sign of Indians about."

Hannah glanced over at Star Path. She and the older Sioux woman had formed a special bond after they had been taken by the Blackfeet and suffered a host of indignities during that time. Hannah was grateful for Star Path's kind words and support, and worried about her though she knew the Indian was well versed in facing the rigors of the wilds. Then she nodded and grinned.

The hunting party rode out — arrogant Li'l Jim taking his two women and two mules — moving slowly, and spotted the herd less than a quarter of a mile west, heading south.

"*Allons-y!*" Squire shouted and kicked *Noir Astre* into a run. He shoved several rifle balls in his mouth as he charged along. The great, black horse quickly pulled up alongside a plump cow. He lowered his rifle and fired. The ball tore through the buffalo's heart and the huge animal crashed forward, sliding to a dusty stop a few yards ahead.

But Squire was long past by then. He poured a dose of gunpowder into the muzzle. It was unmeasured but from experience he knew he it was near exact. He brought the muzzle up to his mouth and spit a ball into it, then slapped the side of the butt stock hard on his saddle several times to settle the ball.

In moments, he was alongside another cow, relishing the action. He had never tired of the exhilaration of running buffalo. There was nothing like it — except battle. The bellowing of the shaggy beasts, the thunder of their hooves, the wind tearing through his long, bushy beard, the dust swirling in great clouds, the feel of *Noir Astre's* powerful muscles bunching and stretching, the rush of adrenaline that coursed through him.

He finally pulled up after downing three more buffalo, having used all the lead balls he had stuffed in his mouth. Both he and the horse were blowing hard. He reached out and patted the massive horse's neck. "You done well, boy."

Squire trotted back to the camp and got one of the

mules. Just as he was riding out again, Hannah came in to get a couple of mules to pack in meat she and Train had taken.

"How'd ye do, girl?"

She looked a bit crestfallen. "Only got two."

"That be fine."

"Abner got three." She sighed. "This lazy horse of mine give up chasin' them buff'lo too soon. Tired out, I reckon."

"We'll be getting you a new one soon's we can. Now go on and butcher up this buffler. Just take the hump and rib meat, and maybe the fleece."

"Boudins?" Hannah asked with a newfound grin.

"Aye! That'll be settin' well with this ol' coon. For certain."

By midafternoon, everyone was back in the camp. Star Path had started three fires while the others were gone and now meat was being cut into serviceable chunks.

Li'l Jim, who had shot four of the great shaggies, sat, relaxing. He laughed a little. "Now, you can see why I have two Injun wives about. Waugh! I can set here on my rump and watch them girls do all the butcherin' and cookin' while ol' Nathaniel there has only one woman to help. And, Abner, you ain't even got that since Hannah ain't about to do no women's chores."

Squire grinned but said nothing. He knew none of it was directed at him, really. Nor did he really care even if it had been.

"Damn right I ain't butcherin' for him," Hannah said defiantly. "I'm doing it for me – and for him. And he's doin' for us both, too."

Li'l Jim just chuckled some more. "Don't look that

way to me. Looks like from here that you're doin' most of the work and he's kind of puttin' on a show of doin' somethin' whilst he ain't accomplishin' much."

Train shot him a wronged look while Hannah glanced over at Train with suspicion. "Why you lyin' snake," Hannah snorted. She huffed a minute, then chuckled herself. "You just want them two women of yours so worn out from skinnin' and butcherin' that they'll leave you alone in the robes tonight because you ain't got the manhood to handle 'em."

Train and Squire laughed, slapping their hands on thighs, as Li'l Jim's face reddened in embarrassment and some anger at having been found out. Star Path joined in the laughter, happy that she had what she considered almost her family back together and making light of each other again, all the while knowing they would be willing to die for each other if set upon.

"Dammit, don't you talk to me like that, little gal," Li'l Jim sputtered. "Or ..." He stopped when all he did was set off another gale of laughter from the others. "Bah!" He spun and walked away, sitting by himself a ways off on the prairie.

He returned when the meat was roasting and the coffee heating. He plunked himself down silently and scowled at everyone.

"I think you went and hurt Li'l Jim's feelin's, Hannah," Train said with a chuckle.

"Nah. Babies don't have no feelin's of those kind to be hurt."

"Damn if I oughtn't to kill the both of you here and now." Suddenly a grin split Li'l Jim's thin, young face. "But I ain't about to waste so much effort on folks I don't care a fiddle about." He ducked when Hannah and Train tossed pebbles at him as all three laughed raucously.

Squire sat with a small smile on his thickly bearded face. He had to admit, but only to himself – certainly not to Star Path – that his woman had been right in urging him to bring these three young people with them. They were deserving of riding with him. He had a moment of regret suddenly in thinking that he should've just gone with Melton and the others, like last year. But it was too late to do anything about that now. And he was not one to worry over things that could not be changed or decisions he had made.

They soon dug in, savoring the juicy, succulent hump meat and fleece.

CHAPTER 5

THE STORM CAME up out of nowhere it seemed. They had seen the dark, thick clouds gathering to the northwest but even Squire, with his sense of country and weather, was caught by surprise when the storm moved much faster than he had anticipated.

"Get the animals together, lads!" Squire bellowed.

It was almost too late. With the mules already roped together in a long string, Star Path and Li'l Jim's two women were able, barely, to get them to circle on themselves. As Squire, Li'l Jim, Train and Hannah raced to try to rope the horses, the deluge began. Torrents of roaring rain pounded down on them, thunder cracked and rumbled, and lightning sizzled and snapped.

The travelers fought to keep the horses and mules under control but it quickly seemed as if it might be a losing battle.

Hannah's horse suddenly bolted, charging off into the storm's darkness.

"Damn," Train bellowed. He wanted to race after her but knew he could not. He had his hands full trying to control his own mount and battle to keep the other bucking, whinnying horses from racing off.

Noir Astre was the only horse not bothered overly much by the storm. With his giant rider on his back, he remained mostly calm. Squire used the massive animal to force a couple of horses to bunch up against each other. Li'l Jim and Train joined him in his efforts.

————

Hannah battled furiously to control the stampeding mount but the horse was having none of it. She was not afraid, just annoyed and enraged. The animal zigged and zagged, screaming in fright with each startling crackle of lightning or each new clap of thunder.

She jerked hard on the reins, trying to halt the stampeding horse to no avail. All it seemed to do was give it more impetus to keep racing through the storm's fury. Finally, the horse seemed to tire a bit and Hannah yanked on the reins with all the strength her small body could muster. Instead of stopping, the animal reared up a little, its hind hooves sliding on the slick, muddy grass — and dumped Hannah on her rear end with a loud splat.

The mount gained traction again and dashed off once again. Hannah scrambled up, thankful that her rifle had slid out of the loop on the front of the saddle.

"You worthless son of a goat!" she yelled into the teeth of the wind. "You're lucky my powder's wet or I'd shoot you right now. dammit. I could hit you from here even as you run, you stupid, wretched, useless, four-legged sack of mule dung!"

She stopped, panting, and looked around and realized she had no idea where she was or how far she had come.

"Well, I'll be stuffed full of tobacky juice and spit out on a saloon floor," she muttered.

In the brilliance of a bolt of lightning, she saw a ridge perhaps a mile away. She tramped off, sloshing through the mud, the rain still thundering down on her now almost mashed flat hat, her rump hurting from the fall, and her anger not ebbing one iota.

As she walked, she cursed the horse and Homer Bellows for giving it to her. She cursed the rain and the lightning and thunder. She cursed the plains and the mountains that drew her. She cursed the tiredness that had suddenly swept over her. She cursed Squire for some reason. She cursed her Abner because he was not with her, though she well knew why. She nearly cursed God, too, but caught herself at the last moment, figuring that in her present condition that would be a very unwise thing to do.

She would not cry, though, she vowed, despite wanting to. She was not prone to doing so but, under the circumstances, she considered it. Then she managed a weak grin. Even if she did, there would be no one around to see it and she wouldn't even notice herself with the deluge of rain still thundering down on her.

She finally made it to the top of the ridge and plunked herself down. A bolt of lightning seemed to snap the ground within a few feet of her. "Damn!" she muttered. She scrambled down the hill, hoping it was better than sitting on the top of a small hill in the flatness of the prairie.

She plopped down at the bottom of the hill, right into a puddle. Not that it made any difference as soaked through as she was. She sat there, glumly pondering her next move. She considered just staying here until she drowned from the downpour. Shooting herself was out of the question with her powder soaking wet.

She decided to risk returning to the top, hoping for a lightning strike — just not so close — so she might get her bearings. It didn't work. With a sigh of annoyance, she slipped and slid back down to the bottom of the hill. With her knife, she began carving out a small cave in the side of the ridge. As she was doing so, she realized the water was rising under her feet. "Damned fool," she muttered. "Ought to know better'n sit in a gully while it's rainin' like this."

She climbed back up a decent way on the ridge and managed to chop out a couple of footholds. Then she cut out her cave and hunched inside it. At least most of the rain was off her for now.

———

Two horses managed to break free and scooted away. Then a mule snapped free of his rope and bolted off, braying wildly, its packs flying off as it ran.

Li'l Jim looked as if he were going to chase the animal but Squire bellowed, "Stay where ye be, lad."

The young man nodded.

Squire grabbed the rope to the rest of the mules from Star Path who was having the devil's own time trying to control her mount. He used his massive strength to keep the beasts from also running off. It was no easy task with the pack mules braying wildly and frantically trying to escape. No one but Squire could have kept them in line.

Star Path jerked her pony out of the way, fighting it the whole time, so none of the other animals would step on the travois' lodgepoles and hurt itself.

Li'l Jim, Train and the former's two wives rode around the extra horses, keeping them in as tight a knot as they could. The animals' eyes rolled, and they stomped and whinnied and snorted wildly. But the four people managed to keep them hemmed in.

Despite the deluge that still poured down on them, the horses and even the mules began to calm just a little. Until another gigantic, ear shattering clap of thunder followed by a string of lightning burst over them. And the fight began anew.

Squire didn't know how long it had been or what time of day it was but the storm eventually began to wear itself out, though it was a long time before it gave up the ghost. The thick, heavy clouds at long last began to separate, allowing small, scattered patches of dusk to make themselves known.

Exhausted, the travelers finally got the animals calmed down.

"We best be movin' on," Squire announced. "There be a place some miles from here where we can find us a bit of shelter. Might be findin' us enough wood to make us a fire and be dryin' out some. Probably have to travel through the night though."

"I'm goin' after Hannah," Train said. Though his eyes were bleary from tiredness and every muscle ached, he was determined to find his woman.

"She'll be fine, boy," Squire said without sympathy. "We be havin' more important things to be doin'."

"But ..."

"Don't sass me, boy," Squire snapped. "She'll be fine, I tell ye. Like as not she be in better shape than we be. We'll find her soon enough. Or she'll be findin' us. 'Sides, you got no idea where she be."

He looked around. The horses were still not eased completely but at least they were not being too fractious. "Li'l Jim, take one of your women and ride out a little that way," he pointed. "See if you can be findin' that mule or the supplies. Don't be goin' too far though. You don't find anything in a mile or so, get yourself back here *vite*."

"What if I find the supplies and not the mule?"

"Put what you can on the squaw's pony and ride double."

"What about takin' one of the other horses?" Li'l Jim was worn out and annoyed. All he wanted to do was rest.

"Can't afford to be losin' another of them critters. Now go on, git."

Li'l Jim nodded wearily. "C'mon, Cloudy Moon," he said to one of the two young wives of his and galloped off. Still looking rather frightened, she followed.

They caught back up with the others a little more than an hour later. Li'l Jim and Cloudy Moon rode together while the woman's horse struggled a bit under the weight of supplies the young mountain man had piled atop it.

"Mule ain't nowhere to be found," Li'l Jim announced. "Hope a griz or the wolves get it, son of a bitch."

It was a weary group that pulled into a clump of cottonwoods as dawn was breaking. The sunshine and cloudless sky that arrived made yesterday's storm seem like a mirage. Except that they were all still soaked through, their powder still wet, and all of them miserable and exhausted.

Squire helped Star Path off her horse, despite her protests. "How be you, woman?"

"I fine. Good."

Squire cast a gimlet eye on her. While not as physically strong as he, of course, her inner strength and will were his equal. Still, she was no youngster and she was pregnant and had done more than her share in keeping the animals in line during the storm. Squire was worried about her.

The woman smiled through her weariness. "I fine. Tired. Like all others. You care for animals. Me and those useless young women will start fires and food."

Squire nodded. He kissed the top of her head and headed off. "Time to be carin' for the animals, lads," he hollered. "Be makin' sure the extra horses are hobbled real well. Same with the mules once we get 'em unloaded."

The men wearily set about their tasks. Train began hobbling the horses while Squire and Li'l Jim unloaded the pack animals. Then they cared for their mounts and those of the women.

Once the mules were unloaded, the women, in between their own chores, shucked their garments and put on old, ragged dresses that they kept for just such emergencies. They ignored leggings. When the men were finished, they too changed, removing the clothes they had worn in St. Louis and tossed into their packs to use as bandages or rags or whatever need might arise for cloth instead of buckskin. Soon the trees around the camp were festooned with drying shirts, trousers, dresses, moccasins and hats.

They finally all sat to a meal of pemmican that had been sliced and fried and coffee, hot and sweet. Afterward, the three men emptied their powder horns, dried them out, and then made sure their rifles and pistols were also dried before replenishing their horns from the tins of DuPont and reloading their weapons.

The women soon lay down on buffalo robes and slept. Li'l Jim was not far behind. Squire rested his back against a cottonwood and closed his eyes. Soon after, he opened them. "Best be getting some rest, lad," he said to Train who was pacing back and forth.

"I can't, Nathaniel. I'm worried sick about Hannah."

"You won't get far before ye'll be fallin' off your horse, Abner."

"Ain't likely. I'll stay awake till I find her."

"The horses need rest."

"Then I'll walk."

Squire was beginning to lose his patience. Despite his great strength and fortitude, he was tired and not of a good humor. "You take one step, boy, and I'll have to rise up from here and thump your ass."

"Best make it good 'cause it won't stop me."

Squire stroked his great beard and almost smiled. "Reckon it wouldn't," he allowed. "Ye're bein' a damn fool, lad, but go on. Take one of the extra horses. It might be some frisky after yesterday's doin's but you can handle it, I reckon."

"Thanks, Nathaniel."

"Just don't go too far. Couple hours at most." He closed his eyes again.

CHAPTER 6

HANNAH CARPENTER STUMBLED into the camp. She stuck the butt of her rifle on the ground and headed her forearms on the muzzle. She waited but a few moments before saying in a rather aggrieved voice, "Well, ain't no one gonna say hello?"

Eyes popped open around the camp. A burst of raucous laughter burst forth from Li'l Jim almost immediately. It was followed by giggles by his two wives. Big Squire grinned. Even Star Path found it hard not to laugh.

"My Little Flower," the Sioux said, pushing herself awkwardly to her feet and headed toward the young woman.

"Little Flower," Li'l Jim exclaimed. "More like a drowned muskrat, only not as purty." He howled with laughter.

"Why you no good, festerin', skunk-lovin', ugly little pile of rabbit droppin's ..." She dropped her rifle and ran for Li'l Jim.

The young man, no fool he, leaped up and took off. Squire, moving quickly, pushed up and managed to corral

Hannah around the waist. He held her easily even as she squirmed and kicked, shouting the most vile imprecations at her taunting companion.

Tired as she was, it didn't take Hannah long to wind down. Finally Squire set her on her feet, then grinned. "You do be a sight, girl."

She looked down at herself. She was covered in dried mud; her hat, she knew was crumbled and filthy; and she knew her face must be a fright with mud and all. She grinned ruefully as she looked up at him. "Reckon you're right, Nathaniel." Suddenly the smile faded and her eyes grew wide with worry and fear. "Where's Abner?" she asked anxiously, stomach knotting.

"He be out lookin' for ye, lass."

"Then get me a horse."

"No." There was no mistaking the hardness in his voice.

"But ..."

"He'll be back soon. I can't have you two lookin' for each other fore'er, one be comin' into camp then ridin' out again just to have the other be comin' in and ridin' out again. You be waitin' here. He'll be back afore long."

"But ..." she tried again.

"No," Squire reaffirmed in no less uncertain terms. "Go on and get yourself cleaned up. Make sure your weapons are ready and then get some rest."

Star Path came up and placed an arm around the girl's shoulders. "Come, Little Flower." She led Hannah off.

Half an hour later, she was clean and clad in a calico dress she had worn in St. Louis. She didn't know how it came to be in her pack but she was fairly certain Abner had done it for some reason. If she wasn't so worried about him not being here, she would have been furious.

Less than an hour after that, an exhausted Train rode into the camp, looking dejected. Until he saw Hannah. Suddenly the tiredness dropped off him. He jumped off the horse, ready to run to her, but he barely had time to alight before she leaped into his arms, legs wrapped around his middle, her mouth plastering kisses all over his face.

"Lawd a'mighty that's disgustipatin'," Li'l Jim said with a shake of his head. But his chest and stomach jerked a little as he held in his laughter.

Chuckling, Squire said, "That be enough you two. You need to, ye can head behind yon bushes and have at each other but I'll not be havin' such frolickin' out here in front of e'erybody. 'Course," he added with another booming chuckle, "was you to decide to put on an exhibition, I would be some curious ol' niggur and would be payin' careful mind to the goings on. Nary can tell, e'en this ol' chil' might be learnin' somethin'."

That brought forth another burst of laughter from all but the two lovers. Hannah slid down off Train and both reddened in embarrassment.

"Much as I hate to admit it," Train said, "I'm too damn tired for such doin's. All's I want is a bite to eat and some shuteye."

"Well go on about it, boy," Squire said. Then he got a wicked gleam in his eye. "But first, don't you want to be commentin' your woman on her dress?"

Train shook his head as if to clear it. He turned. "Damn, you look mighty good, Hannah," he said. "Purtiest I ever seen you since we was hitched. I ..."

The others grinned widely and took a step or two

back, waiting for the explosion which was but moments in arriving.

"Purty!?" Hannah screeched. "Lookin' mighty good!? Wearin' this frilly girly-girly outfit like I was some house-wife back on some farm in Indiana or somethin'. Why in hell did you pack this damn thing anyway?"

"I thought ..."

"No you didn't, damn you. If you had thought for one minute you would've had sense enough to know not to do such a thing. Where the hell was I supposed to wear it anyway? To rendezvous and sashay around for all them mountain boys to ogle over? That what you want? Every man putting his eyes on me, wantin' me?"

"No, but ..."

"'Cause if that's what you're aimin' for, Abner Train, I can full accommodate you. Yes, I can."

"But, Hannah ..."

"Or was you thinkin' maybe I could wear it in the lodge from time to time, pretend I'm that housewife you seem to want? That it? Let me pretend to be some dainty little flower just caterin' to her big, strong man."

"C'mon now, Hannah ..."

"Don't you 'c'mon now, Hannah' me, boy. I'm every bit a mountaineer as you are, you big, stupid ox."

The others' sides hurt from their laughter at the scene. Star Path at one point managed to catch her breath sitting next to Squire. "You a devilish son bitch, *L'on Farouche*," she said as another gale of laughter washed over her.

"That I be, woman. That I be."

Hannah's harangue went on for some more minutes before she ran out of energy. Train opened his mouth, planning to say something now that he had an opportunity but when he saw her face, he turned and slunk away.

Hannah stood there, still red with anger. Then her face dropped and she looked crestfallen. She started after Train, then stopped, uncertain.

"Well, go on, girl," Squire said. "Be goin' after him. He'll forgive ye but it's ye who ought to do the forgivin'."

She shuffled off.

———

"Looks like you'll be ridin' bareback, girl," Squire said in the morning.

"I looked for her horse," Train said, "but it wasn't nowhere to be found."

"Good thing you didn't bring it back," Hannah said harshly. "I would've shot the wretched critter." She smiled ruefully. "I hate losin' the saddle, though. I don't mind ridin' bareback so much but there's no place to hang my possibles sack."

"I reckon Abner'll be happy to pack your possibles, seein's how you two have overcome your difficulties. Now go on and pick yourself a horse."

When she went off, Squire called Train and Li'l Jim over. "Ye boys'll be ridin' out like usual. Buff'lo be getting mighty scare, Li'l Jim, so ye might have to do some ridin'. Abner, we be in Pawnee country now. Keep your eyes alert for sign."

"Always do, Nathaniel."

The big man nodded. As Train walked away, Squire looked at his retreating back as if he had never seen the young man before. Star Path sidled up alongside him and he said to her, "Somethin' be different about that lad.

Can't figure it out, though. Maybe it's just 'cause he be married now."

"Maybe. But more than that. He more confident now. Knows he's a real mountain man, like you, Nat'aniel."

"You be right, I reckon."

"But he grows, too. He not your size but he be bigger'n last year."

Squire watched as Train mounted his horse. The animal looked smaller than he had remembered. "Damn, if you ain't right, woman." He watched a moment longer. Train still missed Squire's great height by a couple of inches or so and his weight by maybe thirty pounds, Squire figured. But he had grown into a very large man. "All right, woman, go on about your business." Squire mounted *Noir Astre* and they all headed out.

The going was at a quick enough pace but dull as could be. Most of the travelers were half asleep in their saddles. Sometime in late morning, Hannah rode up alongside Squire. He opened his eyes ad glanced blandly at her.

She ignored the bored look. "Why don't you ever let me ride out there like Abner and Li'l Jim?"

"Don't be seemin' the right thing to do."

"It's 'cause I'm a girl, ain't it?"

Squire looked at her, realizing with a bit of alarm that it was true, at least in part. Despite the dangers she had faced, the hardships, the battles she had fought, he still looked at her as a daughter. She was younger than his son, Light Eyes. It would grieve him no end should something happen to her. Still, she had done everything the men had done. Only her size and its incumbent lack of physical strength was a hindrance. And a minor one at that.

"No, that ain't it. You be knowin' well as I do that Li'l Jim is the best shot and Abner be the best tracker..."

"He was so good a tracker, he would've found me. And my damned horse," she said with a touch of bitterness.

Squire chuckled. "Big land out there, lass. Lot of places a headstrong lass could wander off to in a storm. And a horse, well, most critters have a mind of their own."

"I still think you figure it's because I'm a girl. Well, let me tell you somethin', Mr. giant galoot Nathaniel Squire, I ..."

"Hush up, girl. You know I be right about their talents."

"Yeah," she grumbled, at least a little chastened. But she didn't let that slow her down. "But I can shoot buffalo. Don't take much to put down one of them beasts. And I'm better at butcherin', too. Might take me a bit longer since I ain't as strong as even Star Path but when I do it, you get the best."

"That be true."

"And, well, I ain't the tracker Abner is but it ain't like I can't find sign at all."

"Reckon that be true, too." He paused. "Let me be thinkin' some on it. Now go on back and help care for the cavvy."

Hannah stared at him a moment, trying to read what was behind the faded blue eyes. She found nothing that would give her a clue to his decision. She finally pulled her horse around and trotted off.

But in the morning, Squire sent out Hannah to do the hunting, much to Li'l Jim's chagrin and anger.

"I didn't hire on to herd horses," the young man snapped.

"Ye hired on for whate'er I be tellin' ye to do. Ye don't like it, ye can head on where'er ye want. Ahead to the mountains, back to St. Louis. Don't matter none to me."

Li'l Jim growled but went about his work.

The next day it was Train's turn to stay behind, grousing as much as Li'l Jim if not more. After all, it was his woman going out there alone and he was worried sick about her encountering some hostile Indians. After what she had been through at the hands of savages, he shuddered at the thought of it happening again.

CHAPTER 7

ABNER TRAIN CHARGED up to the small caravan and brought his horse to a quick stop in a swirling cloud of dust next to Squire, "Pawnees," he said, not seeming concerned.

"How many be they?"

"Eight, maybe nine."

"War party?"

"Don't think so. They was some distance off but they didn't seem painted."

"They be headin' for us?"

"Not directly. But they'll cut our trail a few miles northwest if we keep on the way we're goin'."

"Well, lad, I ain't about to be changin' course 'cause of a few flea-ridden Pawnees. Go on back and watch o'er the horses. Make sure they're all roped together. Don't want any of those critters runnin' off. Get Cloudy Moon or Fox Woman to help."

"What about Li'l Jim?" Train was a bit confused and more than a tad annoyed.

"Send him o'er here."

"What about Hannah?" Train asked, worry suddenly overriding the other emotions. "I need to go get her."

"Li'l Jim'll be doin' so. Your horse is lathered. Now go on."

Unhappy, Train trotted off. Moments later, Li'l Jim stopped next to where Squire was waiting. "Abner says you need me? He didn't look pleased."

"Reckon he ain't," the giant said with a shrug. "Go on out and find Hannah."

"Trouble?" It was Li'l Jim's turn to be confused, wondering why Squire didn't send Train out after his wife.

"Abner saw some Pawnees. Ain't likely to cause trouble but I be wantin' us all here. She headed south but if she turned west, there's a small chance she'd be runnin' into 'em. I don't figure that be the case since she don't usually sit around half the day before huntin' like some other lazy chil' I know." He looked pointedly at Li'l Jim who seemed not in the least abashed. "No gunfire less'n it's necessary. I just be hopin' she ain't found some buff'lo yet and is ready to take a couple down."

Li'l Jim grew serious. "I'll fetch her back here before you know it, Nathaniel," he said solemnly. He turned his horse and galloped off.

Li'l Jim and Hannah rode up sooner than Squire had expected but no more than a quarter-hour before the band of Pawnees hove into view.

"Hannah, be goin' on back with the horses."

"But why ...?" Seeing the look in Squire's eyes, she shut her mouth. Angry, she trotted back beside Cloudy Moon and Fox Woman.

The two groups stopped about ten yards apart and

stared at each other for some seconds, trying to get the measure of each band.

One Pawnee rode out a bit from the others. He was tall, broad and dark-skinned with a pocked face. His hair was roached and he wore a brass gorget around his throat that hung down onto his tattered buckskin shirt. "I am Long Dog," he said in fractured English and in a voice much higher than should have come from his bulky body. "You in our land."

"We be just passin' through," Squire responded evenly. He was flanked by Li'l Jim and Train.

"You must pay."

"Payin' the likes of you for ridin' across open country don't shine with this ol' niggur. You boys can just be on your way."

"You pay!"

"Look, lad, you be wantin' to keep your hair, you best be ridin' on."

While the war chief was thinking that over, Train leaned over and said, "That horse in the back there, the one bein' ridden by the young son of a bitch with the hooked nose and big hoop earrings, is Hannah's."

Squire looked that way and nodded. "Aye, it be." He looked at the chief and pointed. "That horse be ours. We'll be wantin' it back."

"It ours. We find on prairie. No one with it. We take. Ours now."

"Reckon not." He paused. "Li'l Jim, you keep your gun pointed at those boys 'cept for the chief here. Anybody moves, shoot him dead. Abner, go on over there and yank that red devil off our horse. He fusses about it, whack him with your 'hawk."

Train stuck his rifle through the loop on the front of

his saddle and dismounted. Without showing any fear, he marched over to the Pawnee on Hannah's horse.

The Indian kicked at him. Train was able to shift his head sideways and the Indian's foot brushed the white man's shoulder and ear. He whirled and grabbed the Pawnee's ankle and twisted it hard, then shoved.

The Pawnee half fell off the horse. Train slipped under the animal's neck, grabbed the Indian's shirt with one hand and his hair with the other and tugged. The Indian, surprised and well off balance, tumbled to the ground and landed in a puff of dust.

The Pawnee tried to kick Train again but the mountain man stomped on his knee, eliciting a shout of pain. The Indian reached for his knife and tried to scramble up. Train pulled out his tomahawk. "Don't be foolish," he warned. When the Indian stopped and sank back down — anger suffusing his face — Train grabbed the horse's reins with his left hand — the 'hawk still in his right — and leaped onto the animal's back.

The hair rose on the back of his neck some as he rode back toward Squire and the others, waiting for a bullet or arrow in the back. But none came.

"Now, Chief," Squire said when Train had pulled up alongside him again, "you best be on your way. I be of poor humor and be of no mind to set here and palaver with you dung-eatin' *fils de pute.*"

The Pawnees argued among themselves for a bit before the chief chopped off the debate. "You pay for horse."

"Like hell. Now git movin' before I be losin' my temper for real."

The chief glared at him some more, then angrily jerked his pony's head around and started off. The one who had been riding Hannah's horse, gingerly jumped up behind another warrior. One of his men, however, started nocking his bow. Li'l Jim fired and the Pawnee jerked as the ball tore into his shoulder. He dropped the bow and the arrow.

"Aller—Go," Squire said.

As the furious Pawnee rode off, Train asked, "Was that smart, Nathaniel? Them boys don't look to be in the best of humors now that we degraded 'em."

"I reckon they're not."

"Won't they come agin us?"

"Aye." Squire turned his head toward his young friend and gave him a wicked smile. "We'll be waitin' on 'em."

"Wouldn't it've been better just to give 'em some tobacco or somethin'?" Li'l Jim asked.

"Might be. Reckon if they'd be friendlier — and didn't have Hannah's horse and be so ill-tempered about givin' it up — I might've been a wee bit more disposed to part with a bit of somethin'. But when they be so fractious about it all, it don't set well with this chil'."

"Injuns don't set well with you most times," Li'l Jim said.

Squire looked at him, a hard gleam in his eye. "That be true, lad. Best not forget it neither. Well, we best be movin' on. Stay close. Be watchin' the horses and mules close. Be ready."

"When do you think they'll come at us?" Train asked.

"Scared, boy?"

"No, I ain't scared, dammit, and you sure as hell know it. Just be nice to know."

"They'll be comin' agin us when they be comin' agin us. Might be half a mile down the trail. Might be they'll do so when we're makin' camp. Might be just before dawn. Just be ready." He rode off and got the others moving.

Before long, Hannah rode up alongside Squire. She was silent for a spell and the big man finally realized she wanted him to ask first. "Something be on your mind, girl?"

"Why you send me back with the other women 'stead of goin' up with you and the others?"

Ye asked me such a thing before, lass."

"And ya never gave me a real good answer."

"Mayhap."

"Them why'd you send me back this time?"

"It were best."

"'Cause I'm a girl?"

"Aye, that be it."

"Dammit, Nathaniel, I'm as good as any of the others. Well, maybe not you, but ..."

"That be true. You be nearabout the toughest critter this chil' ever knew."

"Then why ...?"

"You remember, don't ye, how Injuns and others be actin' to ye when they learn you be a white woman?" When she nodded, Squire continued. "Well there be no sense makin' a point of you bein' out front less'n it be necessary."

"Can't always be that way, Nathaniel. Not if I'm gonna stay out here."

Squire thought it over a bit, then nodded. "Reckon ye be right. I ain't used to havin' someone like you 'round. It be some strange to me. Even after all this time and even after all ye been through. Reckon I'll be lookin' at it different."

Hannah grinned.

———

The attack came not with a rush and a chorus of war cries but with stealth and a silent burst of arrows. Nor did it last long.

Squire and the others were ready. They had taken refuge on a fair-size island in the Platte River. The land was thick with trees and brush. More important, there were few trees on either bank, offering an enemy little cover for an attack.

The small group had worked the horses into the thickets as best they could and hastily threw up some barricades of deadwood. Star Path and the two Shoshones stayed with the animals. Then they hunkered down to wait.

"Which way you think they'll be comin', Nathaniel?" Train asked from his position behind a half-rotten log a dozen yards in front of the thicket, facing basically north.

"Cain't tell, but I figure they'll've crossed somewhere upriver and be comin' at us from the both sides. That's why you and Li'l Jim be where ye be."

The sun was beginning to dip when *Noir Astre* snorted and whinnied in a way that sounded no different than usual to anyone but Squire. "They be comin', lads," the big man said. "Be ready."

Suddenly a burst of arrows flew from both sides of the river.

Li'l Jim, who was on the opposite side of Train, fired as a Pawnee popped up to fire another arrow. Train did the same. Li'l Jim figured he hit his target but he was not sure and if he did, he was not certain how badly he had hurt the Pawnee.

As Li'l Jim and Train reloaded, Squire and Hannah held off, waiting until a better target showed itself.

Two Indians jumped up and raced for the two trees on the north bank. Train and Hannah fired, and both warriors went down before they reached cover.

Train rose up onto a knee, tracking a Pawnee with his rifle, and an arrow hit him high in the left shoulder.

Hannah gasped and started to bolt forward but Squire grabbed her by the scruff of the shirt and jerked her to a stop. "Nay, lass," he said.

Hannah gritted her teeth but stayed put.

Train winced when the bolt hit him, then steadied himself and swung his rifle toward the one who had fired it. In a moment, the Pawnee was dead.

A few moments later, the Pawnees who were still alive were fleeing rapidly across the prairie.

"Reckon that'll teach 'em," Li'l Jim said with his usual cockiness.

"Aye, lad, that it will," Squire said.

Hannah ran to Train,. He smiled as he easily plucked the arrow from his shoulder, it not having sunk very deeply.

"It be times for some robe time lads. It ain't likely those Pawnees'll be back but we best take turns on guard anyway. Li'l Jim, ye be the first."

"Damn, why's it always me?" Li'l Jim grumbled good-naturedly.

CHAPTER 8

"Injuns comin'," Li'l Jim said.

Squire looked at him with raised eyebrows.

"All right, all right, so you knew it an hour ago," Li'l Jim said somewhat sourly. "Or yesterday. Or maybe last year."

Squire laughed. "It weren't but a few minutes." He grew serious. "Tell the others to be ready. They be Sioux and I think they be from Sky Hawk's village, but I ain't certain just yet.

The warriors pulled up in a eddy of color, noise and dust. "*L'on Farouche!*" one said with delight.

"Four Horses."

The Sioux looked around. "But where are others? Many come with you before."

"They be on their own this year."

"You come to village?"

"Aye, lad."

"We will tell Sky Hawk you come." He yipped, spun his horse and, with his friends, charged off over the broken ground.

Squire and his group moved along more slowly and soon he brought them to a halt. "Horses be needin' water," he said. "Whilst the women be takin' care of that, I be needin' to talk to all of ye."

When they had gathered in the shade of the single cottonwood, joined shortly by Star Path, Squire said, "I been thinkin' some on the ride out here."

"Didn't know you could," Li'l Jim said with a snort.

Squire cast a baleful eye on him but it did not cow the short mountain man.

"I be wantin' to avoid troubles that might rise up because of Hannah."

"You ain't thinkin' of sendin' her back, are ya?" Train asked, half in anger, half in worry.

"Nay, lad. We come too far, both in miles and doin's to do that."

"Damn good thing," the young woman at the heart of the conversation said.

Squire's great beard parted as he smiled at her. "Aye, that it be, lass. Now most of the mountaineers we meet likely'd be treating a white woman with the most politeness."

"But at rendezvous ..." Hannah started.

"That be because of the way ye dress — and the ways them coons found out."

"Well, I ain't wearin' a dress, that's for certain," Hannah said with finality. "I had me more than enough of that frilly foofaraw back in the Settlements.

Squire grinned again. "Ain't no one big enough 'cept this chil' could force you to do so and, though they call me *L'on Farouche*, I ain't that *fou*. Rather be goin' agin a passel of Blackfeet."

When the burst of laughter died down, Squire grew

serious. "It ain't so easy now to hide that ye be a woman." He smiled a touch again. "You've done growed some."

Hannah looked at him in puzzlement for a few moments. When Li'l Jim snickered, her eyes widened. She glanced down at her calico-shirt-covered breasts and her face flushed a bright crimson.

Li'l Jim laughed, Squire grinned, and Train couldn't decide if he should be angry that the others had noticed or smirk because she had blossomed and she was his.

To save her further embarrassment, Squire said, "If we be aimin' to avert troubles, we need to figure somethin' out and that's what I been contemplatin' on. There be some women warriors amongst some of the tribes. Ain't many, for certain, but there be a few here and there. And since Hannah be a fierce warrior anyway, such as she'll be known out here. But I don't think it'll be workin' if she's a white woman."

"Can't help what I am, Nathaniel," Hannah said, confused.

"Reckon that be so. But ye can change."

Hannah, Train and Li'l Jim looked at him as if he had lost his reason.

"From now on, girl, you be a half-breed."

"A what?" she exploded.

"A half-breed."

"But ...?"

"Listen to me, girl," Squire said only a bit harshly. "It'll stave off trouble if you be somethin' other than a white woman in most folks' eyes out here. So from here on, any chil' be askin' about ye, ye be Hannah Carpenter, a half-breed."

"Ain't no one gonna believe that," Li'l Jim said.

"Fer certain they will. Ain't no one gonna get near

enough to check too closely. Any chil' does, he'll have devilish means in mind and he'll be facin all of us."

"I'm purty fair-skinned for a half-breed."

"Ye've darkened up some bein' in the sun so much. So I think ye be the daughter of a Cree — they be somewhat lighter-skinned that many an Injun — and a Scots father. Them Scots're damned near as pasty-faced as the Britishers."

"Might work, I suppose." Hannah still sounded doubtful.

"Aye, it will. Ain't anyone be likely to question ye beyond that. Some hoss does, maybe he be thinkin' ye speak English too well or something. If ye be thinkin' he needs answerin', tell him your ma died when you was just a babe and your pa took you to the city for some learnin'. And he took ye to the wilds with him whilst ye still be a youngster and that's where ye became a warrior — fightin' Injuns."

"Last part's sure as hell true," Train said.

"Aye, it be."

"Won't someone in Sky Hawk's village have somethin' to say about her name when Star Path calls her Little Flower?" Li'l Jim asked. "Ain't much of a warrior name, even for a girl." He grinned at Hannah.

"Ye be aimin' to challenge her?" Squire asked with a grin.

"Hell, no. But some Lakota buck might be willin' to go against her, not knowin', of course, that she's really a she-wolf tryin' to pass herself off as a dainty little flower."

"If I didn't want to get my knife dirty, I'd fling it at you and you know how well I handle a blade." Then she burst into laughter with the others following.

When it had died down, Star Path piped up, "We call her *Ohitekah Winyan*. It means Fierce Woman."

"That fits," Li'l Jim said. "Unless you can call her maybe *L'on Farouchette*, Nathaniel's wild, crazy daughter."

Hannah glared, then burst out laughing again as did the others.

When the laughter had run its course, Train asked, "You think there'll be any trouble in the village?"

"Nay, lad, but best to be ready, of course. Might be a chance some young buck'll try to come agin her to show he's ready for the war path. But I be doubtin' it. Wouldn't be doin' that young hoss any good to get whupped by a girl. If one of 'em be that damned foolish, let him go agin her. She'll be teachin' that coon what a woman warrior can do."

He paused while the others chuckled, then said, "It be e'en more unlikely but there be a possibility some full warrior might take it to mind to show that a woman can't be a warrior."

Hannah pulled a knife and tossed it gently in the air, then caught it by the handle. "He does, he might just find himself no man a'tall after I get done with him."

Train cringed just a bit, Li'l Jim gulped, and Squire just grinned and nodded at her.

Squire rose "Well, lads, we best be movin' if we want to get to the village afore it be dark. Li'l Jim go see that the animals and women be ready."

When the young man walked away, the giant mountain man said to his two companions. "Ye best be takin' these words to your hearts: Ye both got to stop frettin' so much about the other. Won't be easy, for certain, but it's got to be done. Ye keep on worryin' what might be happenin' to the other and ye'll be makin' damp powder for e'eryone.“

"I ain't so sure I can do that," Train started.

"I ain't askin' ye, boy, I be tellin' ye. All your frettin's like as not to get all our hair raised. I know ye got deep feelin's fer each other but there be other folks be carin' for you and e'erybody else. Ye know full damn well me'n and Li'l Jim'll stand with ye agin anyone, e'en if the goddamn devil be risin' up out of his fire and brimstone to go agin us. We done it afore and it be likely we'll have some poor doin's to face again. I expect ye to stand with me and Li'l Jim — and anyone else who be with us. Not just your own selves."

Train looked angry and abashed at the same time and so stayed quiet.

"You're right, Nathaniel," Hannah said. "I don't know what I'd do if Li'l Jim or ..." she smiled just a touch "... you was to go under because my mind was only on Abner. Like as not, I'd stand here empty handed and let every red devil on the Plains and in the mountains come take my hair."

Squire laid a giant hand on one of her small shoulders. "I believe ye, lass."

She smiled grimly. "And I'll make sure this big oaf understands it, too. He already knows I ain't pleased with him treatin' me like I'm some fearful, defenseless girl. The rest might take some work beatin' it into that mulish head of him, but I'll be certain to work on it."

"*Bon*. Now let's ride."

———

An hour later, they rode into the Lakota village. As usual,

the lodges were scattered here and there, seemingly with no rhyme or reason, though every one had its opening facing the east.

While Star Path, Cloudy Moon and Fox Woman took the horses and mules out past where several lodges had been set up for the visitors, Squire and the others stopped in front of Sky Hawk's tipi.

The old man was as regal as ever, the wind ruffling his long, mostly gray hair, and the two eagle feathers tied near the crown of his head. He stood straight-backed despite his age, a red, six-point Hudson Bay blanket wrapped around him.

"*Hau*, Sky Hawk," Squire said.

"*Tan yan yahee ya* – Welcome. I'm glad to see you."

"Aye, It's good to be here."

"Four Horses say the others not come?"

"Aye. The others be on their own, I reckon. Big Chief Melton wasn't figurin' on comin' out here but he was thinkin' of sendin' the others out for him. Don't know if he did, but I reckon son."

"Even *Le Chevals Gardien*?"

"Aye"

"We talk? Eat plenty? Drink plenty whiskey?" The ancient chief grinned, showing some gaps where teeth had once resided.

"*Mais oui*! Soon's we get the horses and such took care of."

"*Bon*. I wait. Not long." He grinned again.

"Not long, certain." Squire swung back into the saddle and led the way toward the lodges.

As dusk began to give way to dark over the village, Squire and Li'l Jim settled in around the fire with Sky hawk, Four Horses and half a dozen other warriors.

Squire had brought a jug of whiskey with him and it was quickly making the rounds while the men gobbled down large chunks of fresh buffalo meat, plenty of which was hanging over the large fire.

"You fought much o'er the summer?" Squire asked.

Four Horses nodded. "Counted coup and took hair against the Pawnees and the Crow. Damn bad Injuns them. You fight?"

"Aye. Raised hair agin a small group of Pawnees a few days ago. Took us all their ponies, too," he lied, then laughed.

The talk, sometimes of importance, sometimes not, made the rounds of the circle with the whiskey and, before long, the glow of alcohol-induced friendship had permeated the group.

Li'l Jim rose after a spell. Squire looked up at him in question though with no concern. The slight young man grinned. "Maybe I can talk one of these ol' coons to take one of them damn women off my hands."

Squire chuckled. "Good fortune be with ye, lad." He turned back to the circle.

CHAPTER 9

"Come to the robes, Abner," Hannah said brightly, lusting for her man.

"Maybe later," Train said quietly.

"Somethin' wrong?" she asked, worry cutting through Hannah's voice.

"No."

"Like hell. Somethin's eatin' at ya. Otherwise, you'd be over here with your naked woman waitin' for ya to cover her."

"Ain't somethin' I'm comfortable talkin' about. 'Least not yet. Maybe never."

"You ain't thinkin' of castin' me out, are ya?" her worry deepened. She sat up, the blanket falling down to Hannah's waist.

"Good Lord, no." Train sighed as if a heavy weight was dragging his spirit down. "I'm just contemplatin' on what Nathaniel said."

Hannah knew that Squire was right in that Train had to be less mindful of just Hannah in dangerous situations.

It threatened them all. Hannah'd feel powerful bad if Train should go under but Hannah knew Train'd feel near as bad if Squire — as hard as that thought was to believe — or Li'l Jim was to be made gone beaver because of his attentiveness to Hannah.

Trouble was, Train loved Hannah so desperately that he could not contemplate not fearing for Hannah whenever trouble arose, which it did with infuriating regularity. And Train was certain he could not change.

"It ain't just you, ya know," Hannah said, sure that she knew what Train was thinking. When Train glanced at her, she continued. "When I saw you take that arrow the other day, I was gonna head for you right off. Wasn't for Nathaniel, who grabbed me by the scruff of the neck and held me back, ain't no tellin' what might've happened."

"That was damn foolish," Train said with a grimace. "It wasn't that bad and I can take care of myself."

"So can I. Doesn't mean I don't fret extra when you're in danger."

"So what do we do?" Train's voice was almost anguished.

"I ain't sure."

"But we gotta do somethin' about this, Hannah. It'd like to kill me was I to disappoint Nathaniel." Next to his worry about Hannah getting killed — or captured by the Blackfeet again — his greatest fear was letting Squire down.

"I ain't ever thought of it that way but it's true. Disappointin' Nathaniel would be worse than death. Worse even than bein' took by Elk Horn again. It'd be downright shameful."

They sat in silence for some minutes before Hannah

said, "We just best try hard as we can to do what Nathaniel says. Ain't nothin' else can be done."

———

Squire sat at the fire outside Sky Hawk's lodge. The old chief look considerably hungover but seemed to be handling it well despite his age. Four Horses and several other warriors showed up and plopped down around the blaze. All but one — a large, particularly unhandsome and unpleasant Lakota – exchanged greetings.

Sky Hawk's three wives began handing around bowls of buffalo stew and mugs of coffee sweetened with a supply of sugar Squire had provided.

Li'l Jim slumped up looking sour and sat next to Squire who looked at him and grinned. "No luck riddin' yourself of one of them damn squaws, that be it, lad?"

"Damn Lakota," Li'l Jim partially spit out. "Don't want Snakes for wives. Maybe for slaves but not for sharin' the robes."

"Could've told ye Lakota and Snakes be enemies."

"Then why in hell didn't you, dammit?"

Squire laughed. "Figured you'd be findin' out soon enough."

"Bah." Li'l Jim was polite enough, however, to nod thanks to the woman who handed him food and drink.

As they ate, Train and Hannah wandered up. The latter sat on Squire's left, the former on Hannah's left. They too began to eat.

Before long, the ugly Lakota pointed at Hannah. "Why white woman dress like man?"

"She be a half breed," Squire said easily but with some bite to his voice.

The man shrugged. "She still dress like man."

"She be a warrior, lad. Ain't no rule says a woman can't be one."

"She too small. She can't fight. I teach lesson: Women not warriors. I teach. She go back to being squaw. Be wife — if someone wants stick woman."

Squire sensed both Hannah and Train ready to rise, and muttered, "Stay put." Hannah looked at the big warrior. "She be named *Ohitekah Winyan* — Fierce Woman, like a she-wolf."

The warrior barked a harsh laugh. "More like *Itukala* — Mouse."

Hannah started to rise but Squire grabbed her arm and pulled her back down. "You be a purty big *fils de salaud*. It gonna be makin' ye feel bigger to take on someone so small? How about Li'l Jim here. He be about the same size as this warrior woman. Ye feel the need to take him on?"

"No. He warrior, not woman. Teach her not to pretend."

"Ye be a walkin' pile of shit, hoss. That your warrior name? Pile of Shit?"

The man's face got even uglier. "I am *Inyan Mato* — Stone Bear." He thumped his chest.

Squire grinned disrespectfully at him. "Ye be a disrespectful piece of coyote dung, boy." He paused, knowing the others were watching with interest. Squire could see little sympathy in the others' eyes for Stone Bear. "Tell you what, hoss, how about ye come agin someone a wee bit closer to your size. Say young Abner there." He nodded at Train. "Or me."

"No. Woman."

"Shit. You so scared that the only chil' ye be willin' to fight is a woman ain't half your size? Seems like ain't much of a man. Like as not, ye ain't got nothing 'tween your legs. 'Leastways nothin' manly."

The other warriors laughed and made a number of rude comments only some of which Squire understood, and which only made Stone Bear angrier.

"How 'bout this. Ye go agin Abner there and if ye win,

ye can have a go at the woman." Next to him, Hannah gasped.

"If ye lose," Hannah shrugged, "well, it be up to Sky Hawk and the others what your punishment be."

"Why would my friends punish me?"

Squire laughed. "From what I be seein', boy, ye don't have any friends here. And they be likely to punish ye for disrespectin' guests in your village."

There were nods all around and murmurs of approval.

"So what's it gonna be, lad?"

"I fight him. Then I take woman."

"Ain't goddamn likely."

Everyone rose and headed for a clear spot. As Hannah and Squire rose, Train said, "Have you gone mad, Nathaniel? Offerin' Hannah to him if I lose?"

"You be aimin' to lose?"

"Hell no. But ..."

"Stop it, Abner," Hannah said quietly. She was worried but her voice was calm. "Nathaniel and I got a heap of faith in ya. Just make sure ya whomp him good." She gave out a nervous giggle.

"Hush now, girl," Squire said. Then to Train, "Don't

be 'foolin' with that chil'. He be big and he be an experienced warrior. Take him down as quick and neat as ye can. Ye remember our first meetin'?"

Train nodded, shuddering at the thought of the punch Squire had hit him with. It was like being kicked by a mule.

"Try'n do the same to him. Don't be givin' him no opportunities but if ye be getting a chance to thump him right good, do so. It'll be endin' this fight right quick."

"I'll see what I can do." He sounded nervous.

"We talked about this just last night, Abner," Hannah said. "Don't ya go worryin' about me and what might happen if ya lose. I ain't a-scared of it. Just put your mind to the task at hand. You go worryin' about me and you'll get yourself killed."

Train stopped and looked at her. Hannah smiled a little and nodded.

People from all over the village had heard and were hurrying up, wanting a good vantage point for the excitement. They formed a ring in which the combatants were to go at each other.

Just inside the ring, Train handed his pistols, knife and tomahawk to Squire. Train pulled off his shirt and gave it to Hannah. He flexed his large, muscular shoulders, ignoring the scratch from the slight arrow wound. He turned and saw Stone Bear partially crouched, holding a knife in one hand and a stone war club in the other.

Sky Hawk spoke sharply and Stone Bear looked angrily at him before tossing away his weapons. Then he charged. Train, momentarily surprised, rushed at his enemy. They slammed together, eliciting a grunt from each.

The two men grappled, each trying to find a purchase on the other's sweat-covered body and gain an edge to toss his opponent to the ground.

Stone Bear suddenly jerked an arm off of Train and swung a forearm at Train's chin. With the Indian's one hand off him, Train was a little off balance and managed to keep out of the way of the warrior's forearm. But it still jolted him when it swiped across his chin

With his two hands still on Stone Bear, he flung the Lakota to the ground. Train paused, breathing hard already, taking a moment to get his breath.

Stone Bear, furious, surged up and at Train again. But the young mountain man was prepared this time. Instead of latching onto the Indian's shoulders as before, he waited an extra second, ducked, and slammed a shoulder into Stone Bear's midsection. Train pushed up and shoved the warrior over his shoulder; Stone Bear landed in the dirt again with a thud. Train spun and went to stomp on Stone Bear's chest but the warrior was too fast and rolled out of the way, coming to his feet.

Twice more, Stone Bear charged at Train only to have the white man dance out of the way and shove him to the ground. The warrior was getting winded now and his anger had him acting without thinking.

As Train stood there a moment to let his breathing return to something approaching normal, he became aware for the first time of the hoots and catcalls, whistles and war whoops coming from the assembled Lakota. He wasn't sure they were rooting for him or Stone Bear.

Then a voice cut through the other noise. "End it, lad."

The Lakota charged again and the mountain man waited, then took a short step to his right. Train swung a ham-sized fist with his large, powerful body moving with it. His knuckles slammed against the side of Stone Bear's jaw, smashing the bone, knocking out several teeth and pushing the bottom of the Indian's face an inch or so to the side. The warrior dropped with a muffled groan.

Silence suddenly came over the tribe and Train had the sudden thought that he and the others were about to be slaughtered. Then the chattering began again with a number of yips.

Four Horses walked up to Train. "You do good," he said. "Mighty warrior."

"Obliged. I think." He managed a grin. He was still somewhat behind on his breathing, his chest was sore from the few shots Stone Bear had gotten in, and his knuckles hurt like hellfire. He hoped he had not broken something in his hand.

Four Horses grinned. "Maybe you become Lakota, eh? Fight the Crows and the Blackfeet?"

"Reckon I would make a good Lakota warrior," Train responded, feeling better about himself. "And I've done more'n my share of fightin' Blackfeet. But I reckon I'll stick with ol' *L'on Farouce, Fierce Woman* and the others."

Four Horses laughed. He went to help Sky Hawk to his feet as Squire, Hannah and Li'l Jim joined Train.

"Hannah be right, Abner," Squire said. "Ye done good." Hannah handed her young champion his weapons; she kept his shirt, smiling proudly at him.

Four Horses and Sky Hawk joined them. "I reckon there won't be any trouble with that ol' *fil de puta* considerin' his condition, Sky Hawk. But if there be — from him or any of his friends, if he be havin' any — they'll be made wolf bait of."

"There be no trouble," the old chief said.

"*Bon.*" He grinned. "Now let's get back to feedin'. This chil's meatbag ain't but half full, maybe."

You stay longer?"

"A night more. We'll be leavin' come dawn."

CHAPTER 10

WITH THE HEAT of a new day rising early, Squire and the others met in Sky Hawk's large lodge the next morning. Four Horses and two other warriors, Eagle and Bull's Tail, both of them grandsons of Sky Hawk, were there. The sides of the tipi were rolled up a couple of feet to let the breeze through.

As they ate, Li'l Jim asked, "I thought the Lakota were mostly against whites. How'd they come to be so friendly toward Nathaniel — and Homer?"

"Many Lakota still unfriendly to the white-eyes," Four Horses said in his stilted, unaccustomed English. "Many others are not. Make friends with white men when first ones come to Lakota land."

"Meriwether Lewis and William Clark," Squire added. They be the first. I was but a boy then."

"Most Oglala — we are Oglala," Four Horses added proudly, "are friends of some white men. Any friends of *L'on Farouche* and Horse Keeper are friends of Oglala."

"How'd that come about?" Hannah asked.

Four Horses smiled and looked at Sky Hawk. "You tell? Or me?"

"No need to tell," the old chief said with dignity.

Four Horses grinned again. "He still ... how to say ...?"

"He be embarrassed, I figure," Squire said. He nodded at Sky Hawk. "No need to be, *mon ami*."

"Tell us, Grandfather," Eagle said in his own language.

"*L'on Farouche* tell," he said gruffly.

Squire grinned. Using a combination of English, French and a smattering of Lakota, translated as necessary by whoever could do so, Squire started: "It were some time ago. This old fart," he nodded at Sky Hawk, eliciting a gasp of shock from the two youngest, though Squire, Four Horses and even Sky Hawk laughed, "was still a strong warrior then, about the age of Four Horses now."

————

"I be with the Missouri Fur Company then, where I had started several years before. It was owned by Monsieur Lisa. But on this trip up the Missouri, Monsieur Lisa had died. Our party be led by Joshua Pilcher. Mostly in those days, we be traders, not trappers, but I knew how to handle traps.

"One day, I went ashore to do a bit of trappin' on my own hook, and to hunt meat for the men."

"Our people," Four Horses interjected, "went northeast to visit and to trade at white man's fort. Did every year. The people were near big river when many Arikara attacked our small hunting party.

"The people fought bravely, especially a warrior

named Badger." He smiled at the confusion on the younger people's faces. "He now called Sky Hawk," he said with something approaching reverence.

"Were you with 'em?" Li'l Jim asked.

Four Horses nodded. "I was a boy, not ready for war, but ready for hunt. But war come."

"He fought well," Sky Hawk said, breaking his silence. "Counted plenty coup. Took a scalp."

"What happened then?" Train asked.

"We began singing our death songs," Four Horses continued. "The end comes, we thought. We would die fearlessly. Just when end seemed near, a whirlwind come. We thought it was what you say is devil, called up by Rees to take the breath from us. But it not devil. Not to us. It was a big white man. Very big white man."

"It was Nathaniel," Hannah said more than asked.

"Aye, lass. It be me. I don't know why I chose the Lakota o'er the Rees but Sky Hawk's people be lookin' like they was getting the worst of things. So I joined in."

"More than join in," Four Horses insisted. "He fought like wild man." He grinned.

"Ah, but 'twas afore I had the name *L'on Farouche*."

"No matter. Without your help, all the Lakota would have gone under." Four Horses glanced over at Sky Hawk.

The old man's eyes were closed but Four Horses knew he was not asleep. He was envisioning the battle. Four Horses did, too:

The battle was filled with dust and war cries, the shouts of warriors, the screeching of wounded and dying men. The Lakota started the battle on the back of their ponies but they were soon being overwhelmed so they dismounted, hoping to use the animals as something of a bulwark against the great numbers of the enemy.

Sky Hawk rammed his lance through a Ree but as the warrior fell, the lance was wrenched from the Lakota's hands. He managed to duck as another Arikara swung a war club at him, and blocked the spear thrust of another with his hardened bull hide shield.

Though Four Horses was still a youth, he suddenly appeared alongside Sky Hawk, a knife in one hand, tomahawk in the other. He had no shield, as he had not yet been to war. Sky Hawk glanced at him and saw the fierce determination on the youth's face. But there was no fear.

The two fought back to back as what seemed an unending wave of enemy warriors slammed against them. Sweat formed on their faces and ran down their sides and backs. Weariness began to make their arms sluggish. Dust choked them and clouded their eyes. But still they fought on.

"Get on a pony," Sky Hawk managed to gasp. "Go. Run. Warn our people."

"I will not leave!" Four Horses retorted. "I stay ..." The stone head of a war club grazed his shoulder and he gasped with the sharp pain though the blow had not been that hard. It only made him more determined to die valiantly.

"Fool!" Sky Hawk muttered but he was proud of the young teenager. He was certain now the end was only minutes away.

Suddenly from out of the dust came ... just what he wasn't sure at first. Then it showed itself to be a man. At least it had the shape of a man. But it was wild, ferocious. A demon with a thick beard obscuring much of his face, a rifle slung across his back and wielding a tomahawk.

A splash of cold fear splattered through Sky Hawk's insides as this raving beast appeared before him, weapon raised in hand. The man stopped before swinging the 'hawk. He nodded once and was gone. But Sky Hawk could hear his bellows of rage as he disappeared into the thick of the dust cloud.

Sky Hawk and Four Horses fended off a couple more attacks but after a few minutes, they were alone. The dust began to settle and the noise dwindled. When he could see clearly again, Sky Hawk was astonished. Arikara bodies were strewn about, a good many of them. All four others who had been with Four Horses and Sky Hawk were down, wounded, one badly but not dead.

Once again, the giant appeared before them but, this time, his weapon was not to be seen. Nor did he seem so fierce. He stepped over the several bodies piled in front of the two Lakota. "Ye be all right, lads?" he asked, his voice a rumble that fit his huge body.

"Yes. Think maybe." He looked at Four Horses for confirmation of the youth's condition. Four Horses nodded.

"Good. Ye be needin' help getting your friends back to your people?"

Sky Hawk shook his head.

Squire nodded. Then he grinned. "Ye want these scalps?"

Sky Hawk's eyes widened in surprise. Then he smiled widely. "Yes. Good. We take."

"Well, be havin' at it, Chief. But I reckon ye ought to be seein' to your friends there first. I'll try to round up some ponies." He looked around. "Ye be a mighty warrior, Chief. You, too, lad," he said, nodding to Four Horses. The two Lakota had killed at least five enemy warriors.

The boy beamed.

The Lakota ponies had wandered back to the vicinity and a number of Arikara horses had followed. Squire had little trouble herding them toward where the Lakota were just finishing up their grisly trophy collecting.

"How be your friends?" Squire asked.

"Hurt. One bad. Others only little."

"Well, Chief ..."

"I not chief."

Squire wasn't sure the Lakota was angry at the notion or just apprising him of the truth.

"Don't ye worry none. You'll be one. I be certain of that. 'Sides, ye be leadin' this here party. That makes ye a chief for now." He turned to walk away, but stopped.

"Where you go?"

"Back to the boat. Reckon there won't be much trappin' here now. I'll do a bit of huntin' on the way."

"Where your horse?"

"Got none. No horses be on the boat."

"You walk?"

"Aye."

"Not good for warrior to walk. You take a horse."

Squire laughed. "Ain't a one of these ponies be able to hold a man big's me."

"Maybe you take two. Ride 'em together," Sky Hawk said, then burst into laughter, too.

"Doubt that'd work, Chief. But thank ye for the offer."

"Take horse to carry meat. Maybe two to ride. One a little, then change. Ride a little, change."

"That be temptin'," Squire allowed. "But I got nothin' to do with the horse once I get back to the boat. I don't want to let it go." He grinned. "Might get stole by some other thievin' warriors."

"I go," Four Horses said suddenly. "I bring ponies back."

"Ain't ye afraid?"

Four Horses pulled himself up a bit straighter. "I am Lakota."

"What ye be sayin' about this, Chief? By the way, what be your name?"

"Badger." Sky Hawk thought that over for some moments, then spoke quietly to the youth in his own language, little of which Squire understood. Then the warrior nodded. "He go. Take two ponies for you to ride, one for meat. He ride another."

"Reckon that'll do. All right, lad ... what be your name?"

"Small Hand."

"All right, Small Hand, pick us out some ponies."

A few minutes later, Squire skeptically looked at a pair of short, powerful ponies, both some shade of muddy gray. "This horse ain't gonna like it none when I climb on him," Squire muttered.

"No matter. He can't throw you," Sky Hawk said with another laugh.

"Reckon that be true." Squire grinned. He went to get on the animal but it skittered off to the side. "Damn horse," he snapped. The more he tried to mount the saddleless animal, the more it tried to get away. It did not improve his suddenly sour humor when the Lakota, including the wounded ones, laughed.

Finally Sky Hawk eased Squire's annoyance. "We mount from other side," he said, still laughing.

"Damn, ye could've told me that before I made a fool

of myself." He ducked under the horse's neck and leaped easily onto the animal's' back. His good humor returned.

They stopped once and Squire shot two buffalo. With Small Hand's help, they butchered out the ribs, hump meat and fleece, liver and tongue from each as well as more meat as they thought the horses — Squire had decided to forgo switching horses and use the extra one as a pack animal — could carry.

They finally caught up to the boat, which pulled to the bank where the meat was unloaded. The traders on the boat looked in surprise at Small Hand and the ponies but said nothing.

When they were done, Squire gave Small Hand one of the tongues. "You be watchful on your way back, boy."

"Yes." He paused, then said, "Badger says you come to village. North of river you call Platte, near mouth of Loup."

"If I ever get out that way, I'll be certain to do so, lad. Now ye best be on your way."

With a whoop and a holler, Small Hand trotted off, herding the extra horses before him.

———

Eagle and Bull's Tail looked both awed and dubious. Seeing it, Li'l Jim said, "I don't know if all them particulars are true, boys, but I've fought alongside Nathaniel and when it comes to fightin', he deserves the name *L'on Farouche*. Just ask the goddamn Blackfeet."

Both boys looked at Four Horses who nodded. "It's true," he said in Lakota. He turned to look at Squire. "Blackfeet may be dealing with American Fur Company."

"Not Hudson Bay?"

"Still them. But move toward Americans. Still not much, but some."

"Shit," Squire muttered. He sighed. "Well, it be no matter to this chil' who those red devils be tradin' with. Any of 'em — or the American Fur boys — get in my way, they'll be payin' a hard price for doin' so."

CHAPTER 11

"ABNER!" Squire bellowed. When the young man trotted up, the giant said, "Go out and find Li'l Jim."

"You think something's wrong?"

"Can't be certain. But he's been gone a heap longer'n usual on a hunt."

"Could be that the buffler are farther away than usual."

"Aye, that could be. It could also be that some Crows or Blackfeet come upon him and raised his hair. But knowin' that scamp, he could be out there takin' a nap. You find he be doin' so, grab that little son of a bitch by the hair and haul his festerin' carcass back here right quick."

"Yessir." Train needed no other encouragement. He dug his heels into his horse's sides and galloped off. He had a general idea of where the buffalo were and he could, even at this speed, catch a glimpse of the prints from Li'l Jim's horse and the pack mule.

He found the sprawling herd in half an hour or so but he could see no sign of his friend. Whatever prints there had been were wiped out as the shaggy beasts had moved slowly across the landscape, grazing unhurriedly.

Train began checking small hillocks and buffalo wallows, looking for one where Li'l Jim would've put his horse and mule while shooting a buffalo or two. Near the top of a little ridge, he found sign that Li'l Jim had been there, lying along the top. But neither Li'l Jim nor the animals were there.

"Damn," Train breathed as he stopped on the ridge and looked around. He saw plenty of bison but no horse or mule. And certainly no Li'l Jim. He pushed forward, walking his horse in a line he thought would have been Li'l Jim's line of fire. Up and down, he rode slowly across the undulating land, stopping at the tops of the rises to search.

Judging by the sun, it was more than an hour since he left Squire and the others when he spotted a mule amid the herd. He trotted toward it and grabbed the rope that hung around its neck. "All right, mule, where the hell's Li'l Jim?" he muttered in frustration. He was worried now, certain that something had happened to his friend. It could've been Indians, or his horse could've broken a leg and dumped him. He could've been snake bit.

Train rode some more, now in a semicircle, wide and farther with each turn. Four hundred yards or so from where he figured Li'l Jim had made his stand to hunt, Train saw a downed buffalo and, nearby, Li'l Jim's animal. He kicked his horse and they raced there. Train stopped in a flurry of dust and was off his horse before it had fully stopped. The buffalo was dead, two bullet holes in it that Train could see. He stood on the carcass. A few yards behind the dead buffalo lay Li'l Jim.

"Oh, sweet jumpin' Jesus," Train muttered as he ran

toward his friend. He knelt at Li'l Jim's side. The young man was in bad shape, one side covered with blood. He moaned and Train breathed a small sigh of relief. At least Li'l Jim was alive. How long he would stay that way was another question.

He continued to kneel there, wondering what he should do. He knew he had to get Li'l Jim back to the others where Squire or Star Path might be able to do something for him. But there was a very good chance that trying to get him there would kill him or, perhaps with the pain, having him wish he were dead. But there was no choice, he knew. It was either try to get him back to the others or let him die out here.

Train rose and got Li'l Jim's horse, which had not wandered far, and brought it back. He took the horsehair rope hanging from the saddle horn and tossed it to the ground. He knelt beside his friend again.

"Can you hear me, Li'l Jim?" he asked urgently.

"Yuh," the young man managed.

"I got to get you back to Nathaniel and the others."

"Nuh. Die here."

"Like hell, I ain't lettin' you die without tryin' to get you fixed up."

"All broke up inside." The words were choked and filled with pain.

"Reckon you are. But you're one tough little critter. Or so you always said." He was pleased when the ghost of a smile flickered across Li'l Jim's face for a heartbeat.

"I gotta be honest with you, boy," Train said. "I reckon it's gonna hurt like hellfire a dozen times over but I got to get you on your horse somehow."

"You carry."

"Don't think I can do that. The jouncin'll hurt all the more."

"Saddle too."

Train thought a bit more. Then he rose and got Li'l Jim's sleeping robe and lay it next to his friend. "Can you put your arms up over your head?"

Li'l Jim did so, gasping.

"That's good, boy." Train spread the robe out. "Get ready, hoss, this ain't gonna be fun."

Li'l Jim looked up at him in fear for a moment, then weakly nodded.

Train grabbed him by the side and rolled him as fast as he could into the robe. Li'l Jim screamed and it made Train wince with the pain he was causing his best friend. He finally had Li'l Jim rolled up on the robe like a papoose. He waited a minute, letting Li'l Jim calm down as much as he could. Then he easily lifted the wounded man and gently placed him face down across the saddle. He tied him there with the rope going under the horse's belly.

"You look pretty good that way, hoss," Train said, trying to sound a bit jovial, hoping it might ease Li'l Jim even a tiny amount.

"Piss on you," Li'l Jim managed to squawk. "Go."

Train mounted up and, with Li'l Jim's horse in tow, galloped off, leaving the mule behind.

———

"Abner's comim'," Hannah said. "But I don't see Li'l Jim. That's his horse, though."

"Aye. But Li'l Jim's across his saddle."

"Oh, Lord," Hannah gasped, panicked and close to tears. "Injuns got him."

"We'll see, lass. We'll see." He couldn't quite keep the worry out of his voice though Hannah didn't hear it.

Train pulled to a stop in front of the two. "Li'l Jim's hurt bad," he said.

"Injuns?" Squire asked, walking to Li'l Jim's horse.

"Don't seem so."

Squire gently lifted Li'l Jim's head and shook his own. "Damn, you be in plumb bad shape, lad," he muttered.

"I know," Li'l Jim groaned weakly.

Squire almost smiled. If Li'l Jim could joke when he was in such poor condition, he might just have a chance. "Hannah!" he snapped, "head on up the river a ways. Should be a fair good place to be stayin' a spell maybe a mile or two. We'll be followin' along a heap slower."

Star Path hurriedly waddled up and saw Li'l Jim. "He will need my help," she announced. "A'ner, you come help."

Train glanced at Squire. "Don't be lookin' at me, lad. Just do what she be tellin' ye."

Within minutes, Star Path, Train and the two other women had the travois unloaded. Train packed what he could on the mules, almost overloading them. He did not care. The rest he tossed aside. If they needed it, he would come back and gather it up.

Squire watched the activity, waiting, unconsciously stroking Li'l Jim's hair. When the others were done, Squire untied Li'l Jim and lifted him as if he weighed no more than a leaf. Li'l Jim groaned, then managed "Hot."

"Got to be keepin' ye wrapped up, lad," Squire said

quietly. "Be protectin' your ribs some. We ain't got far to go, then we'll unwrap ye." Li'l Jim's eyelids flickered a bit and Squire didn't know if that meant yes or no or was just from the pain. He carried the young man to the travois and set him gently down on it. He and Train tied Li'l Jim to the travois around the feet and under the arms.

Then they headed out, moving very slowly. After a few minutes, Train asked, "Wouldn't it be best to move some faster, Nathaniel? Get to where we're going faster so we can care for Li'l Jim?"

"He's been jostled enough with that ride you made getting him here." He shook his head at Train's sudden look of self-loathing. "Ye did well, lad. It was best to be getting him here. But now we go easy."

Before long, Hannah galloped up. "Found us a place. Half a mile or so."

"What took ye so long?"

"Went a bit farther on tryin' to find a better spot but first one I found is best."

"*Bon.*"

They picked up the pace just a bit, with Hannah leading the way. After what seemed like an eternity, they reached a pleasant stretch of riverbank with a grove of cottonwoods, some hackberry and chokecherry bushes and a small, clear path to the water.

With efficiency born of practice, Star Path, Cloudy Moon and Fox Woman set up camp with a minimum of fuss. Squire and Train untied Li'l Jim and unwrapped him, then lay him on the blankets. With his knife, Squire sliced open the front of the youth's shirt.

Next to him, Hannah and Train gasped. "Damn," the former muttered.

"Aye, lass. It be bad for certain and ain't no use in

sayin' nay to it." He touched Li'l Jim's side above the nasty looking wound that was still seeping blood. Li'l Jim sucked in a hissing breath and groaned. "Sorry, lad." He touched the other side which elicited a much smaller indication of pain. "Looks like a buff'lo got him but good. Gored him, as you can see. Must've butted him and stove up some ribs."

"Can we fix him?" Train asked, his worry deep.

"Ain't certain. He be in bad shape. We can be patchin' up that hole. It ain't that large. Them ribs have to be healin' on their own. We can bind 'em up maybe. My biggest worry be about what happened inside him. If something in there got tore up, ain't much we can do."

Star Path waddled up, a buckskin bag in hand. Squire looked up and nodded. To Hannah and Train, he said, "Ye two best be findin' yourselves something to be doin'. See to the horses and mules. Maybe go back and get anything we left behind that we might be needin'. First, bring o'er one of them jugs."

Both nodded and headed off.

Star Path knelt on the opposite side of Li'l Jim from Squire. "We sew up first?" she asked.

"Aye." He took the jug of whiskey Train handed him. The big young man stood there a moment, sick at his friend's condition. Then he turned and hurried off.

"Ye got to be drinkin' some of this, boy," Squire said as he lifted Li'l Jim's head with one massive arm. With the other hand, he poured some whiskey down Li'l Jim's throat.

Li'l Jim coughed, then groaned. "Hurts," he gasped.

"I know, lad. Take some more though." He poured a little more slowly so as not to gag Li'l Jim. It did not take much before the young man was out. Squire set the jug aside and nodded at Star Path. She had a large, sharp, curved needle threaded with sinew.

With Squire holding the ragged edges of the wound together, Star Path swiftly and expertly stitched up the hole as if she were adding beads to her dress.

When she was done, she made up a poultice and slathered it on the wound. She called out to Fox Woman who hurried over, worried to death about her husband, and handed Star Path a long strip of cloth.

Squire and Star Path carefully wrapped the cloth around Li'l Jim, covering the poultice and ribs. Then they sat back.

"Reckon it be up to the Great Spirit now."

"He'll be all right," Star Path said with a nod. "Yes, I think so."

"I hope ye be right, woman."

CHAPTER 12

"You think Li'l Jim'll be all right?" Hannah asked.

Squire had never heard her so shaken and uncertain. "Can't say, lass. Depends how stove up he is inside. He be a strong cuss, that chil'. Mighty determined, too. Still, ain't but so much a body can be doin' when it's been through something so bad. But Star Path says he will." He stretched out his long legs and accepted a refill of coffee Star Path offered him.

"'Course, ol' Hugh was tore up even more'n Li'l Jim be and he made out all right. Certain he did."

"Anything we can do?" Abner asked.

"Mostly I be needin' one of ye to stick close to him most times. Dose him with awardenty now and agin if he needs it. Be helpin' Star Path with whate'er she needs to do to doctor him. If he starts sufferin' too much, come and get Star Path."

"What do we do about them?" Abner asked, nodding toward Cloudy Moon and Fox Woman.

Squire glanced over at the two young women. Li'l

Jim's wives seemed even more forlorn than Abner and Hannah. "Let 'em sit by Li'l Jim if they ain't needed elsewhere. Just don't let 'em go annoyin' him. He needs rest and quiet whilst his body tries to heal."

"I never thought they'd care for him so much," Hannah said.

"Reckon there be no tellin' with women," Squire said, then looked hurt at the hard glance both Hannah and Star Path threw at him. "Well, it be true, dammit," he said just a bit defensively. He stood. "Someone best go out and make meat," he grumbled. "Ye be takin' good care of Li'l Jim. I'll be back before long."

He saddled *Noir Astre* and rode out, towing a mule behind him. Before long, he found the slowly wandering herd. He headed along their back trail and found dead animals, both shot. The second one had blood on one horn. He was a little surprised to see that it was a bull but he figured Li'l Jim had wanted the animal's tough hide for some new trousers or such.

"So ye be the *fils de pute* who tried to put ol' Li'l Jim's lights out. Damn if I didn't wish I could be countin' coup of ye. But since ye be wolf bait already, 'least I can do is be takin' some prizes from ye." He cut out the horns and then the scrotum.

He stuck them in a bag from the packsaddle on the mule, then drifted back the way he had come in the wake of the herd.

He dropped two cows and packed as much of the good meat as he could on the mule and headed back to camp. Hannah and Abner hurried up and began unloading the meat. The two Shoshone women were sitting by Li'l Jim's side looking as mournful as Squire had ever seen anyone. He handed the bull's horns and scrotum to Star Path with a short bob of the head toward Li'l Jim.

Star Path nodded.

———

As the days passed slowly by, Star Path changed the poultice frequently. Every other day, either Squire or Abner or Hannah would go out and make meat. Cloudy Moon and Fox Woman rarely left Li'l Jim's side. It annoyed Squire at first since they did little around the camp. One day, he stomped up to them.

"Ye women best be getting back to your chores. Star Path be needin' your help. Big as she is with chil', she can't do as much as usual. Now git."

But it had minimal effect. They desultorily did some chores, then edged their way back to Li'l Jim's side. Squire finally gave up when Star Path told him, "Let 'em be. They little help anyway. They leave A'ner and Little Flower to do things, not sit by their friend."

"Reckon you be right, woman, as you usually are about such things." He smiled at her.

She smiled back but Squire could see tiredness in her face. He wondered how long it would be before she gave birth. He had no idea about such things. That was women's burden. But he was concerned for her.

The days passed slowly in that Li'l Jim seemed to be making little progress, but quickly in that they were stuck here instead of making their way to the hunting grounds. And the fall would be here before long and hard winter soon after that. But there was nothing could be done about it.

After the first couple of days that Squire went hunting, he said to Train and Hannah at the night's fire, "I've seen beaver sign. Not much, but I reckon it be enough to do some trappin'. I want ye both to go on out tomorrow and be settin' your traps. There's a pond the beaver made about half a mile southwest that should be fruitful."

Both nodded. "You'll be all right here by yourself?" Hannah asked.

Squire offered a small smile. "What do ye think, girl?"

"Well, I ain't sure. We been protectin' ya for a long time now. I ain't sure you're ready yet to be left on your own," she said with a laugh.

"Waugh! Ye be a tryin' woman, lass." He grinned at her and paused to light his pipe. "Now ye mind ye be watchful out there. I seen no Injun sign less'n a week old out there but ye ne'er can tell that there won't be some comin' through. Ye see any, ye hightail it back here straight off if ye can be doin' so. Leave the traps if ye have to."

The next morning, the two rode out. Squire and Star Path practically had to shove the two Shoshone women out of the way so they could look at Li'l Jim.

"He be feverish," Squire said, rather uselessly.

"He be." Star Path gingerly pulled off the bandaging and poultice. "No smell," she said.

"That be good."

"Yes, but fever worries me."

"Anything ye can do?"

"Maybe yes. Need willow bark. And yucca root. You know how to find?"

"Willow be easy. I ain't so certain about yucca though I reckon it be plentiful enough. I'll be findin' some, don't ye fret." He paused. "You gonna be all right here by yourself?"

"Yes. Cloudy Moon and Fox Woman be here. They help."

"They ain't been of much use since Li'l Jim got hurt," Squire said, half in annoyance, half in amusement.

Star Path smiled. "I be all right."

He returned her smile. "I should ne'er have asked. Well, I'll be havin' another cup of coffee before headin' out."

As he had thought, finding willow was easy. There was plenty of it along the river. Yucca was harder but he managed to dig up several roots and hoped it would be enough. Star Path seemed pleased so he figured all was well. He grabbed a piece of cloth cut from one of the bolts to be used as trade goods. Then he went and knelt next to Li'l Jim. He handed the cloth to Cloudy Woman. "Go and wet this in the river."

Looking a bit fearful, the woman took the cloth and hurried toward the water. She returned quickly with a sopping cloth.

"Bathe his face and head with it," Squire said. When the woman seemed not to understand, Squire took the cloth and showed her. She nodded and took over the task. At one point, he lightly took her hand and used it to gently squeeze some water onto Li'l Jim's dry lips.

Squire soon handed the cloth to Fox Woman and had her go through the ritual. By then, Star Path had returned and shooed the other women away. "Must make him drink," she said, holding out a tin cup.

Squire nodded and lifted the top half of Li'l Jim so he was bent at the waist. Star Path brought the cup to the young man's lips and dribbled it a few drops at a time. Li'l Jim managed to lick a little in and then opened his mouth a tad so some of the liquid could run inside.

He swallowed small portions of it and Star Path sat back.

The Lakota woman handed the bandages to Fox Woman and said a few words to her in Shoshone; the younger woman ran down to the river and began washing the bandages. With another wet cloth, Star Path gently washed away the dregs of the old poultice.

With a horn spoon, she slathered on more poultice material of yucca, then re-bandaged the wound when Fox Woman returned with the clean wrappings.

Abner and Hannah rode back in before much longer. "How's Li'l Jim?" Abner asked as he dismounted.

"He be about the same," Squire said. "Wound don't look too bad but he's feverish. Star Path's usin' a new poultice and has a concoction to break the fever."

The couple took care of their horses and then sat at the fire and poured themselves coffee. "Beaver sign looks good, Nathaniel," Abner said. "Might not get the best plews out of it but it'll be some and they should be good enough."

"Ye be soundin' worried, lad," Squire said.

"Worried about Li'l Jim."

"There be more."

"Reckon I'm concerned about the season. We got us a ways to go yet and ..."

"We'll be reachin' trappin' country in time to make a good hunt."

"Reckon you're right. It's just that with Li'l Jim layin' there all busted up ..."

"Star Path be takin' good care of that chil'."

Squire went hunting soon after and returned, as always in buffalo country, with plenty of fresh meat.

When he handed the meat to Star Path, he went to look over Li'l Jim. The young man seemed to be resting fairly well though he still had a fever.

"Star Path's been dosin' him regular with that willow bark brew," Hannah said. "I ain't sure it's workin' but I reckon it ain't doin' any harm neither."

"She be knowin' what she's doin'."

———

Two days later, Li'l Jim's fever broke and the day after that, he even awoke. Squire and Star Path hurried over, kneeling on opposite sides of the injured man after shoving Cloudy Moon and Fox Woman out of the way lest they smother him. "It be about time you woke, lad," Squire said gruffly.

"Needed a nap," Li'l Jim croaked.

"Always knew ye to be a lazy ol' chil'. Always be sleepin' when the rest of us be workin'."

"Shush now," Star Path ordered. She took the bandages off. "How you feel?"

"Shinin'."

"You lie," Star Path said. She was not one to brook any nonsense at a time like this.

"Hurts like the devil."

"It be getting better," Star Path said. "No sign of badness. No more fever."

"Good."

Star Path poulticed the wound and rewrapped him in bandages again. "You sleep more."

"Supposin' I don't want to," Li'l Jim said weakly with a wan smile.

"I can be makin' certain," Squire said, holding up a massive fist but grinning.

Before he could make a retort as was his wont, Li'l Jim was asleep again.

CHAPTER 13

It took two more weeks but finally Li'l Jim was up and about. He shuffled around like an old man with rheumatism but he was ambulatory.

He rode out of camp with Abner and Hannah a couple of times, not doing any trapping but just to get away and try to build up his strength. As they had all thought, there was fair trapping in the area though it petered out pretty quickly. Still, they had the beginnings of the season's catch.

It was yet two more weeks before Li'l Jim thought he was ready to go.

"Ye be certain, lad?" Squire asked, looking hard into Li'l Jim's eyes.

"I am. I might not be as spry as I was but I'm strong enough, I reckon. "'Sides, by my reckonin', even though I was out a spell, I figure winter ain't far off. You can feel it already."

"Ye be right on that."

"Nathaniel, I ain't fully myself agin, I know that. But we been held up long enough because of my damn foolishness. I can't hold y'all up any longer. If I can't keep up, leave me behind. I'll be following the best I can."

"We ain't leavin' you behind," Hannah snapped.

"She be right."

"Well, then let's cut some dust. And if I can't keep up, tie me to my saddle and drag my horse along with the mules." He grinned, some of Li'l Jim's cockiness returning.

"I might just be doin' that anyway," Squire said with a laugh. "That'd plumb shine with this ol' coon."

"Don't you dare do such a goddamn thing, Nathaniel Squire, you overgrowed ox."

"Reckon I won't," Squire allowed. "Be too much for this ol' chil' to listen to ye caterwaulin'. Scare the horses and mules. Hell, even scare off the buff'lo so's we be havin' nothin' to fill our meatbags."

"Then quit flappin' your lips and let's light out, you ol' fart."

"Must be better," Train said sotto voce, eliciting a laugh all around.

They pushed hard but often stopped early. Li'l Jim didn't complain but he was exhausted each evening when they stopped and was often asleep well before the others. Gradually, though, he gained in strength until, three weeks out, he was ready to start hunting again.

"Be takin' Abner with ye," Squire said.

"Reckon I got to be doin' this myself, Nathaniel. Don't you go frettin' about this ol' coon."

"I ain't frettin' about ye, boy. I be concerned with the others. We got no more time to be nursemaidin' ye."

"I don't expect you to, Nathaniel. But I don't need him nursemaidin' me out there neither. I don't come back,

I'll be gone beaver and you can just move on without me. But I don't need someone with me."

The hint of a smile cracked Squire's thick beard and mustache. Li'l Jim was indeed back to himself, at least mentally. Physically, they would soon see. "All right, lad, ye be on your own."

As Li'l Jim forked his horse, he said, "And don't go sendin' Abner or Hannah to come followin' me as if lookin' for Injun sign."

Squire nodded.

"You really gonna be lettin' him go off on his own?" Train asked.

"Aye. 'Tis what he be wantin' — and needin'."

"Ain't you worried about him?"

"Nay. He be ... Li'l Jim." Squire laughed.

Train wasn't so sure but he figured Squire knew best.

———

Li'l Jim felt a little odd being out there alone. He wanted to be — needed to be. But it was somewhat disconcerting nonetheless.

He sat on his horse on a ridge looking out over the scattered herd of buffalo grazing placidly in the warm afternoon sun. He was the least bit reluctant to move closer but he was content for the moment to sit there and watch the great shaggy beasts.

Suddenly, he smiled at the thought of how he had come to be here — a mountain man, expert shot, seasoned Indian fighter.

———

James Ambrose Hawkesworthy — and Squire was the only one of the group who knew that name — had been born into the wealthy Hawkesworthy family of Boston. The family's Beacon Hill home was filled with expensive furniture as well as antiques, most of them passed down from generation to generation in the family. The house that fronted on a narrow cobblestone street was plenty big enough to accommodate the frequent, often large, gatherings of the city's elite.

Young James had all the luxuries a child could want but one. His father was distant and his mother cold; both were stern and had little time for youngsters. As an only child, James was left on his own for much of the time though he had a nanny who watched over him. Still, there were few and infrequent friends to play with and it taught him even at a very young age to be rather independent.

When he was eight, James's father put the boy in his carriage and climbed in after him.

"Where're we going, Father?" James asked. He was full of wonder. This had never happened.

"You will see." The father shook open a newspaper and started to read.

They soon arrived in front of a small brownstone building. Fancy carriages lined the street and children from James's age to teenagers were walking into the building.

Edward Hawkesworthy climbed out of the vehicle and started walking toward the building. The driver helped James down and the two followed Hawkesworthy. The father stopped in front of a stern-looking man dressed in a suit that was as severe looking as he was.

"James," Hawkesworthy said, "this is Master Teagarden. He is in charge of this school."

Scared, James could only mumble, "Hello, Master Teagarden."

"You've learned all you can, I believe, from the governess Miss Walter. So you will be attending this first rate primary school daily," Hawkesworthy said. "Charles will drive you each morning and pick you up each afternoon. You will obey Master Teagarden as you do me. Is that understood?"

"Yes, Father." James was confused, unsure of what to do or how to act.

Edward turned on his heel and, with Charles, walked away. James watched, worried though not particularly sad, as the carriage drove away.

"Inside, young man," Teagarden ordered. His voice was as cold as a Boston winter.

Terrified, the boy complied. He became more so a month later when he was caught talking during class and was paddled for his disobedience. When he tearfully told his father about it that evening, he was scolded by both parents.

There was no real thought on the boy's part — he was too young for that — but over the next year, a resistance to those in authority began to seep into him and he grew defiant bit by bit. That increased the frequency and somewhat the intensity of his punishments. And before the next school year ended, the now almost-ten-year-old James was expelled.

James's father was mortified. This tainted his reputation and that was foremost in the mind of Edward Hawkesworthy and his wife. For much of the next year, he kept James's freedom to a minimum. And when another school term was to begin, James was dropped off at another fancy education facility ruled by a master who was even harsher.

But even as young as he was, James was beginning to channel his defiance and with it came the first vestiges of cockiness. It did not take long either before James was expelled from that school.

In disgust, Hawkesworthy delivered his son — with a small valise — to the Regis Academy in Salem, a small city northeast of Boston. "This is a boarding school," Hawkesworthy announced. "It means — if you do not know — that you will be staying here rather than returning home each day. You will visit home on holidays — if your mother and I decide to allow it. Otherwise, this will be your home for the next several years."

Despite his age, James was intelligent enough to know to behave himself when he got to the academy. For two years, he almost behaved well, only occasionally getting into scrapes. It was enough to get him mildly punished though not nearly so bad as to get him expelled. But all the while, he was building up his arrogance and his impertinence.

Yet another log on the fire of his brashness came from his size — and the way it meant he was treated by the other boys. Almost all of them, even many of the younger ones, were bigger than he. As a result, he was frequently set upon by some boys. His recklessness often provoked it but the confrontations also toughened him.

He learned one day just how tough he could be when one of the upper-level boys named Lafferty called to him, "Hey, Shrimp, go fetch me some bread from the kitchen." He snickered as did some of his cronies.

"You can't be talking to me, you manure pile," James shot back.

"Watch your mouth, little boy," Lafferty said.

"Or what? You and your gang of skunks going to thrash me?"

"I don't need them," Lafferty said, rising.

James did not hesitate. He simply charged forward, surprising Lafferty, slamming a shoulder into the older boy's stomach, pushing him back until he hit the wall. Lafferty gasped and slid down the wall.

"Leave me alone, pus bucket," James snapped.

Then three of Lafferty's friends jumped on him. He got thumped pretty well but the other boys knew they had been in a fight. Two sported bright shiners while another had a broken nose.

The headmaster was beside himself in anger. "How dare you start such an altercation in my school, Mr. Hawkesworthy."

"I didn't start anything, Headmaster. Lafferty started it. He and the others have been calling me names and picking on me for months now."

"That does not mean you should assault them."

"Headmaster, look at me and at them. Do you think someone as small as me would actually start a fight with four boys as big as them? I may be somewhat rash but I'm not a fool."

"That, young man, is debatable. Now, being the kind-hearted soul that I am," the headmaster said with a straight face, "I will overlook this affray. However, you will perform whatever chores I order you to do for the next two months. I can assure you they will not be pleasant ones."

He did his chores without much complaint and he took the abuse Lafferty and his friends forced on him when they saw him at his menial work. But he stored up to all the insults and the humiliation of his punishment.

Once his penance was done, he decided it was time for some retribution. He was fierce enough but when Lafferty and the others had started to bully him a year or so ago, he had taken up sports which also gave him some strength.

One day, James waited around the corner of a hall, knowing Lafferty would be along soon. When the older boy turned the corner, James pasted him one in the mouth, staggering Lafferty and bloodying his lip. James grabbed him by the shirtfront. "Push me again, you dopey bastard, and this will be just a taste of what I will do to you."

Less than a half-hour later, James was in the headmaster's office. "I see that I was far, far too lenient last time," he said. "Much to my distress, but with no regret, I order you to leave Regis Academy immediately. I will send word on the next express to your father. I'm sure he will be rather dissatisfied about this turn of events."

"No need. I'll tell him myself." James rose. "I can't say it's been a pleasure, Headmaster. And I'm damned glad to be shed of this place." He turned and left.

He had enough money to take a stage back to Boston and to get a room at a nondescript inn. There he sat for a day, pondering his future. The next day, he headed to Beacon Hill. His father would be at work and his mother out with her society friends for some luncheon or other. With his key, he entered the house and, making his way straight to his father's den, he managed to open the safe his father thought was hidden. James took out three hundred dollars, closed the safe, and left the house. Not knowing yet what he was planning to do, he went back to the inn.

The next day he bought some clothes and a valise to carry them in, and a stage ticket to Framingham. At fifteen, he was on his own. When he arrived in Framingham, he did not know what he was to do. He was not used to work so he lazed about mostly, then moved on to Worcester and beyond. He kept traveling, moving from one place to another, eventually buying a horse and learning how to ride it well. He also became adept at coarse language. And he found that he could so some work, eventually hard work.

His arrogance often got him into trouble and he learned to deal with it with his fists. He also bought himself a small single-shot pistol to protect himself.

Even supplemented with money earned at various odd jobs, he eventually began to run low on cash. Down to his last few dollars, he found himself in St. Louis and, soon after, an employee of an outfit managed by Colonel Leander Melton and guided by a giant named Nathaniel Squire.

———

Li'l Jim laughed a little at the absurdity of it all. But thinking back as far as he had come, settled what little uncertainty he had. "C'mon, horse," he muttered, slapping the reins lightly on the animal's neck and headed toward the herd. "We got us some meat to make.

Early fall 1834
Fort Elk Horn

"I come to see Herr Murdock," the coarse-looking man said to a servant.

"I much doubt that Mr. Murdock will want to see the likes of you," the servant said, looking with disdain over the crotchety visitor. Meisner was short and blocky with a thick neck and deep-set dark eyes. He wore buckskin pants and a calico shirt, both encrusted with blood, grease, dirt and sweat. His face and hands were filthy and a scruffy, salt-and-pepper beard covered the bottom half of his face. He emitted a stench that followed him wherever he went.

"Herr McKenzie said to meet him."

"Mr. McKenzie has had some ... shall we say problems ... at Fort Union."

"Tell Herr Murdock it's about Squire."

The servant glared at him for a few moments. "Wait out here." He turned and slammed the door. A few minutes later, he returned. "Mr. Murdock will see you," he said with distaste and some surprise. "But don't go touchin' anything."

Rifle resting in the crook of his left arm, Meisner shuffled inside, again feeling as if he had stepped into another world though not as much as at Fort Union. The bourgeois' house here at Fort Elkhorn was far smaller and less posh than McKenzie's at Fort Union.

Still, Alastair Murdock tried to be more of a fastidious dandy than McKenzie had been. He was waiting in his office, sitting behind his desk. When Meisner entered the room, Murdock rose but he did not offer his hand. He simply nodded to a chair in front of the desk and then sat back down.

Meisner felt a surge of anger. He knew he was not in Murdock's class, and certainly not in McKenzie's, but the latter at least acted civilly toward him despite his looks and wilderness manners. Meisner took an instant disliking to Murdock. In just his first action, he came across as imperious. His attitude, displayed on his face and in his demeanor, was about as warm and friendly as a snake's. Meisner leaned his rifle against the wall next to the door and took his seat. Even that was uncomfortable for a man used to the cold, hard ground for a chair or a bed.

"So, just what have you to tell me, Mr. ... Meisner, is it?"

"Ya. Dot is *mein* name."

Murdock shrugged and leaned back a little, crossing his hands over the frilly front of his snowy white shirt. He offered no sign of friendliness or even interest. "Well?" he asked.

"Did Herr McKenzie tell you?"

"About what?" Murdock's tone was cold, patronizing.

Meisner was used to being condescended to but this man's arrogant attitude grated on him. "You got some coffee?" he asked.

"No. Tell me why you are here. And be quick about it. You are wasting my time and, frankly, your presence is an affront."

"Herr McKenzie offered food and drink ven I come always."

"Mr. McKenzie is not in charge of this post. I am. Now tell me what it is you have to say or I will have you thrown out like the garbage you are."

With difficulty, Meisner stifled the anger that rose up in him. "You know of Nathaniel Squire? Der Blackfeet, dey call him *L'on Farouche*. The vild man. Dot he is for sure. Ya."

"I have heard of this man." Murdock found himself becoming a bit intrigued. "But why would I be interested in him?"

"He is the reason vhy ve are havink trouble vit de Blackfeet coming to us for all der business."

"He is the one who has been stirring up trouble with them?"

"Ya. He is der enemy of de Blackfeet. De Blackfeet, dey hate all the American trappers but, Squire, he is der biggest enemy."

"Kenneth did tell me about this man. He said Squire was to be killed."

"Ya. He vas. Ve haf sent men against him."

"Yet this Squire still lives?"

"Ya. Twice ve had men who vas to kill him. Both failed."

"So why come to me? Do you expect me to send my men out after this phantom? If I understand, that is your task."

"He is not a phantom," Meisner snapped. "He is more like a demon."

"I don't care if he is the devil himself in the flesh," Murdock said, voice even icier. "If he stands in the company's way, remove him."

"Dot's vhy I come here. To tell you, so you can get vord to Herr McKenzie dot I vill take care of him *mein* self."

"When will you do this?"

"Soon. Before long, he vill come to Blackfoot country. Ve — I — vill be ready for him. He vill not get away dis time, no matter how mighty he seems to be. I vill kill him and bring his scalp to you."

"That won't be necessary. Just remove this obstacle to the company's business."

"I vill," Meisner said with determination.

"Make sure you do. Is there anything else?" Murdock wanted nothing more than to get rid of this uncouth creature and his fetid odor. It would take days to get his foul smell out of the room.

"I vill need supplies."

"You can pay for them of course?"

"Mr. McKenzie gave us supplies on credit. We vould pay for them in furs."

"Have you any?"

"I brought some. Most are still vit der Blackfeet."

Murdock sighed as if greatly put upon which, indeed, he felt he was. He leaned forward, dipped a pen into a small jar of ink and scribbled something on a piece of paper. "Take this to the trade room. You will get your supplies there. But there is a limit."

"Ya," Meisner said, voice harsher than usual. He was tired of the bourgeois' condescension. He knew that McKenzie had hated him, felt far superior to him, but at least the former factor had treated him with a modicum of respect. But this man ...

"Now get out of here, Meisner."

The German glared at him for a few moments, then rose. "You haf much to learn about der men in the field and der Indians, Herr Murdock."

"I doubt that, Mr. Meisner. I know far more than you think I do. Now farewell to you. I will not be seeing you again. When you have taken care of this Squire demon, you may send word to me. You won't need to come in person. Is that understood?"

"Ya," Meisner said, almost spitting the word out. He grabbed his rifle and stomped out, shoving roughly past the servant who had, he figured, been listening outside the door. The servant flinched as Meisner bumped him in passing.

The clerk in the trade room was barely more friendly that Murdock had been despite the fact that he had dealt with Meisner before in a reasonably affable manner. The German figured that Cumberland had laid down new rules as to how men like him were to be treated. It only increased his anger.

Meisner got no assistance loading the supplies on a mule though the clerk stood leaning against the door jamb, watching, making sure none of the laborers helped.

Finally, the cantankerous mountain man climbed onto his horse. He hawked up a good load of phlegm and launched it toward the clerk, just missing the man's foot. The clerk's eyes blazed with sudden anger.

"You haf made a pact with der devil," Meisner said. "It vill do you no goot to kiss his ass like you haf been doing."

"I'll be better off than you ever will, you scabrous old bastard," the clerk snapped, anger and arrogance mixed on his face.

"I hope you come down vit a bad case of de clap or maybe even the French disease. If you have anyt'ing between your legs, then it vill fall off maybe." He laughed a coarse, humorless laugh and kicked his horse roughly into movement.

CHAPTER 15

FALL HAD ARRIVED which meant that the weather was often erratic. One day it would be hot, dry and dusty; the next, snow spit harshly at them, shoved along by strong, cold winds. The freezing wind and bitter cold plowed over them at times and then was gone in a day or two.

With Li'l Jim recovered, Squire pushed them hard, moving fast to the northwest. After a couple of weeks, they slowed, beginning to trap some of the smaller rivers and streams along their route.

They finally reached Crazy Woman Creek in mid-September and Squire called a halt. "We'll be spendin' some time here," he announced. "Enough grass, plenty of wood, good water. And I reckon there be a heap of beaver about, too. And that's why we be out here, of course. So be makin' camp. I expect ye lads to be settin' traps come mornin'.'"

Pitching camp was so routine to them all by now that it was but a little time before tents were up, fires going and food cooking, and the horses and mules tended. Robe time came early for all.

In the morning, while Squire and Li'l Jim stayed in camp, Train and Hannah set their traps and checked them that evening, bringing in eight plump beaver from their twelve traps. The next day, Squire and Li'l Jim went out while Train and Hannah remained in the camp. Switching kept the traps out but kept the camp protected.

The rest of the days were spent keeping up the supply of wood, water and feed for the animals. And hunting. Elk and deer abounded, and there were buffalo enough to provide more than ample provender for them all.

Two weeks later, the beaver catch was dwindling so the group moved on, heading for the Powder River where they again set up a comfortable camp and resumed their activities.

"I've seen sign," Train said one day when he and Hannah returned from setting their traps.

"Ye be knowin' what kind?" Squire asked.

"Crow, I think, but I ain't sure."

"I reckon ye be right, lad. I've seen sign, too, this mornin' whilst out huntin'."

"Think it means trouble."

"It ain't good. Ye nary can tell what Crows be plannin'. They can be friendly but they be seasoned horse stealers. Steal anything else they can get their hands on if they be thinkin' it's easy."

The others had gathered around. "Should we be set to fight?" Hannah asked.

"Always. Ye should be knowin' that by now. But maybe they'll be passin' us by. Just be ready for whate'er those critters might do."

That afternoon as the small group waited uneasily, half a dozen Crows rode into the camp. They stopped and dismounted. "Ye best be getting back on those ponies,"

Squire said, standing in front of them, rifle in the crook of his left arm. "Ye be havin' no business here, boys, and we got no business with ye."

"We friends," the apparent leader said. "We smoke, talk, maybe make trade."

"Got no reason to smoke, talk or trade. 'Sides, ye got nothin' I'd be wantin' to trade for."

"I am Red Blanket. I your friend," the Crow insisted. He looked around as if curious. "Where are your friends?

"Watchin' ye and the your friends. Ready to shoot your red ass down should you try somethin' foolish."

"We smoke. Show we're friendly.

"I reckon if ye be such a pain in the ass about this, we'll smoke. You and your boys be puttin' your weapons o'er there." He pointed to a large cottonwood."

"That not good."

Squire shifted the rifle a little, letting Red Blanket know that he would accept no argument about this."

All the Crows looked at him, faces determined. Then Red Blanket nodded and removed his bow, quiver, knife and tomahawk.

"Sit, then," Squire said. He called over his shoulder, "Come on out lads."

Train and Li'l Jim marched out from behind the trees.

As Red Blanket and the other Crows sat, the leader said, ignoring the women, "There is another. Where is he?"

"Don't be no other here, lad. This be all of us." He could tell Red Blanket didn't believe him but he did not care. He stared straight at the Indian. He had told Hannah to stay in the brush. She had not liked the idea at all but she understood the sense of it.

Red Blanket said something to one of his warriors

who brought out the long pipe. "Need tobacco," Red Blanket said, trying to sound and looked sheepish. It fooled no one.

Squire tossed a half twist of tobacco to the Indian who quickly wiped the faux hangdog look off his face and began filling the bowl. He got it lighted and passed it to Squire who went through the ritual of offering the smoke to the four directions and then Mother Earth and Father Sky. Everyone else did the same when the pipe came to them.

As he was waiting for the pipe to make its way round, Squire said, "Red Blanket, ye best be warnin' that lad of yours to set himself back down afore I be puttin' a lead pill in him."

The Crow leader barked something at the warrior who had been heading for some supplies setting under a tarp. The warrior skulked back to the circle and sat. He tried glaring at Squire but the huge mountain man's hard stare made him lower his gaze in moments.

"Now that we've smoked, what be on your mind, Red Blanket?" His voice let the others know he was of little patience.

"Now we talk," the Crow said magnanimously as if he had some great information to impart.

"About what?"

"The Blackfeet maybe."

"I suppose you'll be tellin' me ye'll be goin' after them red devils?" Squire smirked.

Red Blanket nodded. "We'll kill many Blackfeet," he boasted.

"You be full of buff'lo droppin's."

"I speak truth."

"I think ye likely be out huntin' and're talkin' big to try'n impress us. Hate to tell ye, lad, but it ain't workin'.'"

Fury crossed Red Blanket's face but he wiped it away almost immediately. "We hunt all right. We hunt Blackfeet," he insisted, throwing his chest out.

"All right, lad, so ye be huntin' Blackfeet. Why'd ye stop here then?"

"Want supplies. You give us some."

"All you'll be gettin' from us be trouble, lads. Now we've had our smoke and our talk, such as it was. Time for ye lads to be movin' on."

Red Blanket and the others started to argue but thought better of it when Squire and the others shifted their weapons just enough to let the Crows know that any aggression on their part would lead to a bloodbath. Grumbling, the warriors left.

As soon as the Crows had left, Squire turned. "Be getting everything loaded up, lads. *Vite!*"

Everyone froze, looking at him in astonishment. "Now, *mes amis!* There be no time to delay."

Suddenly, everyone burst into motion and in less than an hour, everything was packed. As they were working, Li'l Jim suddenly asked, "What about the traps, Nathaniel? You and me got us a dozen of 'em out there."

"Leave 'em be. We got no time for bringin' 'em in. If we can, we'll come get 'em some other time. If not, we'll do without till we can maybe find a few more somewhere."

Sometime before the packing was finished, Squire pulled Train aside. "Take yourself out there just a bit, lad, and find which way those Crows went. I reckon they headed west but we best be certain."

Just as the packing was completed, Train rode in and

stopped in front of Squire. Hannah and Li'l Jim hurried up. "You were right, Nathaniel. They headed west." He paused, then shook his head. "I seen an awful lot of sign though. A heap more'n that group was here would've made. And it was all new."

"Aye."

"That's why ya had us get ready to move right away, ain't it, Nathaniel?" Hannah asked.

"Aye, lass." He looked at Train. "Ye see enough sign for fifty, maybe sixty Crow?"

"About that, yep."

"We're in a heap of buffler shit, ain't we, Nathaniel?" Li'l Jim tossed in.

"That be about the way of it."

"If there's that many of 'em out there, why didn't they just attack us at once?" Li'l Jim asked.

"Crows be fine warriors but they be best when they outnumber their enemy by a heap."

"Like now?"

"Aye."

"Then why ...?"

"I ain't certain but I reckon they had no idea how many of us there be. Could've been just us but maybe they be thinkin' there was a heap of us out on the trap lines or huntin'. So a few of 'em come into our camp to scout us. I'd wager they be thinkin' if there was only a few, they'd overpower us and steal all our plunder."

"And the women and our hair, too," Train growled.

"Aye. But they learned right off we ain't so naïve as to think those critters'd be our friends."

"Won't they come at us now with all of 'em?"

"Might take 'em a bit. I reckon they be arguin' o'er who of 'em's gonna get what of our plunder."

"Countin' their chickens some early, ain't they?" Li'l Jim groused.

"Aye, But in doin' so, it gives us time to be makin' ready. Now let's be movin'. Abner, ride out ahead on scout. Head northwest. Ain't a trail, really, but buff'lo been movin' that way for a heap of years so there should be some way to follow. We be in the foothills. Clear Creek, higher up, ain't but a few miles. There be places there we can use to hole up. We'll be followin' right behind. Don't be takin' no chances, lad. First sign of trouble, ye be getting yourself back to us."

"Right," Train bent and kissed Hannah, then galloped off. Squire got the others on the move.

As dusk began spreading its purplish-grayness over the land, Squire trotted out and caught up with Train. "Follow me, lad," the big mountain man said, pushing his horse a little. Ten minutes later the two stopped. Squire pointed. "Ye be seein' that thicket?" When Train nodded, he continued, "Just the far side of it be another one with heaps of big rocks scattered amongst the trees and thick brush. Get all the animals worked well up there. The women can be keepin' charge of the cavvy. Ye and Hannah can be keepin' watch. Ye be in change, lad."

"What about you and Li'l Jim?"

"Aim to be payin' the Crows a leetle visit. Maybe discourage them devils from comin' agin us. Now let's be headin' back. You can lead the others up here."

———

Squire and Li'l Jim moved as quickly as the swiftly falling darkness allowed, heading southwest. They did not have to go far. By the time dark was full on them, they caught sight of a large Crow camp and pulled to a halt.

"Think that's them?" Li'l Jim asked.

"Aye. Ain't but one Crow camp in these parts that big."

"Why'd they stop for the night?"

"Likely be cheerin' themselves on a wee bit early. Rather'n travel through the night, they made camp and figure to come agin us in the mornin'."

"But we ain't about to let that happen, eh, Nathaniel?" Li'l Jim said as cockily as ever. He had fully recovered, physically and mentally.

"Aye, lad."

"What're you plannin'?"

"Much as I'd like to be puttin' e'eryone of them devils under, I reckon we can't. So I reckon we be runnin' off their horses. Leave 'em afoot. Damn near as much shame to a Crow as losin' his hair." He grinned, teeth shining in the darkness. "They maybe could be gatherin' 'em up after a spell but it'll keep 'em busy plenty long enough for us to be on our way."

"Don't you figure they'll be some unwillin' to part with them animals?" Li'l Jim asked sarcastically.

"Aye. So?"

"Maybe you'll get to kill a heap of them Crows after all."

"Wouldn't bother this chil' none but puttin' 'em afoot is why we be here."

They tied their horses to a western hemlock and crept toward the camp under a bright almost full moon. As they neared the horse herd, Squire stopped his companion, then tapped his shoulder and pointed in three directions, indicating the horse guards he had spotted.

Li'l Jim nodded. "We take 'em out?" he whispered.

"Aye. I be takin' the nearest one. Then we each go for the other. Make it quiet. I don't want them Crows gettin' an early warnin' of what we be up to. Then we be makin' some noise to get them horses runnin'. We be downwind so they won't be sniffin'' us out aforehand. We'll try to get 'em runnin' e'ery whichway 'cept north."

"When?"

"Soon. I want them to be full asleep when we go about our business."

Before long, Squire tapped Li'l Jim. "It be time, lad."

They moved out swiftly but silently. None of the three guards were paying much attention. Squire slipped up behind the nearest, in but a moment had dragged the young man off his horse and snapped his neck. He headed for the second.

Seeing it, Li'l Jim moved quickly toward the third. As he was nowhere near Squire's size or strength, killing the Crow the way Squire had was impossible. But he was fast and agile. He crept up on the horse guard, leaped onto the pony's back, slit the man's throat, flung the body off and kicked the horse into motion.

Squire had easily dispatched the other guard. He, too, leaped on a pony and got it moving. Between the two of them, waving blankets silently and urging the herd with their Crow mounts, they got the cavvyard moving. The animals moved slowly at first, then picked up speed. Within a minute or two, they had the animals racing helter-skelter across the rocky meadow.

The two mountain men drove their ponies between groups of the herd, forcing them this way and that, scattering them in all directions. Finally Squire fired a pistol. Li'l Jim heard it, looked over just a bit worried, then relaxed when he saw that Squire was just telling him to break off more stampeding.

They slowly rode back to their own horses, taking a circuitous route, then hid there for a while as the Crows frantically tried chasing down their horses with the few ponies that had stayed nearby.

"Showed them ol' red critters, I reckon," Li'l Jim said with a grin as he and Squire mounted their horses and headed back toward their camp.

"That we did, lad. Aye." He, too, grinned.

CHAPTER 16

"MOVE YER ASSES, LADS!" Squire bellowed.

At a time like this, the word lad encompassed them all, male or female. The group worked frantically to get their camp set up as they watched the storm bearing down on them. Supplies were unloaded, stacked carefully, and covered with canvas and buffalo hides held down by large stones. Simple hide lean-tos were hurriedly constructed as deeply into the brush as they could manage. Fire pits of stacked stones were thrown together, firewood gathered and blazes started. The men fought to control the panicking horses and mules and get them tied to strong ropes strung between trees.

They had barely managed to get the work done when the storm hit with a fury that awed even Squire. Snow poured down on them in thick, wet flakes that piled up even amid the cottonwoods and willows where they had just made their camp. The wind raged and moaned, sounding like the furious roars of mountain gods.

They hunkered down in their poor shelters. But they

could not stay there for long. Firewood had to be gathered regularly to keep their meager fires going. They spent considerable time peeling cottonwood bark for the horses to eat. And the animals had to be watched over and cared for lest they froze to death.

It was exhausting and they had little fresh meat. But they were well-supplied with fat-rich pemmican. Coffee and tea were plentiful and, when doused heavily with sugar, also served to give them some energy.

"Good Lord a'mighty, ain't this damn storm ever gonna quit and leave us in peace?" Li'l Jim groused the second night. "Another couple hours of this and I'll drown in it 'cause it'll be taller'n me in most places."

Despite their misery, they all laughed.

"Hell, that ain't that deep," Train said. "You bein' a midget and all."

"Bah," Li'l Jim snapped. "You're just another over-growed oaf like Squire there. Think you're special or something just 'cause you're bigger'n regular folks."

"That ain't true," Squire said with a wide grin splitting the great tawny beard and mustache. "We think we be special because we *be* special." He roared with laughter.

"You're specially annoyin', that's certain," Li'l Jim rejoindered. "Even more than all this snow and cold."

"Be getting a bit faint of heart, are ye, lad?" Squire growled.

"Hell, you know better than that, Nathaniel. I'm just tired of all this damn weather."

"It'll be o'er before ye know it, lad," Squire said. "Or maybe it won't. Why I've seen storms like this last weeks, sometimes months. Snow higher'n a lodgepole pine, so high you could use snowshoes and walk on the snow flat across to the top of the Tetons. Wind be blowin' so hard it'd blast the Bighorns into dust and spread it all the way to St. Louis."

"Sounds mighty bad," Hannah said with a smile.

"Ah, that don't be the half of it, lass. When it finally ended after two months and the snow melted, it filled up a whole valley down by those boilin' spots near the Yellowstone. Lake still be there. But more, there be thousands of buff'lo all froze standin' up. All we had to do was be takin' our 'hawks to 'em and we had meat and hides to last us a heap of a time."

"Don't sound like starvin' times to me," Train said with a chuckle.

"That don't be the worst, lad. The worse be freezin' to death, all of us. Me and ol' LeGrand, froze solid as rocks. When the sun come out and the heat rose, we be unfreezin'. Felt some good, too, like we had us a good long rest."

"Well, if it looks like it's gonna get that bad and I'm about to freeze over," Li'l Jim said, "I'm headin' for one of them deserts we heard about."

They all laughed again.

———

The men and Hannah were out seeing to the animals the next afternoon when the wind suddenly stopped. The four quit working and stared around in the silence, as if unsure what had happened. Finally Train shook his head. "Wonder how long it's gonna last," he mused aloud.

"However long won't be long enough," Li'l Jim said.

The others smiled and went back to work. Minutes

later, Train stopped and cocked his head. "You hear anything, Nathaniel?"

Squire nodded. "Aye. A babe in arms. Means Injuns. With a babe, it's like as not a huntin' party or some such. But it don't shine with this chil' to be takin' chances. Li'l Jim, gather up the women and keep guard on 'em. Abner, head out and see who it be. Hannah and me'll be watchin' o'er the animals. *Allons-y!*"

Tense minutes passed and then Train called out, "It's all right." Moments later, he materialized from behind the curtain of the softly falling snow leading several Indians: a warrior, two women and two children, one an infant. One of the women and the older child walked. The warrior and the woman holding the child rode.

Squire walked up with Hannah at his side. "Welcome," he said.

Star Path, Cloudy Moon and Fox Woman hurried forward to the women and children who looked worn, frazzled and half frozen. They helped the one woman off the horse and then hustled all of them to the largest lean-to and fussed over them, pouring them coffee, wrapping them in buffalo robes or blankets.

The warrior dismounted stiffly as if his bones had frosted over and did not want to work. Squire led him to Abner and Hannah's lean-to and got him seated next to the fire. Within moments, Train had handed him a cup of steaming coffee. The warrior took it with trembling hands, drank a bit and nodded.

"What be your name?" Squire asked.

The warrior looked blankly at him. Li'l Jim, who had learned much of the Shoshone language from his two women, repeated the question in the warrior's language.

"Blind Dog."

"How come ye to be here in such a state?" Squire asked as Li'l Jim continued to translate.

Blind Dog's face grew stony. He set down his cup and started to rise, looking as if he was going to call to the women and children.

"Now, hold on there, lad," Squire said not harshly. "Set yourself down again." When the warrior had done so, Squire continued. "I ain't questionin' your honor, Blind Dog. We all come on hard times, starvin' times, now and again. Ain't no shame in that. I be thinkin' you handled yourself right well in whate'er troubles ye faced recent."

Blind Dog began to soften his visage a bit.

"So, Blind Dog, I'll ask ye again. How come ye to be here like this?"

"Damn Blackfeet," Blind Dog snarled in English.

Squire raised his eyebrows at the use of English but said, "Damn Blackfeet be the worst kind of devils."

Blind Dog stared at the giant for a few moments, then, as if recognizing him, said as much as asked, "You're the man they call the Fierce One."

"I be *L'on Farouche*, aye."

"You're much feared by the Blackfeet." He smiled grimly.

"And with damn good reason," Train tossed in.

"Good," Blind Dog growled. "The more of them he kills, the better for my people. And for yours."

"What happened?" Hannah asked.

Blind Dog looked at her in confusion for a bit, then shrugged. "We had been visiting relatives of our people up north. All was good. Then we began heading back to our band near the boiling waters when a party of Blackfeet attacked." Pain began inching its way across his dark-skinned face.

"Some of your people go under?" Squire asked.

Blind Dog nodded, seemingly unable to speak for a moment because of his hurt. "My son, Charging ..." He stopped, not wanting to say the name of a dead man as was the custom.

"He took down some of them Blackfeet, I reckon," Squire said, knowing the man's reluctance to name his son.

Pride wiped away the agony, at least for a time. "Raised hair on two of those devils."

"Two more Bug's Boys won't be going to the Spirit World," Train said with nod. "Those bastards' spirits'll roam forever, never findin' a home."

"*Haa* — Yes," Blind Dog said fiercely. Then the pain returned tenfold.

"He be left behind, wasn't he? And lost his hair?" Squire asked, angry now.

"*Haa.*" He took a moment to collect himself. "My brother's son ... He ..."

"Gone under, too," Squire said, knowing the truth of it. "And after losin' their hair, they be blocked from joinin' your ancestors in the Afterworld."

"Yes." It was as if all the life had left him and he had deflated.

"The woman with the babe be your son's widow?"

"Yes. The other is my nephew's wife and son." His robe had slipped off his shoulder a bit and Squire saw dried blood on his war shirt.

Squire pointed to it. "Ye be hurt."

"It's nothing. A small wound protecting the family. I

fought so they could escape. I finally managed to drive the Blackfoot off so we could get away."

"Ye be a brave and honorable man, Blind Dog."

The Shoshone shook his head, a show of anger and pain and resignation. "If I had been, the two who are gone would be here."

"Your duty be protectin' your family not in raisin' hair on the Blackfeet."

Blind Dog's daughter-in-law hurried up with some pemmican on a piece of bark used as a plate. "*Rechaud*," she said quietly.

Blind Dog nodded thanks and took the proffered food. He began to eat without much enthusiasm.

In the firelight, Squire could see that the woman was worn to the bone, battered by grief and the harsh weather. Her face sagged with tiredness and mourning. Her hair had been chopped short and Squire figured she had hacked deep marks in her arms.

Before she could turn and leave, Squire said, "Ye be safe here, girl. Ye can stay here as long as Blind Dog wants to and ye be under my protection." He stroked his long, bushy beard, then bellowed, "I be *L'on Farouche*! And there be no critter on four legs or two that can be comin' agin my camp and the folks in it and not be payin' a damn high price for their foolishness!"

Blind Dog looked startled for a moment, then offered a half smile. The woman's eyes showed a newfound fright. Blind Dog saw it, too, and spoke to her gently in Shoshone. The woman relaxed and nodded. Then she left.

"You speak true?" Blind Dog asked.

"About stayin' here? Aye. Long as ye like. Be best to

wait a few days at least. Another storm be comin' sure as anything. It be safer for you to wait it out here. We can build ye some shelters. There be plenty of pemmican and dried meat to be feedin' us, and there be more'n enough buff'lo robes and blankets to keep ye all warm. Star Path, Cloudy Moon and Fox Woman'll be of big help to your women.

Blind Dog thought about it for a bit while he ate, then nodded. "*Aishenda'ga* — Thank you. We will stay."

CHAPTER 17

"Where be Abner and Li'l Jim?" Squire asked.

Hannah hemmed and hawed before finally sputtering, "Out huntin'."

"Ye should know better by now to be lyin' to me, lass. And this be a lie sure as rain be wet."

The young woman sighed. "I told 'em I wouldn't tell ya." She looked up at the giant mountain man and almost smiled at the baleful look in his eye. "They went out to see if they could find Blind Dog's men who got put under."

"In this weather?" It had started storming again with the wind kicking up and the snow falling in heavy, wet sheets. "That's a damned fool thing."

"Might be, Nathaniel, but they were determined as all get-out."

"All right, let me go saddle up *Noir Astre* and head on out after 'em before they be getting themselves killed."

"No," Hannah said firmly.

Once again, an annoyed look crossed his face.

"Nathaniel," Hannah said as if she were talking to a

child, "we all been through a heap of hard times. Me, Abner, Li'l Jim. Hard times. And we've all come through it. Got some scars from it all, both where ya can see 'em and where ya can't. But we're still here. Ya taught us all well, Nathaniel. And those two fellas've learned well, too." Her lower lip trembled just the faintest bit.

"Ye be tryin' to tell me those boys'll be fine, are ye?" Squire grinned.

"I am," Hannah responded, her face tightening up again. "Ain't nothin' can stop those two." She shook her head. Despite her knowing in her head that what she had just said was true, her heart was still worried sick for her man and the one she thought of as a brother. "It's time you stop motherin' us all."

"I be doin' no such thing," Squire said gruffly. He didn't see it that way. To him, he was just watching out for their welfare. But her comment was close enough that it hit home. He nodded and offered a slow smile. "Ye be right, lass. I need to be puttin' my trust in 'em more." His grin widened. "Just how in hell did ye get to be so smart, girl?" he joshed.

"Ah, Nathaniel, girls are naturally smarter than boys. You just don't recognize it." She walked away, her laughter cutting lightly through the heavy snow.

Squire stared after her for a few moments, wondering if it could be true. Then he laughed and turned. *Nay*, he thought, *such a thing couldn't be.*" He stopped. "*Could it?*" He shook his great head. "Damn women," he muttered. "Never can understand 'em." He laughed. "Likely she's right. Women be smarter — at least about some things. Men were a heap smarter in others." That settled, he went to work feeding the horses.

"You sure you can find 'em?" Li'l Jim asked. He and Train had been riding only a couple of hours and the small young man was cold and tired of the snow.

"You getting itchy to go back?" his large companion asked. "Nothin' stoppin' you."

"Aw, hell, I ain't complainin'." He grinned into the teeth of the curtain of snow. "I am getting itchy to raise hair on some Blackfeet though."

Train looked over at him, concerned. "You ain't getting to like killin' Injuns, are you?"

"Just Blackfeet. And maybe a Crow now and again." He smiled grimly.

"There's others got more reason to hate Blackfeet than you, Li'l Jim."

"Reckon that's so. But when those red devils try to raise hair on my friends, I take mighty strong offense and it's the same as attackin' me."

"You're a good man, Li'l Jim — despite what Nathaniel and the others say."

"What the hell's that mean? What've they said against me, dammit?

Train laughed a full belly laugh. "To be true, hoss, I ain't ever heard a bad word about you from anyone. Other'n maybe you're a pain in the rump more often than not."

Li'l Jim laughed. "Reckon I can't argue much with that. Thing is, I'm damn good at bein' a pain in the rump."

"We all got to be good at somethin'."

They rode in quiet for a while before Li'l Jim broke the silence. "You never answered me, Abner. Do you really think you can find 'em?"

"I do."

"How?" Li'l Jim waved an arm around. "Ain't a thing to be seen out here but snow. Snow in the sky. Snow on the ground. Wind blowing snow this way and that. Damn, I can't even see more'n ten, twenty feet ahead of me."

Train chuckled. "I didn't say it was gonna be easy."

"How the hell do you do it, easy or not?"

"Just follow the tracks best I can."

"What tracks? Like I said, there ain't nothin' out there but snow."

Train shrugged, almost embarrassed. "I don't know. Guess I just see things others don't. An indent in the snow where a horse might've stepped and it ain't been fully covered up. A faint spot of manure. Maybe a branch broken in just a certain way when we're among the trees. Hell, it likely seems crazy, but I swear I think I can even smell things out there at times."

"Reckon you are crazy for such a notion," Li'l Jim said lightly.

Train just grunted in response, annoyed at trying to explain something he did not understand himself.

"I'm just joshin' you, Abner. You just got a talent for such things." He sounded wistful, almost jealous.

"Reckon we all got talents no one else might have. You can handle a rifle better'n anyone except maybe Nathaniel. And you might even be able to outshoot him you get any better. Homer Bellows with horses — and Cletus shows the same talent. Ain't no one I know can handle a knife better'n Hannah. Some fellers can make beaver come like no others, even in the same area. You can't explain, I reckon, just how you can shoot plumb center every time. It just comes natural to you."

Li'l Jim thought that over a bit, then nodded and said, "Reckon you're right, Abner. I never looked at it that way." He smiled. "'Cept Nathaniel can do it all better'n anybody else."

"Yep, he sure can." Train's voice was distant.

"Something wrong, Abner?"

"No," Train snapped. He moved a little ahead of Li'l Jim.

The latter rode along a bit wondering what had suddenly gotten into his friend. Then a notion occurred to him. He pulled up alongside Train again. "You wish you were Nathaniel, don't you? Well, wish you were like him."

"No," Train growled again.

"Like hell. And I'll tell you this, hoss, there's only one feller can fill his shoes. Maybe not now, but someday."

"And who is this special feller?" Train was defeated, deflated. Li'l Jim had found out his secret and that bothered him no end.

"You, ya damn fool."

Train's head whipped around so fast and hard that for a faint moment, he thought it would go flying off and bounce around in the snow. "Me?" he asked, incredulous. "You're out of your goddamn mind, Li'l Jim."

No, I ain't. You ain't maybe quite as big as him but you're damn close. You can track as well as him, maybe better. You can make beaver come with the best. Shoot right well. Not as good as me, of course," he said with a grin. "But good enough. You get more certainty of your abilities, hoss, and you'll stand shoulder to shoulder with ol' Nathaniel."

"Now I know you're plumb crazier'n a coot." But

Train found himself feeling a little better. "But you're a good friend, Li'l Jim. And a good man."

"Don't you go getting mawkish on me, boy."

———

Train stopped, Li'l Jim right next to him. "See something?" the latter asked.

"More like *tryin'* to see something. Seems like the right place from what Blind Dog said." He moved forward slowly, stopped again and dismounted. He inched ahead, searching, then nodded and pointed. There, among the winter-naked hackberry bushes and scattered boulders, was their objective.

"Damn if you didn't find 'em!" Li'l Jim whooped. He charged forward and knelt at the side of one body. "This ain't no Shoshone," he said. He moved to another. "This ain't either. These're Blackfeet." He moved on. "This here's a Shoshone."

Train had wound his way through the rocks, trees and brush. "Two more Blackfeet here and Blind Dog's other kin. He's still got his hair."

"So's this one. Couple of Blackfeet don't." Li'l Jim sounded rather pleased with that.

"Damn, that shines," Train said, voice frosting in the air. "When we talked about comin' out here for this, I wasn't sure there'd be much left of these boys. But I was certain if they were, they wouldn't have no hair. And bringin' back a couple bodies without their scalps might not be such a good thing for Blind Dog."

"Well, they got their hair. Even better, there's some Blackfoot scalps layin' about."

"Blind Dog'll be happy to have 'em."

Suddenly Li'l Jim stood. "Somethin' strange about this," he said.

"What's that?"

"Why ain't the wolves ate these boys up?"

Train stood there contemplatin' on that, eyes drifting over the area. "I don't see no buffler about."

"So?"

"Since there ain't none hereabouts, I reckon the wolves are where the buffler are. And the coyotes'd follow the wolves lookin' for what's left to pick."

"Makes sense." He looked down at one of the Shoshone corpses. "How're you plannin' to get these boys back to our camp? They're frozen stiff as these rocks."

"Travois. There's plenty of trees here and we can take blankets or hides off the Blackfeet."

"That why you had us bring a few extra horses?"

"Yep. That and maybe needin' 'em if somethin' happened to ours."

"Smart. Well, let's get started," Li'l Jim said without much enthusiasm.

"Too late in the day. We'll camp here. We're both hungry and tired and these boys ain't goin' anywhere on their own. Gather up some firewood while I tend to the horses."

Soon enough, they were sitting around a fire — one as big as seemed reasonable — desultorily eating pemmican and sipping coffee.

"Be nice if some Blackfeet come along and raised our hair," Li'l Jim said with something of a grin. When Train looked at him in question, his grin widened. "I reckon I'd rather go under fightin' some Blackfeet than face Nathaniel after settin' out like this without him knowin'."

"Reckon he might be a little cantankerous," Train allowed with a chuckle.

They were quiet for a while before Train asked, "What'd you mean I ain't got enough confidence? Just 'cause I ain't a cocky little critter like you don't mean I lack gumption."

"You let that little gal push you around a mite often."

"Hannah? She's the best woman in all creation and you damn well know it."

"Don't mean she don't have you dancin' to her tune whenever she wants." He tried to suppress his grin.

"Well, that might be true. Sometimes. But she's worth it."

"Hell, boy, you can't lead a tiny little woman, you sure as hell can't be a leader of men."

"But ... Well ... I ..."

Li'l Jim burst out laughing. "Ah, hell, I'm just joshin' again, Abner." He added to himself, "Mostly."

"Why I ought to come over there and raise your hair myself," Train said. Then he laughed, too. "But it's too damned cold!"

They soon turned in, sleeping as close to the fire as they dared, frequently rolling over as one side of them froze and the other roasted.

In the morning, they went about building travois. Hacking through trees was no easy task but it did warm them up considerably. Before long, they had the two Shoshone bodies tied to the travois hitched to the two extra horses they had brought along. But first they had cut out the arrows and laid them alongside the dead warriors.

"What'n hell for?" Li'l Jim groused as Train started to do that. "They can't feel 'em."

"Leavin' 'em in makes it harder to tie 'em down.

'Sides, no need to have Blind Dog see his kin lookin' like pincushions."

"Damn, I'm an idiot sometimes."

"What do you mean 'sometimes'?" Train grinned despite the gruesome work.

"Bah." Li'l Jim finished tying down the Shoshone and mounted his horse. "Well, then, hoss, lead us home."

They weren't gone an hour when the storm kicked up again, throwing its fury at them. But the next afternoon, they materialized out of the storm into the camp.

Squire. Hannah and Blind Dog came out of the lean-tos to greet them. The women followed.

"We brung back your kin, Blind Dog," Train said, suddenly weary.

The Shoshone women started to howl anew at their grief and Star Path and Li'l Jim's two women gently led them away.

Blind Dog looked from his dead son to his dead nephew. Tears leaped into his eyes and streamed down his weathered face.

Li'l Jim handed him a sack. "Blackfoot scalps," he said quietly. "Your folks kept theirs but managed to raise hair on several of those red devils.

Blind Dog took the sack, looking from Li'l Jim to Train. He tried to speak but words would not come.

"No need to say anything," Li'l Jim said, patting him on the shoulder.

He and Train took their horses to the picket line and began unsaddling them. Squire walked up. "Ye lads be the most foolish critters this chil's e'er seen," he growled. Shaking his head, he turned. As he walked away, a smile of pride spread over his face.

CHAPTER 18

THE STORM BLEW itself out three days later, dying of exhaustion. The cold lingered though the snow stopped falling and the wind had wound down to a light breeze. Relieved, the camp cleaned up. Li'l Jim and Hannah went off to hunt and returned with two deer and a small mountain goat. Squire and Train checked over the horses. One had suffered considerably and had to be put down. The rest would be fine with a little care and some more and better feed. The mules had held up well.

They feasted well that night though blind Dog ate little. After the meal, he returned to pacing about the camp again as he had done much of the day, worry creasing his dark face. Squire kept a wary eye on the Shoshone and finally approached him, dragging Li'l Jim along to interpret. "Ye be concerned about somethin'?" the big mountain man said rather than asked. "I reckon it be about getting your kin back home."

Blind Dog grunted an affirmative.

"Tell ye what, hoss, me and my people'll be helpin' ye do so."

"No," Blind Dog snapped. "You have done too much. I will take no more help."

"Then how do ye be plannin' to get back to your village? Ye got two horses, two women, two young'un and two brave warriors who be gone under."

"I'll find a way. The woman can walk. I will walk."

"That be a plumb foolish notion, Blind Dog. The storm maybe has died out but there be no tellin' that it won't be back. And e'en if not, there be a heap of miles to go and a heap of snow and cold to get through on the way."

"I'll find a way," Blind Dog repeated. "We'll leave tomorrow." He stomped off.

"*L'homme soit un fou* — that man be a goddamn fool," Squire said with a shake of his head.

"You'd do the same damn thing, Nathaniel. A man like him — or you — got a heap of pride. You don't like takin' help. You do, but from friends. He ain't your friend, Nathaniel. You ain't known each other but a few days."

"You be too damn smart for your own good, lad."

Li'l Jim ignored him. "Maybe the women'll help change his mind. Seeing Squire's quizzical look, he added, "I don't reckon his women'll want to walk all the way to their village, wherever that might be. And if my two women add their voices to the pleas, maybe Blind Dog'll come to his senses." He grinned just a bit. "Of course, if he's as hardheaded as you, likely he won't."

"Don't ye be provokin' me, lad." But he chuckled. "So go on and talk to the women."

———

Blind Dog approached Squire the next morning while

the latter was sitting in front of his lean-to casting rifle balls. "We take your help," he said in English, his tone sour.

"That be good. No shame in takin' help that be offered by new friends."

Blind Dog looked blankly at him, so Squire bellowed, "Li'l Jim!" When the young man trotted up, Squire told him to interpret again.

Li'l Jim repeated in Shoshone what Squire had said.

"There is much shame in doing so," Blind Dog spit out.

"Hell, hoss, look at it this way — me and my folks be goin' mostly in the same direction. We just be ridin' together, your people and mine. It ain't like we be goin' far out of the way to have ye throw in with us. We just be travelin' together for protection."

That seemed to salvage much of Blind Dog's disgrace. "When will you leave?" he asked.

"Tomorrow. Next day, if ye be needin' a little more time."

"We'll be ready tomorrow."

"*Bon*." When Blind Dog had walked off, Squire said to Li'l Jim, "Reckon your little plan worked then."

"Seems to have," Li'l Jim said with a touch of arrogance.

"Ye weren't so cocky all the time, ye wouldn't be such a troublesome critter."

"I wasn't so cocky, I wouldn't be me."

Squire laughed. "Reckon that be true, lad. Aye. 'Course, for the rest of us, that might not be such a bad thing." He laughed even harder.

"I got to ask though," Li'l Jim said, growing serious. "Are we really not goin' out of the way?"

"Just a bit, lad. We get them home and it ain't but a day or two ride to the Three Forks area."

"Blackfoot country?"

"Aye. it be. Some of the best trappin'."

"What about Hannah?"

"She be one tough lass, that one. She'll be fine. 'Sides, I reckon she knew we'd be headin' into Blackfoot country sooner or later."

"I hope you're right, Nathaniel, about her bein' as tough as you say." He paused, then went on in a voice that was deep and cold, "'Cause if something happens to her, I will kill you, Nathaniel.

"You can try, lad."

"I'll do more than try. You've been like a father to me but, Hannah, well, she's special to all of us. Even you."

"She be that, aye."

"Then you know I mean what I say."

Squire gave him an enigmatic smile, neither accepting nor denying Li'l Jim's statement. But inside he was pleased. These young men — and the sole young woman — were following his footsteps.

———

The morning was clear of sky, the sun and the sparkling blue sky hurtful to the eyes after all the gloom of recent days. Yet the temperature had not warmed even one degree; it was still frigid. But the travelers were covered well with thick Hudson's Bay blankets and heavy buffalo robes.

Still, the going was slow and difficult. The frigid temperatures — barely above zero during the day, plummeting to well below at night — crusted the snow with ice and, before the first day was over, the travelers had to cover the hooves of the horses and mules with buckskin wrappings to protect them.

Hunting was poor so they had to rely on pemmican again to keep themselves fed. They saw no sign of hostile Indians though Squire had at least two of his three younger companions riding guard all the time, and the horses and mules were protected at night.

Four days out, Squire called a halt and told everyone they would stay for a couple of days. It would give the animals — and the people — time to rest and recruit themselves. Squire, Li'l Jim, Hannah and Train trapped some, pulling in some fine pelts though not too many what with the smaller streams frozen over.

That night, Train broke out the dulcimer he had bought in St. Louis and played a few lively tunes. Li'l Jim and Hannah kicked up their heels as the women, and even Blind Dog, clapped and cheered.

Then it was back on the trail. The temperature during the day rose but once night fell, it plummeted down below freezing again, creating a new icy crust over the snow. Despite Li'l Jim's occasional lament — ignored by all because it was just his way — no one complained. They were all used to such hardships. Besides, there was nothing they could do to change it.

Four days later, judging by the excitement of Blind Dog and the Shoshone women, they could sense that they were close. That night, Squire, with Li'l Jim at his side, stopped by where Blind Dog was sitting at his fire.

"Well, lad, me and my folks'll be pullin' out come mornin'. Ye be close enough to your village to be safe. Li'l Jim will be comin' with ye to bring our horses back."

Hannah and Train ambled up and sat.

"No," Blind Dog said.

"Ye ain't keepin' them horses, lad." Squire face began to cloud up with anger.

"I mean, you not go," the warrior said in his heavily accented, rarely used English. "You come with us."

"Nay. We need to be getting on the move."

"Ah, hell, Nathaniel," Li'l Jim said. "Let's go to the village. A day or two ain't gonna push us back none."

Squire looked at him in question.

Li'l Jim ignored him and spoke to Blind Dog in Shoshone for a few minutes. Then to Squire he said, "Blind Dog feels obligated to you — to us — for helpin' him out. He feels he's got to pay us back. There'll be a feast in your honor and a big dance. He can show his appreciation while regainin' his pride. He's a prideful man, Nathaniel, like you are. And he don't like bein' beholden to no one."

"Reckon that's so and it'd be a shinin' time," Squire said after a few moments thought. Then he cocked his head. "But you be seemin' a mite eager for this."

Li'l Jim's face flushed. "Well, I ..."

Suddenly Train broke out laughing. Everyone turned to look at him. "He just wants to go to the village so's he can unload one of them women of his, them bein' Shoshone and all. Figures somebody in the village'll be glad to have one of 'em."

Everyone else laughed — except Li'l Jim whose embarrassment only grew now that he had been found out.

———

When they arrived in the village, there was a fair amount of howling grief at the loss of two brave warriors. But there was great joy, too, at the return of their people. A large lodge was given over to the visitors and another was set aside for the ritual mourning of the two slain warriors.

The next morning, Blind Dog's son and nephew were laid to rest. That evening, a feast and dance were held around a huge bonfire to ward off the bitter cold. Squire and his people joyfully took part. At times, Train would play his dulcimer which sounded very odd indeed amid the drumming and chanting. Li'l Jim, Hannah and Train all danced — or tried to — much to the amusement of the Shoshones. Squire sat, humored and worried, watching as a very pregnant Star Path joined in. There was some enmity at first when this Sioux woman — an enemy of their people — had appeared in the camp, but Blind Dog made it clear right off that she was a valued guest of his. And when the others heard of how she had helped the Shoshone women and two small children, the host tribe accepted her fully.

Everyone slept late the next day, and Squire and Star path were eating together with Blind Dog and the principal chief, Big Shield, when they heard a commotion outside. Curious, they all stepped outside into the brilliant, brittle day and saw Li'l Jim and a Snake warrior arguing. They walked up to where Train and Hannah were standing, watching the exchange with amusement.

"What be these doin's?" Squire asked.

Train shook his head, laughing. "Li'l Jim's the luckiest man ..."

"Or unluckiest," Hannah threw in.

"... at gamblin'. He was playin' the hand game with

Weasel Tail and won himself another woman!" He could not help but guffaw.

Squire and the others followed suit. "So what be this squabble about?"

Weasel Tail don't want his woman either," Train said, wiping tears of laughter from his eyes, his breath pluming in the cold air in front of him. "I think he found himself some way to guarantee he'd lose so he could get rid of her."

Hannah, who was just about doubled over in glee, managed to sputter, "Li'l Jim don't want any part of her."

"So they be fussin' o'er who gets the poor woman?" Squire asked between gusts of laughter.

"Yep."

Squire's laughter tapered off and he grew more serious. "This be worrisome now. They look like they be set to go agin one another."

"Come, we stop them," Blind Dog said.

The two men headed out and got between the two would-be combatants. Blind Dog spoke harshly to Weasel Tail.

"What's he sayin', lad?" Squire asked.

"Sayin' Wesel Tail's an ass and should be ashamed of himself." Seeing the glare in Squire's eye, Li'l Jim grinned sheepishly. "He is callin' Weasel Tail a fool. But he's sayin' they should go to Blind Dog's lodge — and I reckon us, too — to get this all straightened out."

"Sounds like a right smart idea to me."

Soon they — Li'l Jim, Weasel Tail, Blind Dog, Squire, Big Shield and the woman, Yellow Bells — were all gathered in the lodge. They were joined by Painted Face, a warrior who spoke English well, and the arguing began. The elders sat and listened for a while: Weasel Tail would not take back Yellow Bells, arguing that he had lost and the woman now belonged to Li'l Jim; the latter said the former had somehow rigged the game so he could get rid of Yellow Bells and would not take Fox Woman off his hands if he also had to keep Yellow Bells.

Finally, Squire tired of it. "That be enough, lads," he snapped. "Here's what ye'll be doin'. Weasel Tail'll take Fox Woman. In return, Li'l Jim takes yellow Bells."

Both young men burst out in protests.

"There'll be no more fussin' o'er this, lads. It'll be the way I say."

"But, Nathaniel ..."

"Hush, boy." Then he grinned a bit. "Ye said ye wanted to be shed of one of them two women. Well, now ye be."

"But I ..."

"Ye ne'er said ye wanted just one." He laughed, as did the others except Li'l Jim and Weasel Tail. The former finally shook his head and grinned ruefully. "Damned if I didn't put my foot in a bear trap again," he muttered. He looked over at Yellow Bells. She was not particularly pretty, and she was short and somewhat squat. He nodded to her. "Well, welcome to my lodge, Yellow Bells," he said with a sigh.

She looked blankly at him. He smiled and repeated it in Shoshone.

She seemed to relax a little. And when Squire's group pulled out the next day, Yellow Bells looked every bit as happy to be leaving as Fox Woman was to be staying.

CHAPTER 19

THEY WERE CAMPED along a stream about two miles before it entered into the Madison River when someone called for entrance to the camp. Hannah and Train slipped into the trees while Squire and Li'l Jim sat at the fire looking calm, though they were prepared.

"Come ahead," Squire called.

Four men rode in with half a dozen mules loaded with plews and supplies. "Name's Ben Marks," the one said. He pointed to each of the others. "Felix Phillips, Frenchy Bateau, and Brack O'Sullivan."

Squire nodded at each.

"You mind if we set to your fire a spell? Waugh! But it's cold enough to freeze the nuts off the devil himself."

Squire studied them for a few moments. He had heard of Marks whose name was good in the mountains. He had never heard of the others but they looked as if they belonged in the mountains: Hard, weather-toughened, resolute. He decided they were all right.

"Be happy to have ye here. We got us some fresh elk. Plenty of coffee and sugar."

"Obliged." Marks sighed, his breath a big plume of white frost. "You mind if we stay the night here?" He looked around and pointed. "We can make our camp over there."

"Ye be welcome to it. Unload your possibles, then come on o'er here and break bread with us."

"Obliged again."

While the newcomers were unsaddling their horses and unloading their mules, Train and Hannah moved back into camp and took their places.

The others soon joined them, the last being Phillips.

"So who's this little gal there?" he asked as he took a seat on a log with his friends across the fire from Hannah and the others.

"Name's Hannah."

"What're you doin' out here in these wild places, gal?"

"Same thing you are, trappin' beaver."

The man guffawed, a more annoying sound that a mule's braying. "That's a good one, girlie. Humor always shines with this chil'. I reckon you're really here jist to hump one — or mayhap all—— these boys here. Though what one'd be fool enough to roll in the robes with a scrawny strumpet like you. Hell, I wouldn't hump you with someone else's dingus."

Hannah snorted. "You'd have to use someone else's pizzle since I reckon you ain't got one big enough to satisfy a flea."

"Now you listen here, girlie, You don't watch your mouth, I'll drag you over here and spank your ass till you scream for mercy."

"Only screamin' I'd be doin' is with laughter."

"Goddammit, girlie, I'm ..." He cut himself off quick

and blanched when a knife struck, quivering in the log he was sitting on an inch or so from his manhood.

"See, I told ya it was small. Next one, though, will get it no matter how small."

Phillips regained his composure. He pulled the knife free and rose, tapping the blade on one hand. "Purty handy with a knife, girlie. But now I got it and I reckon it's time to teach you some manners, you little whore."

Abner began to rise but Squire pulled him back. "Wait," he said quietly.

"But ..."

"I ain't gonna let him do her any damage. Ye be knowin' that."

Hannah grinned savagely and stood, pulling another of the several knives she carried in various places.

Phillips's eyes rose in surprise, then he scowled. "Think you're purty slick, do you, girlie. Well now I aim to not only teach you a lesson but I'm gonna take your hair — after humpin' you in front of all these others." He laughed that repellent sound again.

"That's enough, Phillips," Marks said.

"Go to hell. I ain't about to let this harlot treat me in such a disrespectful way."

Marks started to rise but a small shake of the head from Squire stopped him. A question in his eyes, he settled back on the log.

"You gonna talk all day or you gonna come agin me before I'm tellin' my tale to my grandchildren?"

Phillips was of medium height and a bit on the slender side though with a fair amount of bulk. He was strong and vicious, and he knew it. He figured he'd wade in, grab Hannah's knife arm, break it and then do with her what he would.

But he was blind to Hannah's slipperiness and speed. She knew that if she kept out of his grip, she would be all right. But if he got her...she pushed that thought away.

Before he could grab her arm, she had slashed him on his arm and danced out of the way. It went on like that for a bit, with Phillips getting more tired and aggravated. Then he managed to get a handful of her shirt.

With a ferocious jerk, she tore herself away, stumbling a couple feet. Phillips turned his back to her and looked at his captain with a smarmy grin.

Hannah did not hesitate. Taking two steps, she slammed the sole of her right foot against the back of his right knee. Phillips's leg buckled. Hannah immediately jumped on his back, locking her legs around his middle. Her left hand grabbed a handful of the man's hair. The right brought the blade of her knife against his throat.

"Now what, hoss?" she asked, trying and only partly succeeding in keeping the triumph out of her voice.

"Let him be now, Hannah," Squire said.

Hannah glared at him for a moment, then nodded. She moved the knife, slid off his back. Then the knife flashed briefly in the sunlight and she came away with a tiny lock of Phillips's hair, cut from the bottom. She grinned. "Scalped him, I did."

That drew another round of laughter.

Phillips stormed away, back hunched in anger and humiliation.

———

Hannah heard a soft grunt and then felt someone atop her. "Not now, Abner," she said with a small, tired laugh.

"Shut up," the man atop her hissed. He started scrabbling at her clothes, trying to get inside her buckskin pants, reaching for her most private parts.

"Phillips!" she gasped. She wondered where Abner was. Her mind was a jumble, not so much with fright but with surprise and sleepiness. Still, she had the fleeting thought that Abner was outside relieving himself which meant he would be back any minute. But she'd be damned if she'd let this foul scut have his way with her or even get close.

"Damn right, whore."

While the man continued to fumble, Hannah managed to get a hand on one of her knives. "Abner!" she screamed, then stuck the blade into Phillips's side.

Phillips howled and jerked back. Footsteps were coming in their direction. "I ain't done with you yet, you little harlot," Phillips snarled as he bolted out of the small lean-to.

Hannah pushed herself up and felt Abner beside her. "Abner?" she asked quietly. "Abner?" There was more urgency in her voice. If he had not responded through this all, something was wrong. Bad wrong. She rolled onto her side and touched him. Her hand came away wet. Instinctively she knew it was blood. "Abner!" she howled.

Squire barreled up and tore the canvas lean-to loose with one massive hand and flung it aside. Star Path was right behind him. Li'l Jim was only a moment behind, a burning branch he had scooped up from the fire in his hand.

Squire knelt and shoved a crying, screeching Hannah out of the way. Li'l Jim brought the torch to bear. "Damn!" he muttered. Squire looked at the gaping wound low on the stomach, inches from the groin. Train suddenly groaned.

"He's alive!" Hannah said in wonder. "Thank the Lord." She bent to hug him.

Squire pushed her gently away. "Star Path ..."

"You move, I look." The woman had Li'l Jim bring the torch closer to where the young man thought he might end up burning his friend.

"It's bad. Very bad," Star Path said.

"You gotta save him, Star Path," Hannah sobbed.

"I be doin' what I can."

Squire turned as Ben Marks ran up. "What's goin' on, Nathaniel?"

"Your boy damn neared killed Abner and tried to have his way with Hannah."

"Shit. That don't shine with this niggur a'tall."

They heard a horse galloping away.

Squire ignored the comment. He shoved past Marks.

"You goin' after him?"

"Aye. That I be."

"I'm comin' with you," Marks said, catching up to Squire.

"I don't be needin' your help."

"Felix is one of mine, Nathaniel. It don't shine when one of mine turns bad."

"Come along then but don't be getting in my way." He trotted over and leaped on *Noir Astre*. "*Allons-y!*" The big horse bolted forward. Marks was a minute behind and lost ground as Squire's massive stallion thundered along.

It did not take long before Squire spotted the fleeing Phillips just entering the trees on the other side of the glade. He closed the distance quickly, raced around some trees to his left, then pulled out a few yards in front of Phillips and stopped.

The latter's horse screamed and reared in fright, dumping Phillips off on the ground. The horse bolted and, in moments, was lost in the pines.

Squire slid off *Noir Astre* and stalked up to Phillips. The man was just getting to his feet, hand going for his pistol. As he pulled it, Squire slapped him across the face, staggering Phillips whose pistol went tumbling away.

"Ye made yourself one hell of a big mistake here, lad."

Phillips yanked out his blade and, despite his shakiness, lunged at Squire. The big mountain man swatted it away with a forearm and then slapped Phillips again so hard it spun the man around.

Phillips turned back, fear and desperation exuding from him. He bent and snatched up the knife and came at Squire, swinging the blade wildly. Squire suddenly reached out, grabbed Phillips's arm at the wrist and biceps, then brought the arm down and his knee up. Both forearm bones snapped and Phillips screamed.

Marks rode up and stopped. "That's enough, Nathaniel," he said.

"Reckon not, lad. This here feller has a heap to be payin' for." He held Phillips up by the back of his crusty buckskin shirt.

"I'll take care of him."

"Nay, Ben. This be my doin' to take care of."

"Can't let you do that, Nathaniel." He reached for one of the pistols on his belt.

"You pull that piece, Ben, and I'll shove it up your ass and blow your brains out. Now be mindin' your business about these here doin's."

He glared at Marks until the man eased his hand away from his pistol. "Reckon you're right, Nathaniel. After what he done, it's your doin's to handle as you like."

Squire nodded. Then he spun and grabbed Phillips by the neck and crotch, lifted him, took three steps, and hurled Phillips against a tree, cracking the man's back. He grabbed the groaning, limp Phillips and tossed him across *Noir Astre*, then leaped on the horse. "You first," he said to Marks.

They stopped where Star Path was tending to Abner. Li'l Jim was still holding the torch for her to work by and Hannah sat there, sobbing in despair. Squire dismounted and yanked Phillips off the horse with one hand and dropped him on the ground.

Star Path, Li'l Jim and Hannah stared up at Squire. Marks's other two men stayed in the background, curious but, unusual for men who had faced Blackfeet and the other dangers of the wilds, somewhat afraid of Squire.

Hannah sniffled back her crying. "You could've left the body out there to rot, Nathaniel," she said, voice still choked with emotion.

"He ain't dead, girl. Near about, maybe, but he's still breathin'." He smiled a grim, harsh smile. "I was of a mind that you might be desirin' of finishin' the job."

Hannah stared at him in shock and surprise for some moments. Too much had happened in so short a while that she didn't know what to think. But then it became clear to her. "That's right thoughtful of ye, Nathaniel," she said in a voice that seemed to drift up out of a grave. Even Marks shuddered at the sound.

Hannah gently stroked her husband's forehead and hair. "This here's for you more than me, dear Abner." She stood, pulled a knife and walked over to where a semiconscious Felix Phillips lay. She looked down at him and then spit on his face. "Ya know, boy," she said in a macabre tone, "I ain't ever scalped me a white man for real but I reckon this might be the time to take my first one."

She knelt next to him. Staring into his frightened, pain-riddled eyes, she went about her task. After just a minute, she pulled off the scalp and dangled it in front of Phillips's face. "Kind of scraggly," she said in a flat tone. "Likely ain't even worth keepin'." She dropped it on his chest. "That was for Abner. Might be somethin' else for me to cut off, considerin' what you tried to do to me." She turned a little and rested the point of her bloody knife just on his pubic area.

It brought an involuntary gasp from the other men.

Suddenly, Hannah whirled and plunged the knife into Phillips's heart. She stood, leaving the knife in the body, and stumbled back to Abner's side, drained. She slumped down on her buffalo robe and laid a hand across Abner's chest.

CHAPTER 20

"ALL RIGHT, dammit, come agin me, you oversize son of a bitch," Li'l Jim snapped.

"I'll stomp you into a puddle, boy," Train said.

"Have at it, hoss, if that's what it'll take for you to get some sense into that thick head of yours." Li'l Jim pulled out his two pistols and dropped them on the ground. He also slid his knife out of the sheath and the tomahawk out of the belt at the small of his back and dropped them, too. "I'm ready whenever you decide you got the stones to come agin me. I'm waitin'."

Train removed his pistols and tossed them to the ground.

Off to the side, Squire sighed and started to move forward but Star Path grabbed his arm. He looked at her in question. She shook her head. "It be fine," she whispered.

Skeptical, he turned his face back to the two would-be combatants.

Train slid out his knife and dropped it. But that was as far as he got before Hannah trotted up. She had been in the bushes but had heard everything. She stopped in front of Train and slapped him so hard it left a bright red mark on his face. It stunned Train, not so much from the power of it but the anger behind it.

"What in God's earth has gotten into you, Abner?" she demanded. "Have you lost all your reason, you big oaf? You go makin' some damn fool accusations about me and Li'l Jim?"

"But he ... you ..."

"Him and I what?"

"I saw you two ..."

"Saw us what?" Her voice was icy.

"You was there on your back with your shirt up almost to your ... your ... Well, you know." He was embarrassed now, as well as angry. "And Li'l Jim was straddling you and you were both laughing. Like you was enjoyin' it and ..."

"And what?"

"Well, what was I suppose to think? You barin' your whole middle and that skunk over there sittin' on ya ..."

"Doin' what?"

"I ain't certain," Train said, suddenly feeling almost foolish. "But it sure didn't look right. Looked like maybe he was gonna ..."

"Ravish me? Lordy, you can be such a damn fool sometimes, Abner Train."

"But ..." Train's confusion grew.

"As you well know, we was out checkin' traps, you lummox. The bank was a little steep so Li'l Jim offered me a hand. As he was pullin me up, he stepped on a rock and we went tumblin'. When we fell, my shirt rose up some and Li'l Jim landed atop me. We was laughin' at how silly it was."

"Oh ..." Train's discomfiture grew.

"Do you really think Li'l Jim and I would do anything immoral, huh? I'm your wife, dammit all. You've disrespected me and Li'l Jim and I won't stand for it, damn you."

"But ..." Train seemed to have lost most of his power of speech or at least comprehensible speech.

"Dammit, Li'l Jim's the best friend you ever had. Probably ever will have. Do you think he'd try something depraved with me? Or do you think so little of me that I would try something wicked with your friend? If I did, he'd be runnin' for the hills to get away from me. And if *he* did, one or both of us'd be lyin' out there dead along that stream. Now pick up your guns, go apologize to your friend and then go dunk your head in the water."

"What about you?" Train was abashed, face bright red with shame and embarrassment.

"I'll be around camp decidin' whether I gonna forgive you and, if I do, how long it'll be before I do."

Before she could go, he said roughly, regaining some of his composure, "Just one thing, Hannah. Don't you ever hit me again."

"Or what? You'll hit me back?" She was haughty, knowing she had the upper hand no matter what.

"I need to, I'll lodgepole you good."

"Like hell you will." She turned and huffed off.

Train picked up his pistols and slid them back onto his belt. He was afraid to look at Li'l Jim but he could not put off doing so forever. "I'm sorry, Li'l Jim," he mumbled. "I made a damn fool of myself."

"Again."

"Reckon so. Ain't the first time," he admitted sheepishly. "Reckon it won't be the last neither." He sighed and walked off, heading out onto the prairie a little ways to be alone.

Watching, Squire grimaced. Things were, in some ways, getting out of hand and he figured he would have to do something about it soon. Then Star Path pulled his head down and whispered in his ear. He looked at her, thinking over what she had said. Then he nodded.

"Hannah!" he bellowed. "Li'l Jim! Get yourselves o'er here." He sat at his fire with Star Path next to him. When the two young people came and sat, eyes full of questions, Squire said, without preliminary or shame, "How long's it been since Abner covered you, girl?"

Hannah's face flushed red as a bright sunset. "What kind of question is that to ask of a woman?" she demanded, staring at him eye to eye even in her embarrassment.

"It be the kind this chil' wants an answer to." Squire's eyes were stony.

"Well, I ain't gonna answer," Hannah said defiantly.

"It be important, Little Flower," Star Path said. "You answer."

"I ain't gonna answer in front of him," Hannah said, chucking a thumb at Li'l Jim.

The young man started to rise but sat back down when ordered to do so by Squire in a voice that brooked no argument.

"Be answerin' me, girl."

She flushed red again but she swallowed her mortification. "Since just before he got ... hurt." She hung her head.

"And how long was it before you covered one of your women, boy, after you be stove up by that buff'lo?"

Li'l Jim shrugged. He was confused and more than a

bit uncomfortable. "Ain't sure. But it was some weeks after I first got up after bein' so ill-treated by that buffler."

Both Squire and Star Path nodded.

"Your man be hurt bad, girl. And e'en though he be up and around and seemin' full vigor, he be havin' doubts about his manliness. Ain't that right, Li'l Jim?"

The young man thought that over for a bit as Hannah stared at him in confusion. "Reckon you're right, Nathaniel." Now he was uncomfortable, admitting such a thing not only to Squire but in front of Hannah.

The young woman stared at Li'l Jim for a few more moments, then turned to Squire, puzzlement still coursing through her.

"He be afraid he can't cover your properly because he was hurt so bad."

"But that part of him wasn't ..." She stopped mortified again.

"Don't matter none. A man be hurt that bad, he ain't sure he be havin' the strength to do right by his woman in the robes. Might be he feels unmanly 'cause he was hurt so bad and shouldn't have been. Might be that he ain't sure he's really recovered. Especially where he took that knife. Mighty close to what's important to a man."

"He's right, Hannah," Li'l Jim tossed in, suddenly understanding. "It don't really come up in your mind to where you think about it but the feelin's there. Deep down. Like somethin' ain't right but you can't put words to it. I was mighty frightened when Cloudy Moon first pestered me into rollin' in the robes with her after I was stove up. I reckon that's what's plaguin' him."

"Aye, and it likely be why he thought ye and Li'l Jim might be doin' somethin' sinful 'cause Abner doesn't think he can fulfill ye anymore."

"Damn fool ought to know better," Hannah grumbled.

"He should," Li'l Jim added. "But if he's feelin' the way I was, he'd be thinkin' bad thoughts. And if it weren't bad enough that he'd think his wife — and that chil' loves you more'n life, girl — and best friend ..."

"Which you are."

"... would do that, he'd at least remember that I got me two women who I can barely satisfy regular without tryin' to bed my best friend's woman."

Even Hannah joined the others' laughter at that but she was not quite settled about what to do.

"And you be likin' that, eh, Little Flower?" Star Path said, grinning at her.

Suddenly not embarrassed, she grinned back. "I purely do, Star Path." She pushed herself up, thinking and thinking hard. Before she got ten steps, she knew what she had to do.

———

"You look tired, Abner," Hannah said. "Why don't you go lie down a bit. I'll heat up that elk stew Star Path brought over and then come and rub your feet." She tried to keep the anxiety out of her voice.

"Could do with a little rest but I reckon I'll wait till after we eat."

"All right. Food should be ready right quick." She hoped her fretfulness didn't show but he did not appear to notice. He had sounded depressed, listless. She was glad that, now that they had wintered up, they had a closed-in shelter even if it was just a ramshackle little trapper's cabin thrown together of cottonwood and willow logs covered with buffalo hides. It gave them privacy which she welcomed considerably now.

Hannah served them each a bowl of elk stew. Though it was delicious, neither exactly wolfed it down. She was too worried and Train was too despondent to enjoy the meal. Finally, Hannah put down her bowl and took one of Train's lethargic hands.

"Come," she said. "Lay down now."

"Nah. I'll be fine. Eatin' helped a lot."

Hannah bit back the retort she was ready to make and instead said, "You been wadin' around in that freezin' water for a couple hours settin' traps, then come back here and did more'n your share of chores. A bit of a nap'll do you good. And so will my rubbin' your feet. Unless you stopped likin' me doin' that."

"I still do. But it ain't much past noon. Ain't a time to be lollygaggin'."

"Ain't a one here can say Abner Train is a lollygagger. You do more work than anyone here 'cept Nathaniel."

"God a'mighty, Hannah, but you can be an infuriatin' young hen with your peckin' at a man. I'll take a short rest if it'll stop you from pesterin' me all the rest of the damn day."

Once more, Hannah had to choke off a sharp remark — and this time considerable hurt.

"And leave me be." He set his weapons aide and stretched out on the buffalo robe. He tried to rest but his mind wouldn't let him. It just swirled with thoughts — unpleasant ones — and regrets and worries, sadness and despair.

Hannah sat near the fire for a while, gazing out the crack between a couple of logs. Her mind, too, was a whirl. She was worried sick, and fearful. She wondered whether she was doing the right thing here, wondering whether things would ever be all right between her and Abner ever again. She feared never having his work-hardened hands caressing her flesh, his thoughtfulness in the robes. She missed the weight of his huge body on her or his hardness under her. She needed to feel his strength. She wanted to have his rough beard scratching along her skin. Many women would not like that as it could be irritating, but she found it rather ... comforting.

But she knew, too, that what Squire, Star Path and Li'l Jim had said was true. Abner was having doubts. The thought was strange to her in a way. But, then again, it wasn't. Despite his strength of will in most areas, when it came to her, he was sometimes filled with uncertainty. Like when she was rescued from the Blackfeet. But he had always come around. She hoped that would be true here.

She finally rose and went to him. She squatted down on her shins at his feet and began pulling off one of his moccasins.

"What're you doin', Hannah?" he asked, voice betraying anger and a touch of panic.

"Told you I was gonna rub your feet," Hannah said more lightly than she felt.

"And I told you no. Don't you ever listen to me, dammit?"

"Not too often," she admitted. "You should know that. Now hush up." She pulled off the other moccasin as he relented. She began rubbing and kneading his left foot, taking her time, not wanting to spook him any more than he was. He did seem to relax a tad though, she thought. After a while, she moved to the right. Giving it the same amount of time, she then began to surreptitiously move upward on his legs, massaging them with her small but strong hands.

When she got to his knees, Abner's panic returned. "What're you doin' now?" he asked in a whisper.

"Makin' you feel good, I figure," she answered lightly. She squiggled forward, parting his legs a little with her knees.

"Stop it right now, Hannah, dammit all," he said. But something had changed in his voice. There was still some nervousness but there was also a smidgen of optimism.

She reached his thighs and then higher. He squirmed a little under her touch. Suddenly, she touched his crotch. With a smile, she felt his growing hardness. She unbuttoned the buckskin trousers and grasped him in her hand. He drew in a sharp breath of pleasure and relief.

"Ain't nothin' wrong with you, my big man," she said huskily, her own excitement growing. She released him. "Don't you go anywhere," she whispered. She stood and quickly shed her shirt and pants. She straddled him and guided him inside her.

Both sighed with relief and desire as she began moving slowly, then faster.

CHAPTER 21

It SEEMED a long time in coming but spring finally began to rouse itself. It did not wake quickly but slowly threw off its mantle of cold and snow and ice. Streams and rivers became trappable again and Squire's crew took advantage, working the beaver ponds and streams heavily. But in doing so, they emptied out the area pretty quickly.

"It be time to move on," Squire said as March turned to April.

They packed up, moving north. As they traveled, they camped here and there along streams that showed plenty of beaver sign. Their hunting was good, with them bringing in dozens of prime plews.

A couple of weeks on, Hannah started showing signs of nervousness.

"Ye be all right, lass?" Squire asked one afternoon while the two of them were heading out to check their trap lines.

"Yep." She sounded less than certain.

"Bull droppin's."

Hannah managed a weak smile.

Squire patted her slim shoulder with one of his huge paws. "It be because we're in Blackfoot country, ain't it?"

Hannah said nothing for some time, then nodded. "Yep."

"Ye be scared, I reckon, and there be nothin' wrong in that. Not after what ye been through. But ye know this is the best trappin' grounds."

"I know." Her voice was a bare whisper. "And I know you and Abner and Li'l Jim will do all ya can to protect me."

"Aye."

"But we were all neck deep in those damned red devils last year."

"It was poor, aye," Squire said with a grin splitting the big beard and mustache; both were now beginning to show bits of gray, Hannah realized with a little shock.

"Was somethin' a heap more than poor bull for some of us, Nathaniel."

Squire smiled gently and nodded. "Aye, lass. That be true for certain." A glint of impishness crept into the big man's eyes. "Did ye know we spent the winter in the heart of Blackfoot country?"

Hannah's head snapped around, a look of horror — and annoyance — in her own light eyes. "What?!"

"Aye. Three Forks be a big part of the Blackfoot homeland."

"Why you despicable, foul, wretched, evil ..." she sputtered before breaking off, unable to continue. Fuming, she kicked her horse into a trot and pulled ahead of the giant.

He quickly caught up to her and grabbed the reins of her horse. "Now that ye know we be in Blackfoot country, don't go off by yourself."

Hannah glared at him but nodded. "Why didn't ya tell me?"

Squire shrugged. "Didn't figure it'd do any good. Ye'd only be worried all along."

"Damn right I would."

"So by not tellin' ye, I saved ye a heap of frettin'."

"What if the Blackfeet had attacked us?"

"There'd be some dead Blackfeet layin' about," Squire said with sly grin. "Hell, ye know those Bug's Boys be raidin' anywhere they damn well please. Don't matter none whether it be in their territory or if they rode for days to attack folks."

"You are one exasperatin' monster, Nathaniel Squire."

"Ye ain't the first to say such a thing about this ol' chil'." He grinned.

She stuck her tongue out at him. "You weren't so big, I'd toss you over my knee and spank the daylights out of you."

"That wouldn't shine with this ol' chil'." He paused, then offered a great, wide grin. "Nary can tell though. I might just take a shine to it." He guffawed.

"You are absolutely incorrigible, Nathaniel." But she laughed, too.

Then Squire grew serious. "Ye listen to me now, girl. Ye be about the strongest chil' of heart and will this ol' niggur's ary seen. Ye had done to ye the worst that could be and ye come out of it all right. Ain't nothin' else them Injuns — or anybody else — can be doin' to ye that'd be worse. Ye be strong enough to deal with whate'er anybody can toss at ye. Ye have nothin' to be fearin', lass. Nothin' a'tall."

"I think you're just spillin' out hot air from that big

chest of yours, Nathaniel," Hannah said with a small smile. But she felt less worried now. It was if she had been more afraid *thinking* about facing danger than she would have actually doing so. "Just get to pullin' beaver out of this here stream."

"Yes'm, Cap'n Lass."

Both laughed.

———

Li'l Jim had just tossed another beaver up to Squire on the riverbank when faint gunfire came from the camp half a mile away. He splashed hurriedly out of the river, snatched up his rifle and leaped on his horse. Squire was already on *Noir Astre* and galloping along the trail.

They slowed as they reached the camp and slid off their mounts, moving slowly forward on foot.

Train, Hannah and Yellow Bells, the only Indian woman who was not pregnant, were trying to calm the horses, of which there seemed to Squire to be somewhat fewer than when he had left to check the traps. He and Li'l Jim ran in and helped.

When the horses were mostly calm, Squire asked harshly, "What be the trouble here? Who took our horses?"

"Damn Crows," Train spat.

Squire looked around counting the animals left almost unconsciously. "They made off with five ponies?"

"I think so."

Squire nodded. He went and got his great black stallion and climbed aboard. "Where away they be headed?"

"Southeast," Train said. "But I'll be goin' after 'em." He was considerably adamant.

"Nay, lad. I be doin' so."

"Dammit, Nathaniel, it was my fault. I should've never been took by surprise."

"Ye know them Crows be the best horse thieves. Weren't your fault."

"Like hell it ain't."

"I be needin' ye here, boy. Watch o'er the camp. Ye be in charge."

"But ..."

Squire was not listening. He was already galloping southeast out of the camp.

Unusually, Train did not argue. He simply began firmly issuing orders to get the camp prepared for when Squire returned from recapturing their horses which Train knew he would do.

Thinking on it sometime later, Li'l Jim saw Train's action as another instance of growing maturity as a leader.

For Squire's part, he was enjoying gliding swiftly across the mountain meadow on the back of the massive stallion, the feel of the smooth, well-cared-for leather reins in his huge, cracked, work-hardened hands. And he enjoyed being alone again on the hunt.

The trail was not hard to follow, not being very old, so he had time to savor the ride and let his mind wander just a bit. He had come to care deeply for his three young charges but being away from them was a blessing, though blessedly short. He realized he had, indeed, become something of a father to them. And, as such, he feared for them, worried about them, wanted to protect them. Especially Hannah. But recently he was coming to recognize, though belatedly and reluctantly, that they were men — mountain men — even if one was a young woman. It was time, he decided, to give them more independence, to not hover over them like a mother hen. Star Path had been pushing him quietly in that direction for some time now.

He grinned. The great, giant mountain man Nathaniel Squire talking himself, at the gentle persuasion of his woman, into doing something that he never in all his years thought he would have even considered doing. "These be some doin's, ol' hoss," he said into the wind. "Some queersome doin's. Waugh!" He laughed.

———

Three Crows pushed a herd of Squire's five horses and half a dozen Blackfoot ponies, plus a few that looked to be stolen from other trappers. Squire had seen the cloud of dust the animals kicked up and hurried ahead, the anticipation of battle sending a surge of energy through him.

Feeling cocky at having just stolen ponies from the Blackfeet but also a bunch of white trappers, the Crows were paying little attention to their back trail. By the time they realized anyone was there, it was too late.

Leaving his Hawken slung across his back, Squire drew his tomahawk and swept up to the Crows. The first tumbled from his horse, head cleaved, before he even had a chance to know someone was there.

The second warrior sensed someone — or something — coming at him, turning just in time to have his face split vertically by Squire's 'hawk.

Hearing something odd, the third glanced across the herd and saw a huge trapper clad in greasy, dirty, bloody buckskins riding a gigantic black horse. The Crow quickly let loose an arrow, then quirted his pony southeast, angling away from the terrifying creature.

A small, forbidding smile spread across Squire's lips

as he urged *Noir Astre* to even greater speed. Suddenly, the warrior jerked his pony to a stop and jumped off the animal. He hurriedly began nocking another arrow.

Squire slowed his stallion, slid out of the saddle and let the big animal wander sedately off. He strode forward. "Hell, boy, that ain't about to do ye no good."

The warrior, sweating heavily through the thick stripes of blue paint that crossed his face, finally managed to fire. But he fumbled it and the arrow had almost no power.

Squire swatted away the arrow, stalked up, tossed aside his hatchet and grabbed the warrior around the throat. He squeezed. The Crow frantically tried to pull the thick, powerful hands from his windpipe to no avail. He tried to kick, he tried to gouge Squire's eyes. He finally tried to pull the knife he had forgotten about as his mind swirled and black spots appeared.

Squire gave one last squeeze and dropped the lifeless body. "Teach ye to be stealin' this ol' chil's horses." He turned and walked toward where Noir Astre was munching placidly in the new grass. He rode off, now on a mission to gather all the horses.

It took more than an hour but he had the herd back together and moving haphazardly toward his camp. But some strayed and he had to chase them down. He didn't have much rope but he used what he had to link together four of the Blackfoot ponies — the most fractious. He hoped all the others would follow along at least somewhat peacefully.

It was nigh onto dark now and there was still some miles to go so Squire decided to stay the night at a cotton-wood-and-willow-dotted spot along a stream. Finding some rawhide strips in his possible sack, he managed to hobble the last two Blackfoot ponies. He plunked himself down against a willow, pulled out a strip of jerky and tore at it with strong teeth.

In the morning, he unhobbled the peevish ponies and moved out. He rode into camp two hours later. Train rushed up, shouting, "Nathaniel!"

The big mountain man frowned. He had expected to be welcomed back but not with anywhere near such enthusiasm which was vastly unlike Train."

"It's Star Path! She's ..."

Squire vaulted off his giant horse and ran, shoving past his young lieutenant.

CHAPTER 22

"… BIRTHIN'."

But Squire was past him. And only as he stumbled into their lodge did the words actually hit him. "Birthin'! Damn!" He turned and rushed out with a chorus of "Get out!" ringing out behind him.

"Hell, boy," he snapped at Train, "why'n't you tell me she was foaling? A man's … "

"But I did."

"… got no place among such doin's."

"I know. I tried …"

"Foolish chil'," Squire muttered as he headed toward the horses to tend them.

Train, perplexed, looked at Li'l Jim who just laughed. "Best let it go, Abner. There's no talking to him when he's like this. You know that. Does seem odd though. He's been through this before."

Train shrugged, concerned but not too much. It wasn't unknown for Squire to be moody at times. He went over and helped Squire, keeping quiet.

Afterward, the men sat around the fire, sipping coffee

and nibbling desultorily at bits of roasted buffalo. It was evident Squire was nervous so the two younger men remained quiet. Suddenly, Squire asked, "Hannah be in there?"

"Yep," Train answered. "I got to say it surprised hell out of me that she went in there."

"Ne'er can tell about women."

They fell silent again. Squire tried to hide the wince every time a moan drifted over him from the separate lodge they had put up for the birth. Suddenly, there was a long screech followed by a baby's howl.

Squire's relief was visible. Soon after, Hannah came and joined the three at the fire. She looked somewhat pale. "You're a pa again," she said, ignoring the obvious. "You got a shinin', healthy son."

Squire grunted in acknowledgement but said nothing. The others looked at him in curiosity but said nothing. A few minutes later, Squire rose and stalked off without a word.

"What's wrong with Nathaniel?" Train wondered aloud.

"Don't know, but I'm damn sure gonna find out," Li'l Jim said, rising.

"Sit!" Hannah ordered. When an even more puzzled Li'l Jim did so, she said, "He ain't had much luck with young'uns. I reckon he's a mite nervous about such things. I reckon he'll get over it right quick."

"Does seem odd though," Train said thoughtfully. "It ain't like him to be spooked by anything. I mean after all the Injun fightin' and such he's done, it just don't seem right that he'd be this spooked by his woman havin' a child."

"Fightin' off a passel of Blackfeet ain't quite the same

as becomin' a pa. Injun fightin', you can do something. Havin' a child, there ain't much you can do, especially after something like havin' two young'uns die and a son stolen from you like Blue Mountain was."

The two men were silent for a bit, then Train said, "That makes sense. Hope I never get put in that position." He winced, realizing what he had said when Hannah shot him a rather hostile glance.

Squire was his usual self in the morning. They spent another day there despite Star Path's determination to be on the move. Hannah, Train and Li'l Jim chuckled when they overheard the argument. It wasn't often Nathaniel Squire lost an argument, even to Star Path, but this was a losing battle for him and he soon knew it.

The three listeners scattered when Squire came out of his lodge and he growled at them. Soon after, though, he got the three together and warned, "I be catchin' ye listening' in to me and Star Path, I'll cut your ears off so's ye can't be listenin' to things that ain't no concern anymore."

Hannah was the first to break. It started as a giggle, then grew until it was full out laughter. "Damn, Nathaniel, that's the best nonsense threat you've come up with in a spell," she said through the laughter.

The others joined in. Squire just grinned. "Ye three be knowin' me too well by now. Just be watchin' out. One of these here days, I might just make good on one of my threats. Then you'll be sorry." He finally chuckled. "Now get back to your work."

They pulled out the next morning heading east toward the Yellowstone River. They figured to head back to St. Louis along much the same route as they had come out. They moved slowly, in no real rush to reach the city, and there were still some prime pickings of beaver to be had.

They were a week out when Train, who had been checking for sign in a small circle around the group, hurried up to Squire. "Somebody's followin' us," he said though he did not seem concerned.

"Who and how many?"

"Ain't Blackfeet or any others I know of. I figure it's trappers. No tellin' how many. But judgin' by the dust, there's either a hell of a lot of 'em or they've got themselves a large cavvy. Or both, I reckon."

"Aye, could be either," Squire said, tugging on his thick beard for a moment. "If it be free trappers or Rocky Mountain boys, there won't be no trouble. But if it's Company men, I ain't to be trustin' 'em."

"With good reason," Train agreed with a grim smile.

"Well, best keep an eye on 'em, lad. There be a good spot to spend the night maybe eight, ten miles ahead. Should be there in a couple hours since it be all easy travelin' 'tween here and there. We'll stop there. Me and the others'll be ready just in case those boys be thinkin' of causin' some deviltry. Be back with us before dusk."

Train nodded, turned his horse, and trotted off.

———

Camp was made and all was ready when Train rode in. "I got some closer to 'em this time, Nathaniel," he said when he had dismounted and was tending his horse. "I didn't really show myself so I don't figure they saw me. But if they're anywhere near as good as most boys who been in the mountains a while, they'll have known someone was watchin' 'em."

"Reckon ye be right."

"Might think we're Blackfeet."

"That could mean trouble. They think there's Blackfeet about, they'll be on the alert and itchin' for a fight."

Train offered a small smile. "Hell, Nathaniel, we're still in Blackfoot country. Any mountain boys here're be set and ready for raisin' hair."

Squire nodded. "I keep forgettin' you and the others ain't greenhorns no more. Next season, you lads won't be needin' this ol' chil' around whatsoever."

"We still got plenty to learn from you, Nathaniel." He gave out a wide grin. "Besides, you'll be so old you'll need us to be carin' for you, you ol' goat. Instead of bein' *L'on Farouche,* you'll be *L'on Ancien.*" He laughed.

"Any time you want to test yourself against this ol' chil', you just have at it, boy," he growled. "You'll see how old I be." He laughed, too. When that died down, he asked, "Ye be noticin' anything about who they was or how many?"

"I ain't sure, Nathaniel, but I don't think they're Company men. From what I was able to see, they got the look of free trappers about 'em."

"How many?"

"A dozen, maybe a couple more. I couldn't count the animals but I reckon there was a good thirty or forty horses and mules beside the ones they were ridin'."

"Any women be with 'em?"

"Some. Maybe four or five."

"How far?"

"Ain't but two, three miles."

Squire nodded. "*Bon, mon ami.* Go on and get yourself some grub."

"Fillin' my meatbag sounds damn good." He hurried off, heading for the cook fire Hannah had started.

Squire shouted for Li'l Jim. When the young man trotted up, the big mountain man said, "There be a passel of mountaineers comin' our way. Abner says they look like free men but can't be certain. I want you to go on up yon ridge and keep an eye out for 'em. They look like they be goin' past us to the north a bit, just keep watchin'. They look like they be headin' right for us, ye get back here and tell it."

Li'l Jim said nothing, just turned and hurried to the horse herd and began saddling his mount.

———

Though it had not been long, Li'l Jim was already cursing the boredom when the group of men came into view. As they neared his position, one man broke away and started down the trail that would lead to Squire's camp. Li'l Jim slid back away from the cliff edge and scurried down the steep, rock- and scrub-covered slope past his horse. It was not difficult for Li'l Jim to find a suitable boulder for his purposes. It was large enough to hide his small frame but small enough that he could fire over it.

Within a couple of minutes, the rider came into view. "Hold up, hoss," Li'l Jim shouted. When the man did, Li'l Jim asked, "What's your name, hoss? And what're you doin' on this trail?"

"Name's Sam Cotton. I'm lookin' for a place to camp for the night."

"You alone?"

Cotton hesitated a moment, then said, "Nope. passel

of boys're follerin' along."

"You with the Company?"

Cotton leaned over and spit. When he straightened, he said, "I'd as soon kill me a Company man as one of Bug's Boys."

Li'l Jim grinned. He rose and walked down onto the trail. He was wary but not anxious. "Name's Li'l Jim."

Cotton stared at him a moment, then smiled. "You're that little hoss won all them shootin' contests last year at rendezvous."

"That'd be me, yep."

"Hell of a shooter you are."

"The best," Li'l Jim said with his usual lack of humility.

"I see you're still wearin' that badger necklace you won off me."

Li'l Jim stared at Cotton, then nodded. "Thought you looked a mite familiar but there's something different about you."

Cotton grinned. "Didn't have this scraggly ol' beard. It'll come off again just afore we get to rendezvous."

"Maybe you should just keep it," Li'l Jim said with a laugh.

Cotton joined in.

"We got us a camp down the trail here a short ways. I'll take you there and let Nathaniel decide if you and your friends'll be welcome."

Cotton nodded. "Reckon if he's a real mountaineer, he won't have no objections."

Li'l Jim got his horse and the two men rode the short distance to Squire's camp. As they dismounted in front of Squire, who had come up to meet them, Cotton said, "You're Nathaniel Squire, ain't you?"

"Aye, lad. That I be."

"Pleased to meet you, sir." He shook hands with the giant mountain man.

"Sam here says he's with some other fellows who ain't Company men."

"Free trappers?"

"Damn right we are," Cotton said proudly.

"Who's your booshway?"

"Ryan McNab."

"I know ol' Ryan. He be a fine feller. You and Li'l Jim can ride on back and tell him he be welcome in our camp. There be a spot maybe a hundred yards southeast with plenty of water and wood. Good grass for the animals."

———

Two hours later, McNab and several of his friends showed up in Squire's camp after having set up their own. The visitors plopped down around a fire outside Squire's lodge. McNab uncorked a large earthen jug of Taos Lightning.

"You be a right smart visitor, Ryan," Squire said as he grabbed the jug and took a healthy swallow.

"I'd expect the same if you was to come into my camp, hoss. And I know you'd do right, too." He grinned. "Now gimme that damn jug."

Squire did so, then asked, "What're ye doin' this way, headin' east?"

"Figured we'd take the Yellowstone to the Missouri. Take the river down this year."

After a few celebratory swigs by all as the jug made the rounds, McNab said, "I seen that fancy pal of yourn, that colonel feller."

"Colonel Melton?"

"He's the one."

"I'll be dammed, that ol' chil' decided to bring a brigade out here after all. Hope he was farin' well."

"The opposite. That chil's come on some hard times. He and his boys was afoot and lookin' mighty poorly."

"Where?" Squire asked, suddenly worried about Melton.

"Along the Salmon near where it makes that big turn south. They was headin' toward rendezvous. Don't know as if he'll make it seein's how poorly they was doin'. I offered what help I could, which to say weren't much, but he said he didn't want any. Obstinate feller, that ol' chil'."

"That he be. When was this?"

"Couple weeks ago, I reckon. Don't know how far they've got by now. They was movin' plumb slow."

"Blackfeet?"

"That's what he said. Got all their plunder. Lost horse and beaver. Said two men was caught by them devils."

"Who be they?"

"They said but I don't recall. Never heard of 'em before. Couple of Frenchies."

"Dumoulin? Ledoux?"

"First one sounds right."

"*Merde!*"

"Second one don't though. I think it was Gagne, maybe."

"Don't know him but it doesn't matter none. If he be one of the Colonel's lads and be took by the Blackfeet, he be deservin' rescue. Or vengeance."

CHAPTER 23

Interlude

Spring 1835

Jacob Meisner stood outside his lodge in Elk Horn's Blackfoot village, watching as a group of warriors poured in with a large herd of white men's horses and mules, many laden with an assortment of goods.

A tall, broad-shouldered warrior slid off his pony and approached Meisner, who asked, "Do you have Squire's scalp, Gray Thunder?"

"Not have it."

"Is Squire dead?" Meisner asked in a snarling voice.

"Not killed by us."

"Vhy de hell not?" Meisner followed Gray Thunder into the lodge where the Indian slumped down near the fire. He picked up a spoon and scooped out a piece of boiled buffalo from the pot on the fire.

"He was not with the others," Gray Thunder said with a shrug. "We brought all the things from the men we found."

"You sure you got da right vones?"

"Leader was a man dressed like the big chiefs at Fort Union and other trade places."

"You sure he vasn't with dem? Vasn't just out hunting?"

"Yes. We followed several days. Never saw *L'on Farouche*." He sounded both frustrated and relieved.

"You sure?"

Gray Thunder swallowed another bite of meat and took a cup of coffee from Meisner's wife. "He's hard to miss. Ain't gonna mistake him for some other white man."

"Dammit, Gray Thunder, I told you I vanted ..."

"You have much say here, Meisner," the Blackfoot said, voice growing harsh. "You married into tribe - the daughter of a chief - because Elk Horn and others say it's good. You bring us many gifts. And you promise many riches if we do what you say. But you are not Blackfoot. We have many reasons to hate *L'on Farouche* and want him dead. More than you. It's not good you get angry we did not kill *L'on Farouche*. No. You have tried to raise his hair. You have others do the same."

"But, dammit ..."

"No dammits from you, Meisner. There's plenty furs and other things to take to Fort Union."

"But der Company vants Squire dead more dan a couple thousand dollars worth of furs. Those you brought in, dey vill be good, yah. But with Squire running around still, der Company is not happy."

"That's your concern. We killed at least two damn

trappers, stole many horses and took skins and more we can trade at one of your forts."

"*Verdammt*. The bourgeois at Fort Elk Horn is eager as McKenzie to have Squire dead. Until dot son of a bitch is dead, the Company won't be able to control all der Americans' fur trade."

Gray Thunder shrugged. Then he grinned. "Maybe it will help that we brought prisoners. Two of *L'on Farouche's* friends with Fancy Pants. Maybe they tell you where Squire is"

"Vhy didn't you say so already?" Meisner snapped. He rose. "Come, ve talk to dem."

"I eat first. Rest. They're not going away."

Meisner grunted in anger but sat. Soon Gray Thunder rose. "I be back one hour. We talk to *L'on Farouche's* men then."

———

"You didn't rest none," Meisner said when Gray Thunder returned. "You vas humpin' your voman."

The Blackfoot grinned.

They walked to where two men were tied, standing against a cottonwood. "Vhat are your names?" Meisner asked without preliminary."

"*Je ne parle pas anglais*," one man said.

Meisner kicked him in the knee. "Vhat is your name?"

"*Je ne parle pas anglais*," the man repeated.

Meisner turned to the second captive and asked him the same question and, in return, received the same response.

"*Mein* patience is short. Vhat are your names?"

"The two captives looked at each other and shrugged.

"I am Pierre Dumoulin and 'e is Jules Gagne."

"Vell, Herr Dumoulin and Herr Gagne, you should be telling me now vhere is Squire."

"Ve don' where 'e is, monsieur," Gagne said.

"I wouldn't tell you even if I knew," Dumoulin said. "'E left with only a few fellows from last year. We went with Colonel Melton and ze odders."

"I don't believe you."

The two French-Canadians shrugged. "It is ze truth," Dumoulin said. "It don' matter whether you believe or not, whoever the 'ell you are."

"I am Jacob Meisner," he said as if that would explain everything.

"*Zut. Vous êtes la merde qui aide le* Blackfeet — you are the shit who helps the Blackfeet."

"Yah, I help de Blackfoots. Dey trade mostly with de Englishers. But vhen I kill dis Squire, dey vill trade with de Americans."

"You 'ave dreams, monsieur," Dumoulin said. You cannot kill *L'on Farouche*. And ze Blackfeet, zey will not trade with ze Americans."

"Dey vill with de Company. But dey vill not vith Squire alive. He is de devil to dem. Until de devil is remove, dey won't trade with de Americans except me."

"Well, *bon chance*," Dumoulin said. "Now let us go, monsieur. We will go back to ze Colonel. You will 'ave to find *L'on Farouche* on your own. We do not know where 'e is. We cannot 'elp you."

"Ve vill see. De Blackfoots vill encourage you to tell de truth. Yah, you vill be telling de truth soon vhen dey make encouragement."

"Your torture don' scare us none, monsieur," Dumoulin said.

"Torture?" There was fear in Gagne's voice.

"*Etre ferme, garçon. Montre aucune peur* - Be firm, boy. Show no fear. *Mais si vous croyez dans Dieu, vous feriez mieux de prier* - But if you believe in God, you had better pray."

Gray Thunder and several other Blackfeet moved forward, heading toward Gagne who was obviously the weaker of the two French-Canadians.

Gagne said nothing when the Blackfeet sliced off his buckskin shirt. But he howled in pain when a knife sliced a shallow line several inches down his chest followed by a slow cut parallel to that, then two small slices connecting them. One of the warriors grinned as he peeled the strip of flesh away. Gagne screamed again and started to cry.

"*Arrêter cette satanée hurlement, garçon. Cultiver quelques balles et être un homme* - Quit that damned howling, boy. Grow some balls and be a man," Dumoulin snapped.

But the young man could not. He continued to wail as Blackfoot warriors peeled strips of flesh from him. Every few minutes, they would stop and Meisner would ask, "Vhere is Squire?" With the response always, "I don't know," the torture would continue.

Finally, Gagne passed out and the warriors turned their attention to Dumoulin. The mountain man remained stoic, hissing involuntarily on occasion as a knife cut too deep. But he, too, responded in the negative when Meisner asked where Squire was.

"They know nothing," Gray Thunder said after a couple of hours of tormenting the two men. "If they knew anything, the young one would have talked."

Angry, but knowing it was the truth, a grim Meisner said, "Kill dem."

CHAPTER 24

SQUIRE WOKE his group well before dawn the next morning and they were pulling out just about the time McNab and his men were rising. Squire pushed them hard, heading southwest, figuring to encounter Melton still somewhat northwest of the rendezvous at the confluence of Horse Creek and the Green River. If Melton was in as bad shape as McNab had said, it was doubtful he would've made rendezvous by now.

The travel was hard on Star Path and Cloudy Moon, who had given birth to a son two weeks after Star Path, with their infants. Even the others were feeling the strain after five long days. Squire did not care. He pushed more, warning that anyone who could not keep up would be left behind.

There was some grumbling but not too much. Li'l Jim, Train and Hannah all were very fond of Melton and wanted to help him in whatever way they could. So if it took riding from dawn to beyond dusk for a week or more, then so be it. Still, they were all getting irritable.

Four days out, as they wearily set to a poor meal of

pemmican and coffee, Train asked, "Rendezvous is some distance southeast of here, ain't it, Nathaniel?"

"Aye."

"Then why're we headin' southwest?"

"If the Colonel be in as poor straits as Ryan said, he won't be near rendezvous e'en now. I figure Slocum and Marcel, if they be with 'em, will be leadin' 'em through the valley 'tween the Beaverheads and the Lemhis.

"Figurin' to run across 'em there?"

"Aye."

"You think you can find 'em? There's a heap of land out there and you ain't even sure where he is or which way he's travelin'.'"

"Like I said, lad, if Slocum and Marcel be with the Colonel, they'll be leadin' 'em that way. It be the easiest way to get to rendezvous."

"If that's where your stick floats, Nathaniel, then mine does, too."

The others readily agreed.

"And I been thinkin'," Squire said. "When we get to the river, Abner, ye and Hannah will hole up with the women, little 'uns, horses and all the plews and such. Me and Li'l Jim'll move on fast, lookin' for the Colonel."

Train looked a little disgruntled. "You sure you don't want me along 'stead of Li'l Jim? I'm a heap better tracker'n he is."

"That be a fact," Squire agreed. "Hannah, what be your thinkin' on it?"

"I don't mind stayin' behind, I reckon, with Li'l Jim. If that big galoot over there," she pointed to Train, "don't mind. He gets a mite touchy when I'm with Li'l Jim, if you'll remember." She kept her face blank.

Train flushed. "Dammit, don't remind me again of what a damn fool I can be."

Hannah laughed. "Just pullin' your tail, Abner."

Train smiled but it was touched with a rueful grimace. "You don't mind then?"

Hannah grew serious. "If it'll help find Colonel Melton faster and get him some help quickly, I'd let you go even if there was Blackfeet knockin' on our lodge door."

"That suit you, Li'l Jim?" Train asked.

"I ain't so sure," he said with a solemn look. "Ain't certain I can keep my hands off Hannah there." He suddenly burst out laughing. "If you don't know by now, boy, that Hannah's like my sister, you're even a bigger damn fool than I figured."

"I know," Train grumbled.

"I'd purely love to go with you, Nathaniel. But it's a fact that Abner's a heap better tracker than I am. With you and Abner on the trail, you'll be able to run down Colonel Melton in no time. Then we can see about settin' things right."

"So there, it's settled," Train said.

"Nay, lad. I'll be takin' Li'l Jim."

"But ..." Train started.

"Ye be question'n my orders, lad?"

Train hesitated only a minute. "Dammit, yes, sir, Nathaniel, I surely am."

"Well, go on, lad," Squire said as a faint smiled touched his lips.

"Like you and Li'l Jim both said, I'm the better tracker. With me to help, we'll find the trail quicker." He was proud of laying out his objection so smartly but also because of having stood up to Squire.

"Ye also be the steadiest hand, lad. Some Bug's Boys come roamin' around lookin' to be causin' some deviltry, it'd be good to have someone with a steadiness about him to deal with it. Some others here, well, they be a mite reckless."

"You wouldn't mean me by that would ya?" Li'l Jim asked in mock innocence.

Squire chuckled. "Aye, lad. Ye been known to be a bit reckless now and again."

"Now and again?" Hannah laughed.

"Bah!" Li'l Jim said but he laughed, too.

"'Sides," Squire went on with another grin, "despite this young critter bein' a damn poor tracker, I figure the Colonel and his lads be right down the way we be goin'. Shouldn't be hard to catch up to 'em. Unless Slocum and Marcel led 'em some other way, which ain't likely."

———

Five more days of pushing the pace through the Bitterroots via Bannock Pass and then the Beaverhead Mountains and they were in in the vast valley. The grass was tall and green and large patches of wildflowers spread their colors in profusion.

Train, who was out ahead of the group, found a spot along the river with a copse of cottonwoods and willows. There was plenty of grass for the horses, lots of trees for shade and a plentiful supply of loose wood and easy access to water. Train nodded and turned back. Within an hour, he was leading the group to the spot.

By the time camp was set up, it was late afternoon and despite the tension of their mission, Squire figured it was a time to relax as much as they could for one night.

They were all exhausted; even Squire and Train, the two biggest, strongest among them, were showing signs of weariness.

After a hasty breakfast the next morning, Squire and Li'l Jim headed out, moving north up the river, Squire on the east side, Li'l Jim on the west. Less than three hours later, Li'l Jim whistled and waved to Squire. The giant mountain man found a decent ford half a mile up and crossed over. Li'l Jim was waiting for him.

"I found sign they passed this way, Nathaniel," Li'l Jim said, his cockiness even more evident than usual. "Ain't sure, but it's at least a few days old, maybe a week."

"Ye certain it be them?"

"I ain't the tracker Abner is but I'm pretty certain. I traveled with them boys long enough I can tell some of 'em's tracks." He dismounted and directed Squire do the same, then both knelt. Train traced a faint outline in the dirt. "This here is from Homer, I think. He's got that funny little way of walkin' makes a readable impression." He moved a few feet to his right and indicated another mark. "And this here's the Colonel. He and maybe Slocum are the only ones wearin' boots 'stead of mocs. I think they stopped here to water the horses, though they ain't got but three or four far's I can tell from this sign. The Colonel's prints disappear right quick. I can't figure that out." He shook his head in annoyance.

"Ye be right, lad, about them stoppin' here. As far's the Colonel's tracks disappearin', I figure he be ridin'. He be the booshway of this here brigade. Though I reckon it be more than a week since they passed by."

Li'l Jim nodded. "Slow as they're movin', we ought to be able to catch up to 'em pretty quick," he said as he rose and mounted.

"Aye, lad." Squire pulled himself into the saddle. "Now let's make some dust."

They skirted the camp by some distance, not wanting to take the time to explain. They just rode at a good clip down the river. They slowed eventually and moved steadily rather than continuing to gallop along which would have worn the horses down.

They made a quick cold camp that night and the next. Just before noon the following day, they saw dust ahead.

"Reckon it's them?" Li'l Jim asked as he and Squire loped along.

"Aye. I ain't seen no Injun tracks nor those of other trappers."

Before long, they saw a few men straggling along about half a mile ahead. The men turned when they heard horses behind them and then turned back, starting to run.

Squire stood in the stirrups and bellowed, "I be *L'on Farouche*!" He pulled off his cap and waved it.

Two of the men looked over their shoulders, slowed, stopped. The others, realizing their friends were no longer right with them, also stopped. When they looked back, they realized who it was and began waving. One of them spun and raced toward the main group.

"Howdy, Nathaniel, Li'l Jim," one of the young men, Eli Beale, said. He was one of the original group who had gone west with Melton's brigade last year. He was a tall, rangy fellow, usually of good cheer. Now, though, he looked about ready to collapse.

"Eli," the newcomers said, then nodded to the others – Jed Brand, Horace Dawes and Simon Essex, also among the old-timers with the Colonel. Squire and Train pushed ahead, loping toward the beginning of the line.

Within a minute, they pulled up just in front of the only three horses with the group; one ridden by Melton and a pregnant Rising Sun, one by a pregnant Silver Necklace and the third by Slocum Peters. Homer Bellows was holding Rising Sun's reins.

"If you ain't the worst lookin', bedraggled, draggin' ass, starvin' coons this chil's ary seed," Squire said, but he did so with a small smile.

Slocum Peters and Melton sat on their horses facing Squire and Li'l Jim. Marcel Ledoux moved up on foot to stand between both horses.

"Well, we been dawdling for a spell now," Peters said. "jist waitin' on you and your boys to appear so's we could help ye git to rendezvous."

"Well, I be mighty glad ye found us, lad." He looked over his friends. Melton was usually a large, slightly chubby man, jovial in general, except where business was concerned. Now he was gaunted down considerably, his skin seeming to sag off his face. He had a hangdog look about him and defeat in his eyes. Peters was in somewhat better shape. More inured to such hardships, he had weathered it all with a little more success. Bellows looked to Squire as he always had — thin as a rail with a prominent Adam's apple. But he had a beaten look in his eyes, something Squire had never seen before. Marcel Ledoux had lost some of his blockiness and had a considerable amount of gray now in his thick beard.

Squire grinned a little. "*Ah, mon ami, Marcel, pourquoi marches-tu pendant que ce vieux réprouvé être à cheval?* - Ah, my friend, Marcel, why be ye walkin' while this old reprobate be ridin'?" He indicated Peters.

Ledoux smiled though not altogether happily. "Me and Slocum, we change. Sometimes 'e rides and I walk, sometimes ze other way. But Slocum, 'e rides more often. I t'ink it is because I am young and strong. And 'andsome, too. *Mais Oui*! It is a curse sometimes to be un *si grand homme* - such a great man.»

They all chuckled but then Squire grew serious. "Ye lads do look like you encountered some mighty poor doin's. Ye know where that ol' campsite be, Slocum?"

The other mountain man nodded. "About five miles down the river here, best I can figure. It was where I was figurin' to stop, maybe rest a couple days, get some strength to push on to rendezvous."

"Well, let's be getting all these folks down there. Homer, you think you can be getting those fleabags another few miles?"

"Reckon I can," he said without much enthusiasm. "Ain't many of 'em left."

To Squire, Bellows had the right words but the fervor of old was not there. Squire wondered whether it would ever return and hoped deeply that it would.

"Where are the others, Nathaniel?" Melton asked. "Surely Abner and Star Path and Hannah are with you."

"Aye, they be. Set 'em up in a camp couple days ride north of here whilst me'n Li'l Jim be lookin' for ye."

"They'll join us, I assume?"

"Aye. Li'l Jim be haulin' your ass back up the river and get the rest of our people. Push 'em hard."

I'd rather stay, Nathaniel," Li'l Jim interrupted much to Squire's annoyance. Before the giant could stop him, the young man charged on, "I'm the best damned hunter of the lot and these boys look to be nigh on to famished. They like as not could use some fresh meat and ain't no better for makin' it but me."

Squire's annoyance faded. "Damn, lad, where did ye

get some sense? I would've nary thought ye'd be capable."
He grinned and the others chuckled. "What be your
thinkin' on this, Colonel?"

"It does make sense but is your camp hard to find?"

"Nay, Colonel. Marcel, ye remember that place we
stayed one time near where Mud and Birch Creeks be
meetin' up."

"*Oui.*"

"Ye be willin' to go?"

Ledoux stood there, running a hand across the
immensely thick beard as if thinking. Then he nodded.
"*Oui.* I can do zat." Then he grinned. "But only if
Monsieur Afraid to Walk gives me his 'orse."

"You're an evil cuss, Marcel," Peters said as he slid off
the animal, taking his rifle and possibles bag. "Hope the
Blackfeet raise hair on ye. Long's they don't steal
the horse."

"*Et j'espère que ta bite ne va plus marcher. Si vous en
avez un, mon ami* - And I hope your cock falls off from
walking. If you have one, my friend."

The two men clasped forearms before Ledoux
mounted the horse. "Good luck, ol' hoss," Peters said.

"*Merci.*"

"Be ridin' hard, lad," Squire said. "I be wantin' 'em
here quick as possible. They've had a few days rest so they
ought to be rested enough to push themselves. Ye be in
charge."

It took several more hours but with Peters leading the
way and Squire herding the laggards, the Colonel's
motley brigade finally managed to straggle into a shining
spot. Like the campsite where Squire had left his people,
this one had plenty of wood, shade, grass and easy access
to the river.

"Some of ye lads fetch up wood and get fires goin'," Squire ordered as Ransom led the horses to water. "I ain't got much but there should be enough jerky for all of you to get bite or two. And mayhap enough coffee for e'eryone to have at least a sip."

There were a number of women along, some of them pregnant. Squire did not know them but, like all Indian women, they were efficient in setting up what camp they could manage.

When the time came, Squire rationed out the coffee and jerky. There was enough — barely — to give everyone a taste. Even that small bit brought a modicum of cheer to the scruffy, trail-weary men.

In the morning, Squire sent out Li'l Jim, leading one of the group's three horses. Game was scarce but he finally managed to scare up a deer. He easily dropped it and tossed it over the extra horse. In camp, he turned it over to some camp helpers who showed some enthusiasm with the thought of fresh deer meat to be had soon.

CHAPTER 25

"So what happened, lads?" Squire asked when they had eaten and sat back with tin mugs of the scarce coffee and their small clay pipes loaded with dwindling tobacco.

"Had us a hell of a shinin' fall hunt," Peters said. Had us two thousand, maybe three thousand plews all pressed into nice tight bindles. I figure about four thousand pounds or a bit more. It were lookin' like we was gonna be plumb rollin' in cash money."

"Be a heap of money for certain," Squire said through a cloud of smoke. "Nearabout twenty thousand ye be figurin', Colonel?"

"Thereabouts, yes. Likely a little more if merchants there are still paying five dollars a pound."

A couple of the younger men whistled at the amounts being discussed. With their two hundred fifty dollars or so for the year, twenty thousand dollars was money they couldn't even really contemplate.

"Would've been makin' your backers more'n happy, Colonel."

"That it would."

"And the spring hunt shined damned near as well, this chil' says," Peters offered. "We brought in another couple thousand pound. The Colonel and his backers was going to be rich, and me and the rest of us ol' coons was plannin' to have us one hell of a spree down to rendezvous. Or maybe in St. Louis." The thought excited him. Then reality sent his joy crashing to the ground like a landslide.

"That's all gone now," Melton said, dejection weighing heavily on his face. "It will take me years back in the States to make up what I have lost here."

"Don't ye be thinkin' such things, Colonel," Squire said.

"I know you are a man of infinite hope and strength. Alas, I am not. I am a man of practicality. There is no time to trap those many plews again even if I could find the supplies and horses and mules."

"More'n one way to bring in plews, Colonel," Li'l Jim said. "Might just find us some mountain boys wanderin' 'round not payin' much heed to their plews and such."

"We will do no such thing," Melton thundered, looking stricken at the very idea.

"Just a thought, Colonel," Li'l Jim said. He sounded not in the last bit contrite.

"And a bad one," Melton grumbled.

Squire laughed. As did Peters. "Ain't changed a lick, has he?" the latter said.

"Nay."

"Never will neither," Li'l Jim snapped, sticking out his chin in defiance. Then he, too, broke out in laughter.

Moments later when they had calmed down, Squire said, "Ye ne'er did tell yet what happened to put ye in such straights, lads."

"Like I said, we had us a shinin' fall hunt," Peters said. "Found us a fine winter camp up near the Smoke River. Stayed near Risin' Sun's people." A smile teased at Peters's lips. But he said nothing more.

Instead, Horace Dawes said with a chuckle, "It were a good place. The Colonel especially liked it 'cause Risin' Sun's family spent considerable time in our camp visitin'."

"Pesterin' is more like it," Melton snapped. "Damn family is like a tribe of leeches." He looked around hastily to make sure Rising Sun was not within listening distance. He sighed. "That does not matter either now."

"Sounds like ye be missin' 'em," Colonel."

"No, Nathaniel, not missing them. At least not much. Rising Sun was mighty happy when they were around and when she is happy, that's always pleasing to me. But what I miss is the time spent at that spot when we did. As Slocum said, we had many plews and the expectation of plenty more in the spring hunt. The winter camp was comfortable. As comfortable as any I've heard of. But ever since that time ..."

"Yep, they were shinin' times," Peters jumped in. "Spring started out the same way. Streams up that away was teemin' with beaver. Traps full damn near all the time. Camp hands and the women were curin' 'em fast as they could. Hell, we had willow hoops festoonin' the camps by the dozens if not more all the time. Looked like some queersome festival back in the States."

That brought a chuckle from the assembled men.

"Trappin' was so good, we had to stay a while each place we trapped so the plews could be took care of proper. Usually the beaver run out before that. Occasionally, men moved off a little farther and placed their traps but, eventually, the plews'd be bundled up and off we'd go to another shinin' site."

"Then the Blackfoot came," Squire said more than asked.

"That they did," Melton said with some vehemence, regaining a spark of his old self though it lasted but a moment. "Hard to tell how many there were but it seemed like a hundred."

"Ye exaggeratin', Colonel?"

"No, Nathaniel," Melton said with a shake of his head. "You should well know by now that I'm not given to such a thing."

Squire nodded.

"We gave back as best we could," Peters said. "Waugh! It was some doin's it was. Like last year at that big battle in the grove after rendezvous, these boys shined, they did. Couldn't ask no better of 'em. Lost one camp hand. Simon and Mel Eaton — he's one of the new boys we hired on for this season — was wounded."

Squire looked around at the small circle of men. All were stony-faced, haunted, determined. They were a far cry from barely fuzz-sprouting boys who didn't know their asses from a tea kettle that had set out the year before or this year. These were men — tough, fearless, inured to hardship — and thirsty for revenge.

"I ain't seen Pierre here," he said, jaw tight, hoping that his friend had simply left the group sometime.

"Pierre and Jules Gagne, a new man hired in St. Louis, was taken," Peters said, voice filled with anger.

"We gonna try'n save 'em, Nathaniel?" Gideon Hook asked, surprising himself at calling Squire by his first name instead of Mr. Squire.

"It be too late for that, lad. It be a month, two mayhap."

"Closer to two," Melton said.

"Them lads be dead now, lad." He was saddened. One had been a friend and while they had had disputes, they were still friends. And as he had told McNab, if the other was one of Melton's men, he was a friend, too.

Hook nodded. He had come to like the pair of irascible French-Canadians, one older, one not much past him in years.

"It seemed like them red devils weren't so interested in killin' as they were in stealin' our plunder, though," Peters went on.

"That be seemin' rather odd to this ol' chil'," Squire commented. "'Specially after all the troubles we be givin' Bug's Boys."

"Thought the same," Peters said. "But ol' Gideon and ol' Jed there managed to latch their paws on one of those demons. Asked him why his people done so."

"Ye asked politely, I reckon?" Squire said with a hard grin.

"We certainly did," Hook said, his grin as harsh as Squire's.

"*Bon.* That be his hair on your rifle there?"

"Yep.

"*Bon,*" Squire repeated. "And what did this talkative ol' hoss be tellin' ye?"

"Said they was lookin' for you, Nathaniel," Hook said. "Ol' hoss named Meisner wanted his boys to bring you back with 'em."

"That so. Well, seems like those damn fools nary did learn their lessons."

"Seems like," Peters agreed. "That ol' chil' said they

wanted to take you, whether it was puttin' you under or trussin' you up and haulin' your overgrowed corpus to their village. Seems like this Meisner son of a bitch wanted to make sure you was wolf bait. And since you weren't there, I expect they figured to take all our plunder. Reckon they figured they could trade it somewhere."

"And since you weren't there," Hook said, "they figured you'd come after 'em when you found out."

"Those sons a bitches'd be right," Squire said with a cold, hard voice.

"'Sides, I reckon they figured we'd go under soon, what with us havin' not a damned thing to keep us from starvin' times."

"Would have done so in another day or two, too, you hadn't found us, Nathaniel," Melton said. His voice was torn between despair and anger.

"Well, I reckon you be a bit better off now that I'm here. Be e'en better once Marcel brings the others in." He looked at Hook. "And Bug's Boys be right. This chil'll be goin' after 'em."

They all sat in silence for a moment, then Squire looked at Bellows who sat with a hangdog expression on his face. "You be mighty quiet, Homer. Ye be all right?"

Bellows looked up with anguish in his eyes and on his face. He pushed himself up. "Reckon I got some chores to tend to." He shuffled off, looking a lot older than his age.

"Cletus?" Li'l Jim asked. "You been quiet, too."

The young horse-keeper also stood. "Reckon I need to go help Homer." He, too, walked off, shoulders slumped.

Li'l Jim started to rise, ready to head off and talk to his friend, but Squire stopped him. "Let him be, lad." he said. "Both of 'em."

"But somethin's bad wrong with 'em."

"Aye, there be. But now ain't the time to be pressin' 'em on it."

"You know what's wrong?" Li'l Jim asked as he sat again, uncomfortable and annoyed.

"Reckon I do, lad. He been like this all along, Colonel?"

"Yes. It pains me to see him so miserable." He almost managed a wan smile. "He hasn't even cussed out any of the men in some weeks."

"What's wrong with him, Nathaniel?" Li'l Jim demanded.

"That ol' hoss be heartbroken, I expect. And he be filled with shame at himself."

"What'n hell for? I mean everybody else here's been through the same hard time. And everybody here ain't so cheerful. But Homer, he seems like he's the worst off. And Cletus ..."

"The horses, lad," Squire said quietly. "The horses all been took except the three. He feels it be his fault. Ye know how he be about them animals. They be like his children, nearabout. And he's taught Cletus to be the same."

"But he can't blame himself for the Blackfeet stealin' all them animals. The red bastards took everything else was in the colonel's camp, too, and all the boys couldn't stop that." He suddenly looked just a bit abashed. "Sorry, Colonel, Slocum. I didn't mean to seem like I was placin' any blame on you. But from what you said, I reckon there wasn't anything anybody could do with your small force against that many Blackfeet."

"No offense taken, son," Melton said sadly.

Peters said nothing but he nodded ever so little.

"It don't matter to Homer that nothin' could be done,

lad," Squire said. "He still blames himself. Thinks he could've done somethin' more even though he knows that don't be true. Them Blackfeet takin' all his horses was like they tore out his heart."

"But ..."

"Look, lad, them plews and traps and such, they can all be replaced. They meant money to the colonel and a heap of hard work to all the lads. But like I just said, them animals be like Homer's children. And that be a far harsher thing to a man like him than just losin' a pile of plunder."

Li'l Jim looked around. The others nodded at him. He knew it was true but still didn't like it. His shoulders slumped and sagged, too, knowing he could do nothing for his friend Cletus and the young man's mentor.

Gloom suddenly spread over the camp again.

CHAPTER 26

"WE'RE GOIN' after those murderous red niggurs, ain't we, Nathaniel?" Li'l Jim asked, once the tale had been told.

Squire looked at the young man as if he had lost all his senses.

"Then I best be getting some robe time so's I'll be ready to leave come first light."

"Nay, lad, we'll not be leavin' at first light. Not tomorrow anyway."

"But ..."

"Be usin' your head now and again, dammit. Colonel Melton and all his boys are plumb wore down to next to nothin'. They ain't had nothin' to fill their meatbags, hardly, and no horses to ride. They be needin' time to rest."

"Well, that's true, I reckon," Li'l Jim said, looking somewhat abashed.

"And we have to wait for Marcel to bring the others. They could catch up to us but leavin' here to march ten or maybe twenty miles down the trail don't make much sense. We be havin' good water, wood and feed here. No need to push on now."

"But they're getting away, Nathaniel." Even as he said it, he knew it was foolish.

"Them boys be long gone, lad. Ye be knowin' that."

"Yeah, I know. Just feels like we ought to do something,."

"We will, lad. Ye be knowin' that, too. Ye need to be patient at times like this."

"You ain't so patient when it comes to fightin' Injuns."

"Reckon that be true, lad. Mayhap I be needin' to learn to have some, too, leastways in cases like this. In the meantime, ye need to bring in some meat for these lads. It's why I brought ye along."

———

"So what will we do, Nathaniel?" Melton asked when they had all gathered the next morning.

"We be continuin' on to rendezvous."

"How long will it take us afoot and overextended as we are?"

"We got some horses with the others. Mayhap not enough for us all to be ridin' but we can mayhap make do." He grinned grimly. "And mayhap we might be getting a heap of 'em elsewhere."

"Where?" Melton looked confused.

"Crows," Peters said. "Saw plenty of sign last day or two."

"Aye."

"But we have nothing to trade."

"Who said anything about tradin', Colonel," Squire said more than asked.

Melton sat there a moment, then a cold grin spread across his gaunt face. "A splendid idea, Nathaniel," he said with a bit of renewed enthusiasm. "They have been known to steal white men's horses, after all."

"That be true."

"But whatever good will going to rendezvous do? We have no plews, nothing to turn into goods of any kind." His zeal faded as quickly as it had come.

"Now ye be hurtin' my feelin's, Colonel," Squire said. "Ye be thinkin' that I'd be makin' a fall and spring hunt and not have any plews?"

"Damn fool notion, isn't it?"

"Aye, Colonel. I don't reckon we be havin' as much as ye did, considerin' we didn't have the number of men ye did. But it should be enough to get us supplies to last a couple months. And if we be takin' a heap of horses off the Crows, we can mayhap be tradin' some of them in, too."

"Do you really think you can get enough horses from the Crows?"

Li'l Jim snorted. "Here I thought I was the only one dumb enough to say something so foolish."

Melton managed a small grin. "Was rather idiotic, wasn't it?"

"Yes, sir, if you don't mind my speakin' the truth."

"Don't mind at all, especially when it's well deserved." He sighed. "What then, Nathaniel?"

"Then we go chasin' after those snake-humpin' red bastards."

"That sounds better. I ain't killed me one of Bug's Boys in a long time," Li'l Jim said vehemently.

"You'll be getting your chance, lad. But it be time ye

take one of the boys and one horse and go out and make meat. We be havin' a heap of hungry lads."

"You don't need to tell me that, dammit."

"Just get goin', lad," Squire said with a grin.

"What're you planning for today, Nathaniel?" Melton asked.

"Figured Slocum and me'd be takin' a little *promenade* — stroll — out that away," he pointed vaguely to the northeast, "and see if we be learnin' anything about them Crows."

"And what about me?" Melton seemed put out that he was being left out.

"Ye be restin' for the day."

"I am perfectly fine, Nathaniel," Melton said with some heat.

"Reckon ye might be. But ye was abused somethin' awful last year and I ain't sure ye be recovered fully, especially after what you been through the past month or so. Ye be restin' for a day or so. There'll be more'n enough for ye — and the rest of us — to do soon enough."

"I guess you're right, Nathaniel," Melton responded though he didn't seem happy about it.

———

"Since when does the great Nathaniel Squire need help trackin' some Crows?" Peters asked with a grin.

"Since I figured ye'd be itchin' to get outta that camp and be doin' something."

"You ain't so foolish as some folks make out you are," Peters said with a laugh.

"And who 'sides you would be sayin' such a thing?" Squire laughed, too.

"Well, let's see. There's Abner and Li'l Jim and Hannah and Marcel and the Colonel and ..."

"Reckon I'll be raisin' hair on the lot of 'em then. Be teachin' 'em to watch their manners."

Peters grew a little serious. "Tell you the truth, Nathaniel, you might have a hard time raisin' hair on those ol' coons."

"Maybe, ol' hoss," Squire said, also seriously. "But that time ain't here yet."

"You taught them boys — and Hannah, too — well, Nathaniel. I'd throw in my lot with any of 'em."

Squire glanced over at him and nodded. "They be a fine group of young mountaineers, that be sure. I ain't certain, though, that I had much to do with it."

Peters chucked. "Humility from the great *L'on Farouche?* Such a thing don't suit you."

"Reckon not. But them young folks might be just as good now under your teachin', as poor as that be."

Both laughed again.

"I'm plumb glad you did get me out of that damn camp. Don't get me wrong, hoss, it ain't that I dislike any of them fellers. Nope. Like 'em all. But things was gettin' mighty fractious after a couple months of such hard doin's as we went through."

"And ol' hoss like us be needin' to get out from under the closeness of a camp full of folk. 'Specially after such a time. Mayhap I'll be takin' the Colonel out with me, give him a bit of relief."

"That'd shine with him. He's a shinin' feller, that one. Never let the hard times get him too melancholy except maybe once or twice. He kept the men together and kept us pressin' on no matter how tough the goin' was. That ol' hoss got more sand in him than many a mountaineer."

"That he does, lad. Knew it right off. It be why I signed on to take this motley brigade to the mountains last year, against my better judgment."

———

A couple hours later, they found sign of a sizable party of Crows and followed it for a spell.

"Looks like they had themselves a good time raidin'. There be a heap of horses with 'em," Squire said.

"Yep. If we can get most of 'em, we should have enough animals for everybody to set to saddle." He chuckled. "Well blanket maybe. Ain't a saddle to be had hardly beyond what you got."

"Them boys'll be getting used to ridin' bareback like many of the Injuns or they'll be walkin'. By themselves. I ain't aimin' to be waitin' on no laggards."

"Sounds about right." Peters paused. "Them Crows don't seem to be in any hurry. Just moseyin' on."

"Aye. I hope they figure they be far enough from whoever they raided to be slow movin' all along. I'd plumb hate to have to be followin' 'em all the way back to some village near the Bighorns."

Finally, they headed back toward camp. Along the way, they spotted a small bunch of buffalo. Each shot one, though Squire got a laugh when he dropped one with a single shot while Peters had to take two. Peters shook his head ruefully. Then he cheered up. They cut out the tongues, livers and a small bit of the meat, considering they couldn't carry much, and left the rest to the wolves and coyotes. On the slow ride back, they shared and enjoyed the raw liver.

"That's some shinin' eatin'," Peters said. "Ain't had me some of this since them red devils come against us."

"Ye can thank me later," Squire said with a grin.

"I'm thankin' you now, hoss, and that's all the thanks you'll get from me." He smiled.

"Were it that bad?"

"Mostly. Not as bad as last year in that big fracas along the Green. But we was some fewer than we was last year and some of those boys are still a bit green. Accounted well of themselves though. Still, you weren't there with your little band of warriors. 'Tween you and those three, it would've been like havin' a dozen more fellers."

Squire nodded, accepting it as the compliment it was and as a fact.

They arrived back at camp and turned their horses over to Cletus Ransom. The young man was trying to keep up a façade of at least some cheeriness but it was obvious he was glum.

"Where be Homer?" Squire asked.

"Ain't sure. Up the stream a ways, I think. That's where he's been spendin' a heap of time."

Squire nodded. "Tnings'll be gettin' better soon, lad."

"Yessir, I expect they will." He was not convincing.

Peters wandered off to talk to Melton. Squire moved quietly up the stream where he found Homer Bellows sitting with his back against a cottonwood. Squire plopped his great bulk down next to the horse handler.

"Ye can't be fishin' without a pole, lad," Squire said.

"Ain't fishin'. Just thinkin'."

"I reckon that be a heapin' pile of buff'lo shit. You be pinin'."

"So what if I am. Ain't no business of yours."

"Aye, it be. Look, Homer, it ain't your fault them horses was took by those rabbit-humpin' bastards. Couldn't nothin' been done better."

"Piss on you, Nathaniel. What the hell do you know, dammit." He looked at Squire for the first time. His eyes were sunken, haunted, pained. "They was under my care and they was took. Nothin' else to say. It were my fault. Worst thing that could happen, havin' my whole cavvy snatched out from under me." He turned his head to stare back across the stream again, shoulders slumped.

"Ye best be getting o'er this damned melancholy, lad," Squire said, not harshly.

"Bah."

"Best be doin' it, lad. I be needin' ye to take o'er the new cavvy we'll be havin' soon."

"Leave me be, Nathaniel. I'm a useless feller. Nothin' but a drain on all the others."

"Ye stop on talkin' that way or I'll be cloutin' ye o'er the head to knock some sense into ye."

"Won't work."

"Mayhap I should try and see." He paused. "I be needin' ye, Homer. Ye will be havin' a new cavvy soon."

Bellows's head whipped around. "Don't you lie to me, Nathaniel Squire," he snapped but the faintest glimmer of hope had touched his eyes.

"I ain't e'er lied to ye, lad. And ye be knowin' that." He smiled a little. "First thing, Marcel will be bringin' the others'll here soon and they be bringin' a fair number of horses."

"Not that many, I reckon."

"That be true. But there be some Crows with a heap of horses less'n a day's ride from here."

"And they'll just give over those horses?" A smile crept across his face.

"Aye." He grinned. "So best be carin' for the animals we got. Me and some of the boys'll need 'em come mornin'." Squire turned his face away, a bit embarrassed at the look of hope and relief in Bellows's eyes.

CHAPTER 27

TRAIN, with Ledoux and the others, pulled in that afternoon with a small flourish accompanied by whoops and hollers. Train stopped and slid off his horse in front of Squire.

"'Bout time ye got here, lad," the giant mountain man said. "I didn't know ye'd be dillydallying."

"Wasn't me," Train said with a laugh. "It was Marcel. That ol' Frenchie's slower'n a three-legged turtle."

"Merde! Listen to zis nonsense from zis overgrown pup. *Sacre Bleu*! It took me two hours to raise zis boy from 'is slumbers."

They laughed. "I think ye both be tellin' false," Squire said.

"Hell, Nathanial, you just missed our company is all," Train said.

"It be good to see ye, lad. Ye and all the others."

"It's good to be back. We made meat this mornin' so there's fresh buffalo."

"Ye best be havin' a heap of coffee left."

"Enough for everyone, at least for a couple days."

"*Bon*. Go turn the horses over to Homer. He'll be happy to see ye. He's been mighty melancholy since the Blackfeet run off with all his horses."

Train started to grin but it fell off his face when he saw Squire's look. "You're not joshin'?"

"Nay, lad. He be blamin' himself for the red devils runnin' off all the stock."

"That's mighty foolish. He couldn't have stopped it."

"Aye. He be knowin' that. But it don't matter. That be the way he feels. He brightened up some when I told him you were comin' with a heap of horses, so he'll be glad to see ye."

Train nodded and walked off.

"Well, don't ya say hello to a purty young gal?" Hannah demanded with a wide grin.

Squire returned the grin. "I'll be doin' so soon's as I be seein' one." He burst into laughter.

So did Hannah. She reached up and ran a small hand across the big man's fuzzy face, then she turned and headed off.

Star Path dismounted as Hannah took the reins to her horse. She waited, silently but smiling. Squire moved toward her, grin widening. He was about to haul her into his strong embrace when he realized their baby, Mountain Bear, was riding on her back in a cradleboard. He settled for pulling her toward him by the upper arms. She wrapped her arms around his middle and hugged him hard.

They released each other. "I missed ye, woman," Squire said. He grinned again. E'en if just for your cookin'. These boys here can't cook worth a damn."

"No other reason?" she asked, playfully running her

hand from his beard, across his chest and down to his stomach where she stopped.

"Well, now that ye be mentionin' it, ye do warm this ol' chil's robes right well." They laughed. "How is the chil'?"

"Good. Like you, he hungry all the time. Or maybe he just likes my ..." she flushed a little in embarrassment as she jiggled her breasts a bit.

"Either way, woman, he be like me." Squire laughed. "How about ye? Ye be well?"

"Aye. Baby's not fussin' much. I eat good."

"*Bon.* Ye go on and rest now. She started to argue but he cut her off. "It be a long ride ye been through. Rest a little."

She smiled up at him. She looked tired but only a little. She placed a hand on his chest. "You gettin' a soft heart."

"Only for ye and Mountain Bear."

Before long, the women had the camp more to their liking, fires were going and meat cooking. Squire, Train, Li'l Jim, Hannah, Peters and Ledoux were sitting at Melton's fire. Even Homer Bellows and Cletus Ransom were there.

Train quickly filled in the others on the humdrum trip, the only event being an overprotective grizzly sow taking run at one of the horses. It was quickly disposed of.

Because Ledoux had explained most of Melton's perils to Train and the others on the trail, it took almost no time for Peters and Melton to fill in the rest.

When the tale was told, Train asked, "So when're we goin' after the Blackfeet?"

"Nathanial says we got to go to rendezvous first," Li'l Jim said with some derision.

"You mean to have a spree after what was done to the Colonel and the others?" Hannah asked, incredulous.

Squire glared at her and then Li'l Jim. "Look around ye, lads. The Colonel's men be beaten down from hard times. They're plumb wore out. We got near no supplies. We get to rendezvous, we can be usin' our plews to be getting some supplies. And it'll be lettin' these lads here reconstitute themselves. Then we be trackin' down those red niggurs."

"Reckon that makes sense," Train said. "We ain't got enough horses for everyone which'll slow us down considerable."

"We'll be havin' us an increase in the number of horses soon, lad. I be aimin' to appropriate a large number of 'em from Crows."

"I'm in," Train said.

"Me, too," Hannah added.

"Nay, lads. Ye just come off the trail. Me and Slocum, Li'l Jim and maybe Gideon or Billy Van Eck'll ride on out in the mornin'."

"Hell, Nathanial, I want to go."

"Nay, lad. Ye be needed here. While me and Slocum be gone, ye and Marcel be in charge here."

Train nodded. He didn't like being left out but he was pleased that Squire thought enough of him to leave him in charge.

———

As they finished up breakfast, Squire said, "Li'l Jim, go fetch Billy." When the young man left, Squire looked at Train and said, "I decided to take Billy instead of Gideon. Gideon be your best hunter after Li'l Jim. Don't let him be goin' out alone. Always have someone with him. And keep a good watch out. We ain't seen sign except for them Crows we be about to call on but ye ne'er can tell."

"Want me to milk the cows, too, Pa?" Train said sarcastically.

"Ye can find some, certain," Squire said with a laugh. "I just want to be makin' certain."

"I know what needs to be done, Nathanial," Train said a bit stiffly.

"Reckon ye do, lad." He shook his head, realizing again that he had still not reconciled himself to the fact that these young people did not need his constant instruction.

In half an hour, the small party rode out, moving at a good clip. Figuring they were getting close but not enough to keep going for the night, they made a cold camp amid some willows. They were back on the trail at first light and, before noon, they caught sight of a large cloud of dust in the distance.

They dismounted and climbed up a ridge. In the distance, they could see the Crows. The Indians were not moving very fast, the horses doing almost as much grazing as walking. Two Crows were behind the herd, about ten yards apart, lazily pushing it along. The other two rode on to each side of the horses, keeping them in line.

"Must've been a hell of a raid," Peters said. "Only four braves and looks like thirty, forty horses."

"We don't need that many," Van Eck said.

"What we don't need we can sell to rendezvous."

"Oh," Van Eck said, abashed.

"Don't be worryin' about it, lad. Ye can't be learnin' ye don't ask."

"How you want to work this, Nathanial?" Peters

asked. "Wait till they're bedded down or just take a run at 'em now?"

"I say we just ride on down there, shoot the bastards and run off the animals."

"Ye be worryin' me, lad, with all this talk of killin' Injuns. I don't hesitate but ye seem a mite too eager lately."

"Ah, hell, Nathanial, I'm just shootin' off my mouth again." He looked a little abashed. Then he grinned. "Of course, was they Blackfeet, I'd mean it."

"They was Blackfeet, there's be no question about how we'd do it," Peters said.

"Reckon Li'l Jim's mostly right this time. Can't see no reason to wait. Might be a heap more miles before they be stoppin' for the night."

Squire sat for a few moments, thinking, then nodded. "Slocum, ye mind runnin' off the horses? You and Billy?"

Peters looked over at the young man who seemed nervous. "Shines with this chil'."

"*Bon*. Li'l Jim, ye and me'll chase off those warriors while our friends here turn the horses back this way."

"Can I shoot one, Nathanial? Please? Can I?" Li'l Jim said in a mock whine.

"Ye keep this up and I'll be shootin' *ye*." But he grinned. Then he sobered. "Li'l Jim, you take a run at that lad on the right there. I'll head for the two who be pushin' the animals along. Slocum, ye and Billy run up 'tween me'n Li'l Jim on the right side of the herd and turn it to the left."

What about the Crow on that side?" Van Eck asked.

"Either he'll skedaddle in a hurry or he'll be gettin' himself run over by all them horses. None of 'em should cause us any trouble. Their bows all be unstrung in their cases."

"We aim to kill 'em all?" Van Eck asked.

"Be best," Peters said. "We got us enough troubles helpin' Colonel Melton without some of these shit eaters gettin' word to their people and have a passel of them critters come after us."

"Reckon that don't put me out none," Squire said. "We ain't had as much trouble with these niggurs as we have with the Blackfeet but they ain't been exactly friendly to us neither."

"We best move up a bit if we're just gonna shoot 'em down," Li'l Jim said.

"Waste of powder and ball when we can use our 'hawks," Squire said. 'Sides, we be doin' it from a distance, we just might be scatterin' them horses from here to the Musselshell. Then we be havin' to chase 'em all down." When everyone had nodded in agreement, Squire said, "*Allons-y.*"

They moved forward, barely trotting, unconcerned that they would be seen. The Crows were too busy herding their stolen horses. And with the sound of so many hooves pounding on the ground, the warriors wouldn't be able to hear Squire's group either.

At fifty yards or so behind the Crows, Squire's men kicked their horses into a run. Squire galloped toward the warrior on the right side at the back of the herd. Li'l Jim dashed ahead, to his right. Peters and Van Eck followed, just a bit slower.

Squire's target never knew of his impending doom. He was simply riding slowly along, thinking of the second wife he would be able to acquire with his share of the horses when he got back to the village. The thought was pleasing. His thoughts ended abruptly when Squire cleaved his head from crown to neck. He wobbled a moment and then fell.

His companion sensed something was wrong and looked toward his friend. His eyes widened with surprise as he had no notion that enemies were about to attack. He had little fear, though, until he saw the giant on the massive black horse turning his way. He pulled the horse's head around and kicked it hard.

But his pony was no match for *Noir Astre*. Squire easily caught up. The Crow frantically swung his own tomahawk at the mountain man who brushed it aside as easily as he would a gnat. Then he swung his own hatchet backhanded. It split the warrior's chest.

Squire pulled *Noir Astre* to a halt and looked around. Peters and Van Eck were easing the horse herd toward him, though a little ahead. Li'l Jim had taken care of the Crow on the right side and was galloping furiously around the front of the herd, chasing the last warrior, the one who had been on the left side of the herd. Squire considered going after him, too, but Peters and Van Eck had the herd moving around past him and it was in between. He was unconcerned though. Li'l Jim could handle himself. He joined the others in moving the herd back to their camp.

Li'l Jim soon rode up, his horse breathing heavily. "Looks like we done right well," he said, nodding at the horses.

CHAPTER 28

THE FOUR OF THEM, driving thirty horses ahead of them, arrived in Colonel Melton's camp a day and a half later to some fanfare.

Homer Bellows and Cletus Ransom were nearly beside themselves with joy. The two immediately took control of the animals.

"Some of you boys get over here and help out, ya no-good, no-'count lazy buggers. But don't you scare these animals, you shiftless bastards. Come on, now, let's get 'em goin'. Yep. Right now. Be careful."

The two horse handlers and a couple of camp helpers drove the horses toward a clear spot near the stream where they could drink and there was still grass. Squire and the others laughed as Bellows and Ransom kept up their stream of inventive and often profane commentary.

"It sure is good to see those two back to themselves," Melton said.

"Aye, that it be, Colonel. Tell the truth, I was some worried about those lads. And we be needin' 'em. Can't nobody be handlin' horses like them."

"That might be," Hannah said, "but I don't know if I can take all that hollerin' and profanity from them two." After a moment, she burst into laughter.

"Ye be glad they be themselves again, ain't you, girl?"

"Damn right I am. Things just ain't the same without them two cussin' their way around the camp all the time."

"I heard that," Ransom said, walking up and taking a seat at the fire with the others. He, too, was laughing along with the others. "And you're a fine one to talk, Miss Hannah. You're as foul-mouthed as any of us." He grinned.

"Oh, so now that ya got yourself a woman ya think ya can talk to any woman in such an unmannerly way?" Laughter bubbled up out of her again.

"What?" Squire asked, surprised.

"Nary did get a chance to tell you," Peters said. "What with getting settled in and then us ridin' out right off, Ol' Cletus there got himself a woman. Flathead gal named Blue Smoke." His face split in a grin. "Took me in a Flathead, too. Green Robe's her name. Even Gideon wrangled himself a woman. Another Flathead. Sun Goes Slow."

"Well, I'll be damned." Squire shook his head. "I seen those women putterin' 'round camp but didn't know who they belonged to." He lit his pipe, then asked, "How many horses we have?"

"Countin' yours and the three we had left, we got forty-five head of horsebeast plus your eight mules."

"*Bon*. Colonel, how many people?"

"Let's see. There's your seven, counting the women." He smiled. "Not countin' your little one though. With us," he counted silently for a moment, "Fifteen, plus five women and five camp helpers. Thirty-two."

"Got plenty of horses," Ransom said. "We didn't keep any extra, we'd have ... um ..."

"Eighteen," Melton helped.

"Yep. Sure as can be. Eighteen critters we can sell, though I say we keep at least a few extra."

"Ye be right on that. With maybe a dozen horses to sell and what plews me and my lads be havin', we should be able to outfit us pretty well. What be the animals like?"

"They're all in good health, far's me and Homer see. Ain't sure how many, if any, is broke. There's a couple shod ones in that remuda but the rest are Injun ponies. Whether our boys can ride 'em ..." He shrugged.

"They'll be learnin' to ride 'em right quick or they can be walkin'," Squire said.

"We leave in the morning, Nathaniel?" Melton asked. He seemed eager.

"Nay," Squire responded after a moment's thought. "Best wait a day, let the men get used to ridin' them Injun ponies." He grinned. "And let them ponies be getting used to those lads."

"I t'ink is you needs ze rest, Monsieur L'on Farouche," Ledoux said with a laugh.

"Did ye need to be listenin' to such nonsense since leaving St. Louis, Colonel?"

"Well, I wouldn't say that exactly."

"Hell, Colonel, tell the truth," Peters said. "That scabrous little fart was whinin' every damn minute."

Laughter made the rounds. When it had ebbed, Squire said, "While we be talkin' about St. Louis, what brung ye out here, Colonel? When me and the others left, ye was figurin' on just sendin' Slocum and Marcel out to lead this ragged bunch of lads."

Melton grew rather somber, and rather embarrassed,

at preparing to admit this in front of his men. "When I thought about it, I realized I had been afraid of going west again."

"Can't nobody blame ye for that, Colonel," Peters said. "Not after what ye went through at the hands of those devilish red critters."

"That may be, Slocum. At least for some. But I found I could not. I was afraid, yes, but I could not have faced myself if I could not face that terror. I just had to test myself again."

"And ye did so when ye faced them red devils again, didn't ye?" Squire said.

"If 'e won't say so, I will," Ledoux said. "'E show no fear when zem Blackfeets attack us, 'e just stand tall."

"*Vous êtes un grand homme, Colonel, et je suis fier de te soutenir*," Squire said. "You be a great man, Colonel, and I be proud to stand with ye."

Melton's discomfiture grew as nods of agreement made the rounds of them.

"And Risin' Sun?" Squire asked a minute later with a twinkle in his eyes.

Melton just harrumphed, but Peters threw in, "He wanted to be with her somethin' awful. And be free with her, unlike he could in St. Louis. That gal got her hooks in him but good."

Another burst of laughter rippled through the camp.

———

It was a rather happier procession that pulled out. Melton's men were a sight cheerier now that they were riding again, even if it was bareback and even if they were mounted on occasionally fractious Indian ponies.

Still, supplies for so many men and women were short. Except for Squire's group, the others were almost out of powder and ball so most of the hunting was done by the giant mountain man's small group. That kept them in meat though some still grumbled because there was no coffee or sugar or flour. The Indian women, however, were proficient gatherers and at that time of year there was a large variety of fruits and berries to be had. Plums and cherries, raspberries and strawberries all went a long way to satisfying the men's hunger.

With everyone mounted, the moved at a quick pace, making good time. On the third night out, sitting around the evening fire, Squire asked, "Ye know what day it be, Colonel?"

"I can't be certain, Nathaniel. When those damned Blackfeet made off with everything we had, my pack was taken, too, of course. In it was the calendar I'd been keeping. But by my reckoning, it's late July. Maybe early August. Will that be troublesome?"

"Might be. Rendezvous often be in July. Sometimes it lingers on a spell or starts late. If it be the former, we might have trouble gettin' supplies. Won't be much left. If it be the latter, we'll be fine."

"Then we shall press on with all speed. With horses and full bellies, the men will be able to handle long days in the saddle."

"I be thinkin' the same."

A week and a half later, Squire called a stop. "We be getting close now. Horse Creek be about three miles southwest and the Seedskedee about a mile from there."

"Then why're we stopping?" Melton asked.

"I reckon it be wise for us to learn what be goin' on down there before we ride in. Slocum, ye mind ridin' in?"

"Reckon not." He grinned. "'Course me and ye would have to be havin' a spree, no matter how short."

"If there be anything left, I might be takin' me a sip or two. Abner, ye and Marcel be in charge again. Ye make certain Homer and Cletus be havin' enough protection for them horses."

Train nodded.

"And if any of these lads takes it to mind to sneak out yonder to be havin' his own spree, shoot him."

"Sure, Nathaniel," Train said with a small laugh.

"I be serious, lad," Squire responded harshly. "We don't need some goddamn fool getting addle-pated by *awardenty* and start jabberin' about our business."

"We have no business that concerns others or that we must hide, Nathaniel," Melton said.

"That may be, Colonel. But ye be forgettin' what your captive said to ye — that Jacob Meisner be wantin' me. He be connected to the Blackfeet and from what I figure, he be connected to The Company. Neither of which be shinin' with this chil'. And I sure don't need someone here talkin' about anything concernin' us."

"I see."

"Things might be just fine over there in those camps and tomorrow we'll ride on in there nice as ye please and have us a small spree."

"Reasonable again, Nathaniel."

"Course, things might be a mite slow o'er there with little supplies to be had so we might have to be lookin' elsewhere."

"Ready, hoss?" Peters asked.

"Aye, lad. Abner, Marcel, Colonel, be makin' a comfortable a camp as ye can. It ain't likely we'll be back before mornin'." He and Peters rode off.

There were plenty of folks in the camps along the rivers but there was no sign of any supplies. "This be strange," Squire said.

"Seems so." They stopped in front of one fellow wandering around. "Hey, ol' hoss," Peters said.

"Slocum, how ye been, ol' coon?"

"Right as can be, I reckon. Ye?"

"Shinin'. 'Least I will be the damn supply train ary shows up."

"Ain't been here then?" When the other nodded, Peters asked, "Ye know when it's comin'?"

"Some of the boys said Fitzpatrick was on his way. Expected to be here in a couple, three days."

"Obliged." When the man had wandered off, Peters turned to Squire. "So what now, hoss?"

"Head on back to our camp, I reckon. No use in stayin' here. Hell, I don't e'en see a jug around."

———

"This is getting to be a regular thing, Nathaniel," Train complained after Squire had told him again that he would be in charge of the camp.

"Shows I be puttin' my trust in ye, lad."

"But I'm getting tired of settin' in the camp all the time."

"Reckon ye be. But I ain't takin' Hannah o'er there. It be too dangerous. And she ain't about to stay here without ye. 'Sides, there's no one else can be handlin' these folks. E'en Marcel be a bit too lazy at times. Keep your eyes open. There be a heap of folks wanderin' about. Have the lads be careful if ye send 'em out to make meat. Ye got a heap of women and a couple young'uns under your care, lad, but ye got help. Ain't no better'n Li'l Jim and Hannah, of course. And Gideon be a damn good man for certain. I ain't too sure about those new lads but Slocum says Mel and Clay be steady hands along with a few others. We'll be back in a few days."

Squire led the way out of camp, flanked by Melton, Slocum Peters, and Billy Van Eck. Two new men — Sam Livers and Maurice Plante — herded a dozen horses ahead of them. One of the camp helpers rode in the rear, holding the rope to the eight mules laden with packs of plews.

It had been more than a week since they arrived in the vicinity before the rendezvous started but it was in full swing when they rode though one camp and into the middle one a mile or so up the river. Squire and his men herded the horses off to a rope corral stretched between willows and cottonwoods.

Livers and Plante were wide-eyed and slack-jawed at the antics around them, just as Melton's brigade led by Squire had been the year before. And as Squire had the previous year, he suggested that Melton give the two young men a few coins so they could have themselves a good time even if brief.

"Remember, lads," Squire said, "ye be keepin' your traps shut about anything that has to do with me or the Colonel. Anything! Ye lads understand?"

The two nodded. They had heard of this giant and how much of a wild man he could be. They had mostly kept their distance from him in the few weeks they had been together and hadn't thought he was so savage. But seeing the light in those faded blue eyes above the full beard and mustache gave them pause.

"Yes, sir," both said as they darted off.

"Billy, ye want to be joinin' 'em?"

Van Eck licked his lips, wanting to go, but then he shook his head. "Reckon not, Nathaniel. I seen all these doin's last year and I don't have no money."

"I'll advance you some ..."

"No, sir, Colonel. I ain't earned anything. Not after what happened."

"As you wish." Melton was proud of the lad but also saddened some that the young man would place any blame for what happened on himself.

"I'll watch over the horses and mules," Van Eck said.

"Slocum, ye be knowin' Fitzpatrick a heap better'n I do. Ye go and help the Colonel here handle the business doin's."

Peters nodded. "What're ye gonna be doin'?"

"Moseyin' 'round, see if there be anything to learn about anything. Might get word on the Blackfeet or Jacob Meisner."

"Ye figure to ride through The Company's camp?"

Squire grinned a little savagely. "Can't be sayin' I'll do so. Can't be sayin' I won't neither." He tugged slightly on *Noir Astre's* reins and walked off.

CHAPTER 29

"WE BEST BE GETTING BACK to camp soon," Squire said as he, Melton, Peters and Van Eck sat around a small fire.

"Ye hear somethin', hoss?" Peters asked.

"Aye. Meisner and them shit eatin' Bug's Boys still be after me. I reckon they figure I be comin' here or goin' after 'em if I learned about your plight. Or likely both. From what some boys around here be sayin', them red devils ain't far, just waitin' on another chance. They seen plenty of sign. I be trustin' them red bastards about as much as I be trustin' I'd survive a winter out here naked and without supplies."

"There's more, isn't there?" Melton asked.

"Aye, Colonel. I be concerned about our women. They be mighty vulnerable, e'en though Abner and the others be mighty fierce."

"Those snake humpers get wind that our women are out there, they'll take a run at 'em, sure as hell," Peters said. "And if there be a passel of 'em ..."

"Aye."

"When do we leave, Nathaniel?" Melton asked. "We

can be ready rather quickly if we all pitch in loading our supplies."

"How'd ye fare with getting supplies?"

"Better than I expected," Melton said.

"Plews were bringin' just about three dollars a pound," Peters threw in. "But the horses, now, they brung in a fair good price. Ol' Broken Hand dickered a heap with us over everything but he come off pretty square after all was said and done."

"So we're pretty well supplied, all things taken into account," Melton said. He grinned sourly. "I'm afraid my backers won't be very fond of me after this."

"To hell with 'em," Peters snapped. "After what we been through, those fancy pants bankers and such ought to be glad you come through with your life."

"Those men don't think that way. They wouldn't care if I was a skeleton when I got back as long as I had enough plews to make them a handsome profit."

"Money-grubbin' bastards," Peters spat out. "Worse'n the damn Company traders."

"It's the way of the business world I'm afraid, Slocum." He turned his attention back to Squire. "So, Nathaniel, when do we leave?"

"Reckon as soon as we be ready. It still be early in the day and camp ain't all that far off. Billy, you go on and fetch up Sam and Maurice. Tell 'em to be gettin' themselves back here. They argue, tell 'em I'll come fetch 'em. And I won't be in a good humor if I have to be doin' so."

Van Eck grinned. "I don't reckon I'll have trouble with those two.

Squire nodded. Van Eck was of medium height and weight, much like Peters. But he was strong and as tough as a bull hide shield. The two new men were a bit larger but not as well-hardened as Van Eck who was toughened by the ferocious battles of the previous year.

Squire, Peters, the camp helpers and, unsurprisingly, Melton began loading their supplies on the mules. Van Eck and the two other young trappers were back quickly and threw in their help.

"Ye boys had yourself a shinin' time?" Squire asked as they worked.

"Wasn't time for much of a spree," Livers said, partly in sadness. "But it was somethin' just bein' here. Won me a fine knife at 'hawk throwin'. Maurice there, though, he weren't near so lucky."

"I 'ad more sense than to go against those *fils de pute*. You just 'ad *bon chance*."

Two hours later, the group was riding out. Without all the horses, they could move faster and they were back in camp before nightfall.

"That was a mighty quick visit to rendezvous," Train said as they started to unload the mules. "I figured you'd be there a couple days or more."

"There be Blackfeet about, lad."

The ones lookin' for us?"

"Aye, lad."

"Where are they?"

"Can't be certain. But they ain't too far, I reckon. We be needin' to know for sure. So first light, ye and Li'l Jim need to be takin' a looksee, try'n find 'em. I figure they ain't more'n a day or two ride."

"We'll find 'em, Nathaniel."

"I be sure ye will, lad. Just be doin' it without bein' took or scalped."

"I'd favor that myself."

———

"They're gone, Nathaniel," Train said as he and Li'l Jim climbed off their horses. They were tired and frustrated.

"They be gone?" Squire was surprised.

"Yep. We found where they were and tracked 'em for more'n a day but they were movin' fast."

"That don't make no sense."

"Me and Li'l Jim didn't think so neither. But we run across a couple boys from rendezvous. They said a bunch of Bridger's and Fitzpatrick's men had heard there was a camp of Blackfeet about and took off after 'em, fixin' to raise hair. Since the boys we talked to didn't go along, we don't know for certain but we figured Bug's Boys found out the mountaineers were comin' and lit out. We followed 'em for another day, then figured they weren't planning to stop anytime soon 'specially since we cut sign of the mountaineers drivin' 'em on."

"Which way they be headed?"

"Mostly north, some east."

Squire nodded. "Ye lads done good. Go on and fill your meatbags, then get some rest. We be leavin' at daylight to hunt those bastards."

They pulled out just after first light, driven by anger, a desire for revenge and renewed optimism. With everyone mounted and with a sufficient amount of supplies, they were encouraged.

Squire pushed them as hard as he could, but with several women and now a few children — Yellow Moon and Rising Sun had recently given birth — plus laden mules, the going was rather slow. The Blackfeet, on the other hand, unencumbered, could move fast.

"You think they'll double back, Nathaniel?" Hannah asked.

"Reckon not. I be thinkin' they'll head to their village for a spell, rest up and celebrate what they done already, then come lookin' for us. It also be possible they think the Colonel and his boys've headed back to the States with the supply train. They ain't so interested in him, maybe, but they might be thinkin' we threw in with 'em to get back there." He shrugged.

"There's a heap of fellers with that supply train. Good men, all of 'em," Li'l Jim said. "Might give them Blackfeet pause."

"Reckon that's be so. 'Specially if they learn I ain't with 'em."

"So where do we go?" Train asked.

"Keep on the way we be goin'. We're still followin' their trail though it be growin' faint by now. And I still figure they'll be headin' for their village sooner or later. We be getting lucky, mayhap we'll be waitin' for 'em when they get there."

"Or maybe they'll just swing around and come up behind us in a day or two," Li'l Jim offered.

"I reckon ye just volunteered for ridin' our back trail to be keepin' an eye out for them skunk consorters."

"Damn."

"You best learn to keep your trap shut now and again," Hannah said with a grin.

"He ne'er has in all this time," Squire said with a chuckle. "Ain't likely to do so now."

"Go to hell, all of you," Li'l Jim growled, then grinned. "You can depend on me, Nathaniel."

"I know, lad."

———

"Six horses're gone, dammit all," Homer Bellows said without preliminary as he plopped down at Melton's fire, joining the usual members. "Goddamn horse-stealin' bastards. no good camp helpers. Ain't worth a shit for guardin' horses. Not a'tall."

"Quit your blabberin', old man, and be tellin' what ye know."

"Damn boys we had guardin' the horses last night weren't payin' enough attention and six horses was took. Weren't for Tom Douglas, more might've been took."

"Who done it?"

"Hell if I know. Ain't my job to identify horse-thievin' Injuns."

"Abner, go and see if ye can be pickin' up their trail. Don't follow it. Just find out who they be."

Train nodded and headed off.

"Who was guardin' 'em, Homer?"

"Clem Dirks and Smiley Bogard."

"Pork eaters?"

"Yep. Worstest of the worstest them boys. They ain't worth ..."

Squire cut him off. "None of the mountaineers be on duty with 'em?"

"Tom. He was off takin' a leak when he heard a ruckus. He run back and chased off them shit-swallerin' red devils. He's a useless damn feller. Can't understand why I put up with him and all the others."

"Tom's a good man," Melton said.

"Hmmph."

"Was he doin' his job?" Squire asked.

"Yeah."

"The others?"

"Can't say so."

"Be dealin' with them two howe'er ye think best. Short of puttin' 'em under."

"Well if I can't shoot 'em, I reckon floggin'd be best. Damn no-good, worthless bastards deserve it."

"You're not serious, are you?" Melton demanded, affronted.

"Aye, Colonel. It be common."

"We've never resorted to such a thing."

"Ne'er had reason to, I reckon."

"Go light on 'em, Homer. We can't be havin' 'em unable to do their work."

Bellows rose and walked off, muttering curses as was his wont.

Melton was about to protest again but thought better of it

Train returned minutes later. "Ye weren't gone long, lad," Squire said.

"Hell, didn't even need to saddle my horse. Just a looksee for a bit. Weren't hard to find. Crows. Weren't more'n four or five of 'em"

"Damn Crows be getting near as vexatious as the damn Blackfeet. Slocum, ye feel like chasin' after some horse-thievin' red critters?"

"Wouldn't put me out none," Peters responded with a savage grin.

"Pick a couple boys to go with ye. Ye be needin' Abner to go along? He be the best tracker we got."

"Reckon I can find 'em without his help."

Train, watching Peters, wasn't sure whether the old mountaineer was insulting him but he said nothing.

"I reckon Marcel be ready to go, eh, Frenchie?"

"*Mais oui!*" The French-Canadian was already saddling his horse.

"Douglas is a pretty good feller," Peters said, "and I expect he'll be half froze to pay them Crows back. I'll take him if he's willin'. Essex'll do, too. Should be more'n enough to deal with a few Crows." He rose. "They can't be too far. I expect we'll be back before dark." He rose and headed off.

"Are we staying here, Nathaniel?" Melton asked. "If not, we had better ..." He stopped and winced when he heard the scream from the other side of the camp.

"Nay, Colonel. We be movin' on. I don't reckon those boys bein' punished be lookin' forward to a day in the saddle but I ain't lettin' them slow us down none. They can't keep up, they'll be left behind."

Melton pushed himself up. "Then I'll see to getting things moving."

Squire nodded. As Melton walked off, Squire said, "Abner, I want ye to be ridin' out toward the east and north ahead of us today."

"Will do."

"What about me?" Li'l Jim asked.

"Ye offered your services to keep an eye on our back trail." He smiled just a bit. "Abner, what be your thinkin' on Gideon's trackin' skills?"

"He ain't near as good as me but he's better'n Li'l Jim."

"Like hell."

"Shush, Li'l Jim," Hannah said. "He's tellin' true and you well know it."

Squire looked at Train. "Before saddlin' up, go tell Gideon to do the same on our left."

"Done." Train half turned and only a bit self-consciously kissed Hannah lightly. She touched his cheek as he began to stand.

When Train had left, Hannah looked at Squire. "Ya need me for anything special, Nathaniel?" She looked almost disappointed.

"Nay, lass. But it's shine with this ol' chil' was ye to be ridin' alongside me."

A smile brightened her face. "Reckon that's shine with me, too."

CHAPTER 30

THEY WERE LUCKY, making the cover of the copse of cottonwoods, willows and aspens moments before the clouds split apart and sent a deluge down on them. Moments after thundering into the copse, they were rushing to get camp set up. They had managed to get a rope corral made and the mules unloaded when the hail started. Chunks of ice the size of Hannah's fist pounded down on them, slowed some but not stopped by the overhanging tree branches.

The women hung their babies — still in their cradleboards — from low branches close to the tree trunks. Some hurried to get tents or lean-tos put up, others to gather up what dry wood they could find. The men helped Bellows and Ransom control the horses and mules that were panicky in the weather, especially when the thunder cracked and rolled. Others hurried to cover their supplies with tarps. Then they all hunkered down to wait it out.

It was a long wait — almost two full days. The hail stopped within an hour or two but the rain never did though it eased up now and again for a short while. It made for a miserable camp; keeping fires burning was difficult and they had no fresh meat to cook anyway. They subsisted on pemmican and jerky but at least they did have coffee.

The next afternoon, Squire wandered about the miserable camp. A number of young men were huddled in a lean-to that was less than substantial.

"Ye lads be lookin' mighty glum," the big man said.

"Nae much to cheer about, Mr. Squire," Gus Macgregor said. "I nae seen this much rain since I left Culloden."

"Ye been out here long enough to be used to such doin's."

"Aye, that I have. Just seems worse this time for some reason I cannae put my finger on," he added, his burr still rich and strong.

Squire plopped himself down. "Well, lads, I mind the time I was trappin' up near the Bitterroots. I was havin' a fine season. Aye, maybe the best I e'er had. I be pullin' in so many plews I had to hire me near a hundred squaws to work 'em for me and fifty mules to carry 'em all. Damn, it were some doin's tryin' to herd all them mules. And all them squaws. Got to the point where I was spendin' a heap of time huntin' just to keep those damn women fed.

"Then one day it started to rain. I ne'er thought much of it. Rains all the time. Nothin' unusual about that. So we made camp, figurin' the rain'd be gone in a day or so and we could all be restin' up a bit.

"But damn, that rain ne'er did stop. Day after day, it come down. Then the river started risin'. Rose up over its banks. Deeper and deeper it was gettin'. So we moved up the hill some. Next mornin', that ol' river be lappin' at our toes again. E'ery day we had to move higher 'cause of that river. Hell, it seemed like that thing was trackin' us like a coyote huntin' a rabbit.

"Farther and farther up we went, finally past the last of the trees. Weren't much more we could go. I put all the women on horses and sent them packin' down the other side of the mountain. I stayed there with all them plews, thinkin' it sure be certain the rain'd stop any minute and that damn river'd start shrinkin'.

"But nay, lads. I didn't think the heavens could hold that much water. Seems like it picked up e'ery drop in the ocean and stored it up till it got to my camp and decided it be time to let it go. By now I be at the very tippy top of the Bitterroots, feet straddlin' that peak, one foot on the west side, one on the east. It be some predicament. Had all my plews stacked up high. Then I realized that there river weren't gonna stop and I be thinkin' it were time for me to skedaddle down the other side of the mountain.

"But damn if that water didn't grab me by the ankles before I could move and dragged me down off that peak. My plews was next. Down that mountain we went, me fightin' like a wounded griz to swim out. That water wouldn't have none of it though. And e'en quicker than it had rose, it shrank. I be thinkin' it gets low enough, I could be makin' my way free of it. But it ne'er got that low. Stayed about half the mountain deep and swept me along.

"It finally spit me out along the Platte. Lost e'erything. Plews, gun, horse. I be some starvin' chil' by the time I made it back to the States."

The young men sat there for some moments, wondering at it all. Then Hart Crandall said, "Wait a minute. There ain't no river starts up in the Bitterroots that enters the Platte."

Squire rose to his full height and grinned. "Mayhap ye be thinkin' I were stretchin' the truth a mite but it makes this here storm seem like a summer shower back in the States. Now ye lads quit your bellyachin'. Things could be a heap worse." He strode off.

Eventually, though, the rain ceased, the wind died down, and the sun shyly poked its head out from behind the clouds. They took another day to let everything dry out. Li'l Jim and a couple other men went out hunting and came back with two elk which was enough to feed them all for the day.

With fresh meat, good fires and pleasantly warm sunshine, their gloom lifted and, with refreshed spirits, they pulled out.

Another storm several days later caught them in a wide mountain valley and all they could do was ride on, enduring it through the rest of the day and the night. It was not nearly as bad as the other storm but it was still soggy and dismal.

"At least," Train muttered to Hannah as they rode, "there ain't no hail this time."

They ended up stopping a ways back from the bank of what had been a stream but now was a raging torrent fed by the hellacious rains. It took another day before the water receded somewhat and they found a place to ford it. It was tough going but they lost only one mule with its panniers of supplies.

They moved on, not stalling but not pushing too hard either. It was slow enough that Squire began to chafe. He hid it well from the men but not Star Path.

"Why are you so sad, my man?" she asked one night.

I ain't sad. Nor melancholy."

"Angry?"

"Nay. More like aggravated." He shrugged his great shoulders.

"Why are you like this?"

"We be goin' too slow. Losin' time. We'll ne'er catch them Blackfeet. 'Least not before winter sets in."

"Then we will find them in spring. Or maybe they find us first. They want *L'on Farouche* and they will look until they find him or he finds them."

"Ye be right, I reckon."

———

It was edging into October when the first real snowstorm hit. They had faced a few short squalls but this one looked as if it was going to last a while. They had known it was coming and had found a good place to wait it out, a dense collection of cottonwoods and willows backed up against a bare hill. It had wood, water from a small stream that flowed nearby, and enough forage for the horses for at least a little while. Li'l Jim, Gideon Hook and one of the camp helpers were out hunting and came back with a goodly supply of fresh meat. So they were settled in when the snow began, big, fat wet flakes that fell in a silent curtain.

The snow piled up but the temperature never fell much below freezing. The men went about their work, even trapping a little.

The third night there, the usual members of the group gathered in Melton's tent. After they had all eaten and were sitting back with coffee and pipes, Melton said hesitatingly, "I think we should give up this quest, Nathaniel."

"This be no time for joshin', Colonel."

"I am not joking, Nathaniel. I have come to realize

that this isn't the time to keep on with this mission. I don't say we give it up entirely. No, sir, not by a damn long shot. Lest you've forgotten, I got plenty of reasons for hunting those bastards down and putting an end to their atrocities. You aren't the only one who has suffered the torments inflicted by the hands of the Blackfeet."

"That be true, Colonel. It be even more reason to keep after 'em."

"Nathaniel, look around you," Melton said, weariness in his voice. "This storm is a harbinger that winter is near. With this many people, we are already starting to run low on supplies. Our men are having more trouble hunting because of the weather and the scarcity of game."

"This be something that's got to be settled. And the sooner the better to be doin' so."

"The men are tired, Nathaniel," Melton said with a combination of weariness and anger in his voice. "They have been through hard times. Had everything stolen out from under them. Fought Blackfeet. Traveled for miles on foot, often without food and sometimes without water. They are plumb worn out." His tone softened just a little. "Not everyone has your strength, Nathaniel. Physical strength or strength of will. These fellows here are just men. Yes, they are tough, hard men, inured to most hardship. But they are still just men." He half-heartedly smiled. "They are not immortal, as you seem to be."

"Bah. I be just a man, too." He did not believe that, really.

"Like hell," Li'l Jim said.

"Besides," Melton continued, pressing his case, "there are the women and children to consider. Mountain Bear is but a few months old, Li'l Jim's youngster and mine are younger than that. Silver Necklace will drop any day.

Blue Smoke and Sun Goes Slow are due to produce their offspring within the next few weeks. And Slocum's woman likely will be ready to foal in a couple months at most. Yellow Bells is the only one not carrying a child."

Hannah was about to offer a snide comment on Li'l Jim's potency but when she saw the look on Squire's face, she wisely kept her mouth shut.

"Injun women been doin' so in all weather and situations, Colonel. Ye should be knowin' that by now."

"I do. But your women have not suffered so much. The women with us have endured much hardship and they, too, are tired."

"I think the Colonel's right, Nathaniel," Train said. "But if you're hell bent on goin' after Bug's Boys right off, I'll go with you. Li'l Jim and Hannah will, too, I reckon."

Both nodded.

"You want to do that, I figure we can take a wee bit of time and get the Colonel and all the others set up in a winter camp, then head on our own way. But, like I said, I think he's right."

"Somethin' else you might want to consider, hoss," Peters interjected before Squire could respond, "is trappin'. We done a day or two here and there but not much for real. In case you forgot, we lost all our plews and such. Be nice if we could make some now, at least cover the cost of what the Colonel's backers put out. The ones was took from us're long gone but we got plenty of time for a fair fall hunt."

Squire sat there thinking for a spell. He knew that everything the others had said was true. He even agreed with it somewhat. But damn if it didn't go against his grain to just give up the hunt for his enemies. It was no wonder he had spent so many of his years trapping alone or with just one or two well-known partners. Such a large party was nothing but trouble. He had learned that last year but had pushed it out of his mind when he heard of the Colonel's woes. He sighed, then nodded.

"Ye be right, lads, much as I don't like sayin' it. I reckon those red devils can wait till spring. Mayhap we'll be getting lucky and they'll find us o'er the winter. I know of a couple of places not more'n a couple, three days ride. Slocum, ye mind moseyin' on up toward the Three Forks."

"Shines with this chil'. I know of a couple places up thataway would do well."

"Good. Pick someone to be goin'.'"

"Li'l Jim, ye think ye could put up with this ol' coon for a spell?"

Li'l Jim looked like he was thinking it over, then shook his head. "I don't rightly know, Slocum, what with you bein' such a cranky ol' critter." He burst out laughing. "'Course I'll ride with you, hoss."

"Abner, you and Hannah head to the northwest a bit. I know a couple places might do up there. I'll draw ye a map."

"If you and Slocum know some good winterin' places, why don't you pick one and we'll just go there?" Train asked.

"Though it still be some early, might be some ol' boys already stakin' out such a place. Some of 'em might be trapped out already."

"I should of thought of that," Train said, somewhat abashed.

Squire shrugged. He noticed that Hook looked disappointed. "Somethin' be stuck in your craw, Gideon?"

"Nah."

"Reckon ye be feelin' a bit left out that Slocum didn't pick ye to ride along." He saw he had hit home by the look in the young man's eyes. He smiled a little. "I'll say this for ye, hoss, me and the Colonel there have come to rely on ye a heap. Billy, too."

"It's true, Gideon," Melton said. "It's mighty comforting to know you two are with us."

Hook shyly grinned. "Don't know if you mean that, Colonel and Mr. Squire — Nathaniel — but it's sure nice hearin' you say so."

CHAPTER 31

PETERS AND LI'L JIM RODE in less than an hour after Train and Hannah four days later. Within half an hour, the usual group of leaders——which now included Gideon Hook and Billy van Eck——met outside the Colonel's tent. At just past noon, the day was pleasant and warm enough but another storm was building to the north.

"So what did ye lads find?" Squire asked.

Train shook his head. "Can't say as we found anything that might do. One hole was already bein' took over. Couple others looked like they was pickled over pretty well. Didn't see much beaver sign. Me and Hannah'd be willin' to ride on out and look elsewhere if Slocum and Li'l Jim ain't found anything suitable."

Everyone turned their eyes toward Peters. "Couple seemed all right, mayhap, but one's a heap better. Bull Mountains, near the Yellowstone, a ways northeast of Pompey's Pillar."

"That be Crow country."

"Near enough. But I don't reckon those critters'll be roamin' that far west come winter."

"That'd shine with this chil'," Hook said. "We had enough trouble with those devils already. Don't need them and the damn Blackfeet comin' against us."

"Aye, both those things be true. Ye say there be a good hole there that'd be meetin' our needs, Slocum?"

"Ye be thinkin' the same, Li'l Jim?"

"Reckon I do." A small smile just touched the outer edges of his lips. "Even if I didn't, I wouldn't want to go against what he said lest he start whinin' all the time like he usually does when things don't go his way."

"Damn, boy, you and I are gonna lock horns but good one day, you keep smart mouthin' this ol' hoss. And you don't want that, boy. You'll be some hurtin' after I get through with you."

"I ain't afraid of you, Gramps. Dried up ol' bag of wind."

"Well, mayhap I am a mite old——but only a mite, mind you——but I can still shoot plumb center. And even as tiny as you are, I could still put a lead pill in your brisket without hardly tryin'."

"Well, you just go ahead and ..." He burst out laughing, joined in by Peters and almost all the others.

"I may have to be shootin' both of ye, ye lads keep up this foolishness," Squire said through his laughter.

"You will do no such thing, Nathaniel," Melton said rather huffily. Then a burst of laughter bubbled up from his belly. "But if you do, you better make sure I'm around to watch it."

———

They pulled out the next morning —— thirty-two people, including eight Indian women, three of them pregnant, and four half-breed infants, Silver Necklace having given birth the night before —— forty-seven horses and ten mules. They made an interesting procession though a slow-moving one. It took the group longer to reach their winter home than it had for Li'l Jim and Peters to check the place out and return.

They had been lucky, though, with only one minor snowstorm along the way. They arrived in late afternoon. Squire rode around the valley, making his own survey of the valley's appropriateness for wintering. Satisfied, he ordered a simple camp set up.

It started snowing again in the morning as they began putting up a more substantial camp. The men would go out by twos or threes and set their traps, then return to do their share of the work. Trees were cut for a few shacks some of the men would use. Star Path, Rising Sun and Silver Necklace, along with the other Indian women, sewed buffalo skins together to make tipis. Men took the horses to graze, always watchful. Cottonwood bark was stripped and stored for later forage for the animals. Other men hunted. Some of the meat was eaten fresh, some was made into jerky and pemmican to last them over the winter.

Within a week, they had a place that was as comfortable as one could make there in the wilderness. And it was time for some serious trapping and hunting. The beaver were plentiful so the women and camp helpers had more than enough to do curing the hides, along with those of buffalo, wolves and the occasional bear they came across. Game was abundant, too, though it soon began to dwindle with the weather and the men's hunting.

Blue Smoke and Sun Goes Slow gave birth within days of each other, sons both. Squire caught Hannah looking somewhat wistfully a few times at the women and their newborns. He was a little surprised that she hadn't gotten pregnant by now but he shrugged. It would, he figured, happen sooner or later. He wondered if perhaps Star Path had given the young white woman some secrets in how to prevent becoming with child. Indian women had their ways, he knew, though he did not know what they were and he, as with any man, wanted no such knowledge. That was women's doin's.

She had the same look, though, when Green Robe also birthed a son a month later.

―――――

Billy Van Eck stuck his head into Squire's lodge one afternoon. "Someone's comin', Nathaniel," he said.

"Injuns?"

"Ain't sure. They was comin' from the northeast. Gideon saw somethin' and sent me back here to let you know. But he didn't seem too put off by it. If they're Injuns, can't be more'n a few of 'em."

"All right, lad. Ye go on out to rejoin Gideon. Marcel, go with him, make certain all be well."

"*Oui.*"

The two men ducked out.

Squire hurriedly donned his buffalo coat and bobcat cap. He threw his shooting bag and powder horn over his shoulder and headed out. It was below freezing though not by much. It would get much worse before long, seeing as how it was only November. He walked toward the rough center of the camp and waited. Moments later, he was joined by Colonel Melton, Train, Li'l Jim, Hannah and Peters.

Before long, Hook and Van Eck camp into camp, trying to help two hobbling mountaineers.

"Slocum, Abner, go help them lads. Bring 'em to my lodge. *Vite!*"

Within minutes, everyone had crowded into Squire's lodge. The two newcomers were sitting by the fire, thick buffalo robes around their shoulders, bowls of rich buffalo stew and mugs of hot, sweetened coffee in their hands.

The two ate and drank a little, and some color started to return to their gaunt faces. They were weary, their eyes sunken. Under the robes, their buckskins seemed to hang off them as if they were mere skeletons.

They finished and seemed to relax a bit. One started slapping himself around the chest and side as if looking for something. He shook his head. "Damn," he muttered.

Squire nodded at Star Path and she grabbed something from a pack and quickly returned. She handed each newcomer a small pipe and twist of tobacco. The men brightened even more. "Thank ye, ma'am," one said. The two lit their pipes and sucked on them almost blissfully, eyes closed.

Finally, the one opened his eyes. "Lawd almighty, it's plumb good to see you boys. Damn if it ain't."

"*Oui*," the other said, more of a grunt that a word.

"Looks like ye lads seen some hard times," Train said.

"That we have." He took another couple of puffs. "I'm Hoke Williams."

"I'm Vachon," the other said. When Squire cocked an eye at him, he added, "No other name. Just Vachon."

"I be Squire." He pointed to each of his companions. "That be Colonel Melton, the leader of this here outfit;

Slocum Peters, Marcel Ledoux, Li'l Jim, Abner Train, Hank Carpenter ..."

"Hank?" Vachon questioned.

"Aye. Among outsiders she be Hank. And that there's Gideon Hook, Billy Von Eck, and that scrawny chil' there be Homer Bellows, feller thinks he knows horses."

"Damn right I do. Bestest horse handler ever was. And it's a good thing I am, too, with havin' to put up with the likes of this rascal." He chucked a thumb at Ransom. "He's damn near the worstest but I put up with him only 'cause the others are even worster than he is. So he's the least worstest of the worstest. Yep. We was back in the States, I'd have him muckin' out the barn. About all he's good for. Yep."

"Just shut your pie hole, old man," Ransom shot back. "As good care as you give those poor damn animals, if it weren't for me, they'd all be wolf bait. Be best for them animals——and us, too——if you was back in Missouri. And about all you'd be good for there would be milkin' cows."

The two new men looked on in confusion as the others laughed. "And that chil'," Squire said, "be Cletus Ransom, second best horse handler west ..."

"Or east," Ransom interjected.

"... or east of the Mississippi."

"And I won't be second best for long," Ransom said with a grin. "Soon's I can get rid of this ol' coot, I'll be the best."

More laughter sputtered around the skin lodge. When it died down, Squire asked, "So how'd ye lads come to be in such a condition?"

"We was figurin' to winter up near the Crows," Williams said. "We've done a heap of tradin' with them boys. Never did trust 'em fully but they always treated us fair. So we plunked ourselves down in some hole about two miles from a village of 'em. We was settlin' in just fine when a couple of them red devils tried runnin' off our horses."

"Can't trust them Crows for a minute, you can't," Bellows said. "Yep. Not when there's horses about."

Williams shook his head sadly. "Damn I should've knowed better. I went to talk to the chief——feller we call Skunk; never could pronounce his Crow name——and he said he'd tell them boys to leave off botherin' us. But damn if two nights later, a few of those manure piles come at us again."

"*Oui*," Vachon tossed in. "And we kill two of zem."

"Should've killed 'em all," Bellows muttered darkly.

"Me and Vachon figured it'd be a good idea to get us out of there. Didn't figure the Crows'd take too kindly to what we done."

"I wouldn't think so," Peters said dryly.

"So we skedaddled. And damn if we didn't run into some Blackfeet a couple weeks later."

"Big group?" Squire asked. "Was there a white man with 'em?"

"Nah. Only five or six warriors. Why'd ye asked if there was a white man with 'em?"

"Feller named Meisner's been tryin' to bring the Blackfoot trade to the Company. McKenzie was tryin' for a few years. I heard at rendezvous that he be gone from Fort Union. I ain't sure that be true but no matter. Word be he sent some duck humper named Murdock to run a new post called Fort Elk Horn. It seems he be continuin' that quest."

"Damn, what's this country comin' to," Williams said

with a shake of his head. "Anyway, those damned Black-feet took us horse and beaver. Left us with nothin' but our guns and the clothes we was weaarin'. Been staggerin' 'round ever since, hopin' to find us a fort or somethin' where we could put up for the winter."

"Well, ye be welcome to join us," Squire said after a moment's thought. "That shine with ye, Colonel?"

"It does, long as they follow the rules."

"What rules are zey?" Vachon asked, sounding a little surly.

"None you wouldn't be following elsewhere. You do your share of the work," Melton said. "We'll provide you with traps, powder and lead. And a horse each though you'll be riding bareback unless you make yourselves saddles. You can negotiate for better clothes and such but we'll provide a buffalo robe and a blanket."

"Sounds fair enough, I reckon," Williams said.

"We frown on fighting amongst ourselves and you'll leave others' property alone. You will answer to me——or more important—to Mr. Squire. Or to anyone else we designate."

"And," Squire added. "Ye be leavin' the women alone. They be spoke for. One of the men wants to sell one to ye, or e'en to share one, that be fine. One of the women seeks ye out, ye talk to her man before ye do anything. *Comprenez-vous?*"

"Does zat include her?" Vachon asked, pointing to Hannah. "Ze one you call Hank. She looks to be free."

"She be Abner's woman. Ye try to force yourself on that gal, ye will be in a heap of trouble."

"He's a big *homme*," Vachon said, pointing to Train. But maybe I can take him." He sounded cocky.

"It ain't him ye have to be worryin' about, lad."

"You? Zat big fellow can't take care of himself or his woman?" Now there was disdain in his voice.

"Lad, that chil' will tear your head off and be shovin' it up your ass. The real one ye got to worry about be Hannah."

"Zat *petite femme*?" Vachon snorted.

"Aye, lad. She has more Blackfoot scalps than ye'll e'er have. Ye go against her and she'll cut your pizzle and stones off and put 'em in your possibles sack so ye be havin' 'em with ye all the time, though they won't be of much use to ye."

Vachon blanched a moment, then his color returned. He suddenly laughed, then grew serious. "You don't need to fear me, *mademoiselle*. I, Vachon, say dis to you——you are safe from me. Always." He looked at Squire. "I just test you, to see if you 'ave courage. You pass." He laughed again.

The others did, too, though somewhat nervously. Squire merely glared at him. Vachon gulped a little.

Winter 1835-36

Jacob Meisner pulled into Fort Elk Horn during a snowstorm. The weather did little to improve his humor. In addition to his usual surliness, he was bitter at having missed killing Squire yet again. He had to admit, though, that it brought some small measure of pleasure that the Blackfeet had come in with the haul of plews and plunder taken from Melton.

The fort was still run by Alastair Murdock whose demeanor toward Meisner had not improved one iota. Meisner clumped into the small, tidy office in the bourgois's house and eased himself into a chair, rather ill at ease.

"So, what have you to tell me, Mr. Meisner?" Murdock said in that cold, distant tone. "Have you conquered this mythical giant?"

"*Nein,*" he snapped. "He vasn't vit' de same brigade as last year. But the damned Blackfeet attacked anyway and came away wit' all dere plunder——horses, plews, everyt'ing."

"And where is all this bounty?"

"De Blackfeet vill bring in soon. They vill expect much in trade."

"I'm sure they will," Murdock said dryly. "And we will treat them well."

Meisner did not believe him but it was not his concern.

"And what of this legendary giant of a mountaineer?"

"I vill get him for certain," Meisner said, almost spitting out the words in his anger, "in der spring. I know dis man und he vill come after der Blackfeet. Yah, he vill, for sure.

"Why do you hate this man so much?"

"I vas friends with the Blackfoot for a long time, since I was wit' der Hudson's Bay. One of few white men who liked to stay in der villages. Der British had much of der trade wit' them, too. Then Herr McKenzie ask if I can bring the Blackfoot trade to der American Fur Company."

"Why you?"

"I t'ink maybe because I vas not happy wit' der British. They don't treat us Germans or any odder folks not British very well." He shrugged. "Und I know der Blackfeet. Und I know der Blackfeet don't like Squire. When I learned he vould be coming to the mountains vit a new group, I make plans vit two of the men going vit him. I think they would kill Squire. They vas supposed to. He is a big enemy to der Blackfeet so, if he is dead, they vill be happy and bring der trade to the Company."

"That did not work out well, eh?"

"*Nein!*" His voice was bitter. "Und vhen he and the

odders attacked Elk Horn's village, *mein* vife vas killed. I vas at Fort Union und vhen I learned of it, I swore that he vould die. I vas busy wit' other things so I talked to another Britisher who had plans that did not include der Hudson's Bay und asked him and his friends to take care of Squire. This man Carney and his friends had their own reasons for hating Squire."

"That didn't work out either."

"*Nein*. And neither did der Blackfoot attack. But I vill do it next time by *mein* self. Then you vill haf all der Blackfoot trade."

"You said that the last time you were here. You had better get it done this time," Murdock said harshly. "We have other ways of making inroads into the Blackfoot trade. We have lost patience with you."

"Yah, I understand." Meisner was not happy about the ultimatum, or the implied threat, but there was nothing he could do about it — except bring the Blackfoot Squire's scalp.

CHAPTER 33

"It be times to leave, lads," Squire announced. It was only early March but he felt they had waited long enough.

"Where away we headed?" Slocum Peters asked.

"Fort Elk Horn. We'll be takin' care of business there first, then go after the red devils who caused us all this trouble." He grinned harshly. "'Less we find Bug's Boys first."

"What about trapping?" Melton asked.

"We're pretty close to trappin' this place out, Colonel. We'll give it a day or two more to set the traps while we be getting ready to move on. We can be trappin' while we travel but I don't figure to be dallyin' too long in any one place. And once we be takin' care of the Blackfeet, we'll have a heap of time to be havin' us a shinin' hunt."

"Then we best start getting things ready," Train said. He and the others drifted off to their various tasks.

Three days later, they pulled out, heading mostly north. They rode boldly, showing little fear of the Blackfoot. They traveled a couple of days, then would spend a couple in a camp to trap, then push on. They were slowed several times by snowstorms but otherwise made good progress. Just before the middle of April, they were in sight of the fort.

The large group stopped just inside the trees. Ahead was an open space of perhaps a hundred yards in a semicircle around the fort. Behind it was the Missouri River.

They all dismounted and Squire gathered his usual "council" together, plus the two newcomers. "Ye two lads been inside the fort?" Squire asked the latter.

"*Oui*," Vachon responded. "Not long."

"Same here," Williams added.

"What's it like in there?"

"Typical of such places," Williams said. "Hundred and fifty feet or so along all sides, blockhouses on diagonal corners. I heard tell there's a couple cannons in each. Blacksmith shop and such along the back wall. Storerooms and livin' quarters along the right wall."

"Ze bourgeoisie's house is in ze middle of ze left. On zis side of it is ze trading room. On ze other side is ze kitchen and place to eat."

"Nothin' to be causin' us trouble?"

"*Non.* Not for some ol' mountaineers, eh. Zey will welcome us wit' open arms."

"*Bon.*" He thought for a moment. Then he shrugged his great shoulders. "There be no plannin', I reckon, lads. We ride in there like we was just some mountaineers comin' to trade for some supplies. Then we take it o'er."

"Just like that?" Melton asked.

"Aye, Colonel."

"Whatever for?"

"Might be that Meisner be here. E'en if he ain't, there be e'ery chance that this be where all our plunder was taken. It be unlikely these folks'll give it back just cause we ask."

"So we just go in and drop anybody we see?" Hannah asked, horrified. The thought of just going in and killing a bunch of white men — trappers and traders all for the most part — did not set well with her at all. If they were talking about Blackfeet, she would have no problem with that. But this? Looking around, most of the others seemed to feel the same way.

"Not unless we have to. I figure we get the drop on 'em, most of 'em'll be quittin' without much fuss. Most of 'em's just lads workin' there or some trappers who won't much care long as we leave their plunder alone."

Hannah nodded, relieved.

"Me and the Colonel'll mosey on into the headquarters. Rest of you lads who'll be with us, just spread yourselves out some and keep an eye on those lads. We be getting lucky, me and the Colonel'll get Murdock to hand o'er things. I figure to leave some of the lads and many of the animals behind. Cletus, you stay here with those animals. Half the men'll stay here, too, to watch o'er the women and young'uns. But they best be ready if we be needin' help inside, though that be unlikely. Mr. Van Eck, ye be in charge here."

"Yes, sir." There was pride in his voice.

"Hannah, ye be stayin' behind."

"But I can handle myself, dammit. You know ..."

"Aye, lass, I know that. I ain't questionin' your ability or your bravery. But we don't need a white woman with us."

"Oh, hell, Nathaniel, everybody in the mountains knows about *Ohitekah Winyan*, the white woman warrior, by now."

"She's right, Nathaniel," Melton said, surprising everyone including himself.

Squire looked thoughtful for a moment. Then he laughed. "Mayhap we'll be leavin' e'eryone behind, 'cept Hannah and Li'l Jim. Them two and me ought to be able to take o'er that fort e'en if they be puttin' up any fuss."

Everyone joined in the laughter.

"All right, lass, ye be welcome. Besides me and the Colonel —— and Hannah, of course —— Abner, Li'l Jim, Slocum, Marcel, Gideon, Vachon, Eli and Horace will be joinin' us."

"Not me?" Williams asked.

"Nay. It'd be good to have another steady ol' hand here. Ye be all right with that?" It wasn't really a question.

Williams nodded.

"Ye mind takin' orders from a young feller like Mr. Van Eck?"

"Not 'less he tries to ride me too hard." He grinned at Van Eck.

"*Bon.* Homer, ye be comin', too. Need ye to be takin' care of what animals we go in there with."

"Ya sure?" Bellows asked, grinning. "Means I got to leave that no good little snot Cletus to watch over most of the animals. Don't know if I can trust him to do that. He's not the worstest I ary saw but damn near it. Why ..."

"Oh, close your fly trap, old man," Ransom shot back. "Only reason Nathaniel's takin' you along is so Slocum can keep an eye on you, make sure you don't fall dead from old age. I reckon he's even considerin' tyin' you to your horse just so's you won't fall off."

That drew another burst of laughter.

"All right, lads," Squire said after a few moments, "best be getting ready."

Within a quarter-hour, the group was moving out, heading slowly across the grassy sward. As they rode, they were wary, especially after seeing the glint of a small cannon being swung their way. Four riders trotted out of the wide gate and stopped thirty yards out and waited.

Squire's men halted. Neither group said anything for some time before the leader of the fort employees asked, "What's your business here?"

Squire started to say something but Melton laid a hand on his arm, stopping him. "I would think that you are an uneducated man," the Colonel said. "But that doesn't necessarily mean you're stupid, though I have my doubts about that because that was a mighty damn fool question."

The man looked both confused and angry.

"What's your name?" Melton asked.

"Leo Hopper."

"Take a look at my little caravan, Mr. Hopper, and what do you see? A small group of mountaineers, yes?" When Hopper nodded, Melton went on, "And several mules carrying several packs of plews, yes?"

"Well, yeah."

"Then what the hell do you think we're here for?" Melton thundered.

"Tradin', I reckon."

"Brilliant, Mr. Hopper. Brilliant. And here I had doubted your intelligence. I apologize. Now, what say you and your boys there get out of our way and let us go on to the fort where we can conduct business." It was a statement, not an inquiry.

"Can't say as I like your tone, mister. And by the looks of all of you, I don't figure you to be Company men and we ain't about to do business with no damned opposition boys. Now turn your asses 'round and ride on back from wherever you came from."

"Ain't very hospitable, lad," Squire said. He was fidgety, not used to letting someone else take the lead.

"Breaks my heart that you think so." He sneered, then pulled off his hat and made something of a show of wiping his forehead with his sleeve.

Squire raised his rifle from where it rested across his thighs, thumbing back the hammer as he did. He leveled it and fired, blowing Hopper out of his saddle.

Peters, Li'l Jim and Vachon fired a heartbeat later and the other three men from the fort went down, dead.

Then Squire bellowed, "Ride!"

Within a moment, they were all racing for the fort's gate. Seconds later, a small cannon shell burst some yards off to their right and another just behind the galloping group.

They charged into the fort and slammed to a stop. The men tumbled off their horses. Gunfire broke out as fort employees poured out of buildings.

Over the new din, Peters bellowed, "Li'l Jim!" He pointed toward the front bastion where the two men were having trouble getting the cannon around since the weapons were meant to be fired at an outside opposing force, not one inside the fort. Li'l Jim couldn't believe these fools were about to turn cannon on their friends. But he nodded and took aim.

Peters then roared at Hook and pointed to the other bastion. He turned just in time to take a lead ball across the top of one shoulder. "Son of a bitch," he muttered and shot the man who had shot him.

Bellows was having a devil of a time trying to keep the

horses and mules from bolting. Eli Brand hurried over to help though it was still mostly a hopeless task.

"Colonel!" Squire thundered. "Get the booshway. "Hold him!"

Melton nodded and headed toward the chief trader's home/office.

A clerk came out of the trade room and fired at Squire, hitting him a glancing blow off one hip. As he frantically tried to reload, the giant charged over there. At the last minute, the man ducked back inside. But Squire followed. Grabbing the man by the seat of his pants and nape of his neck, he smashed him face first into the log wall. The man crumpled, dead or dying.

Squire popped back outside and took a swift glance around. He spotted Vachon fighting off four burly trappers. He raced over and flung one man away, then grabbed another and snapped his neck.

"*Merci*," Vachon grunted as he smashed a forearm across one of the two last attackers and kicked another in the stomach.

Squire turned to see where else he would be needed most and grinned as the rest of his crew galloped into the fort and threw themselves into the battle.

In minutes, it was mostly over. A few fort employees still tried to cause some damage but they were being subdued. Train had five of them sitting with their backs to the wall of one of the storage rooms.

Hannah joined him, breathing a little heavily from the fight she had just had with one man. Suddenly, she doubled over and vomited.

"What's wrong, Hannah?" Train asked, panicking. He was stopped at the sound of a gunshot. He glanced up to see Li'l Jim standing there with a smoking pistol in his hand. One of the men against the wall was groaning, having just been shot.

"I'm pregnant, ya damn fool," Hannah snapped as she swiped a dirty sleeve across her mouth. "And I shouldn't have to tell ya not to take your eyes off an enemy for anything!"

"Pregnant?" Train asked, befuddled, glad that Li'l Jim was keeping an eye on the other prisoners.

"Yes, pregnant. As in with child. As in carryin' a child. As in ..."

"I know what it means, dammit, woman. I just didn't know. You never said anything."

"I wasn't sure till a couple days ago." She suddenly sounded a little frightened. "You ain't mad are ya?"

"No, I ain't mad. Surprised, mostly. Concerned. Worried." He went to hug her but she doubled over again.

CHAPTER 34

IT DID NOT TAKE LONG before the fort was completely in the hands of Squire and his men. Most of the living Company men were lined up sitting against walls under the watchful eyes of some of Squire's men. A few of the employees —— tradesmen mostly —— had not fought and were leaning against their workbenches.

"What should we do with them boys, Nathaniel?" Peters asked, pointing at the latter.

"Reckon they won't cause any trouble but mayhap ye best go on o'er there and talk to 'em. See if they be havin' any deviltry in mind. If ye be thinkin' so, bring 'em o'er with the others."

Peters nodded and strolled off.

"Simon, where be Billy?"

"He stayed with Cletus and the women and young'uns. Gus and a couple others, too. Gus said he thought it best they be on hand there lest some devils from here in the fort come out there and thought to cause some trouble."

"That be good thinkin'." He had a sudden thought.

"Where be Hoke? He was with ye and I ain't seen him here."

"Went out with the others to help in the attack."

"That be strange," Squire muttered. Then he shrugged. With all the confusion, he could be anywhere. "All right. Eli, go on and bring all them folks, lad."

"Women and all?"

"Aye." He turned "Eli, go on and fetch the Colonel. He be up in the big house, probably with the booshway. Tell the Colonel to bring that ol' chil' with him." He sent others to take over the guard duties from Train, Li'l Jim and the others in what had firmly become the leadership group. They all migrated to a spot near the factor's house under a large tarpaulin. Some stood, some squatted, some sat on a few tree stumps littered about. Colonel Melton came out of the house towing a medium-size, well-dressed man with him. Two nicely clad servants followed.

Simon Essex came along dragging a chair from inside. He set it in the center of the group of men under the tarp. Melton shoved Alastair Murdock in it.

"Where be Meisner?" Squire demanded.

"I have no idea."

"I ain't about to ..."

"Nathaniel, please, if I may?" Melton said.

Squire's eyes rose in question. This was the second time Melton had taken the lead from him. It was not something he was used to, liked, or generally accepted. Then he smiled inwardly. It was about time Melton showed some real gumption in such situations. "Have at it, Colonel."

Melton nodded. "Now, Mr. Murdock, first things first. Where are our plews?"

Hoke Williams strolled up and stood near the corner of the shelter.

Squire marched over. "Where ye been, lad?" he asked.

"Thought I saw a couple boys tryin' to run off and chased 'em. They disappeared though."

Squire saw something he didn't like in the man's eyes but shrugged it off. It was quite plausible and there were more important things to worry about. He walked back to where the Colonel was questioning Murdock.

Murdock shrugged. There was no need not to answer. "Gone downriver."

"All of them?"

"Yes, all of them we had. Six bateau worth."

"That would include ours, I presume, then."

"All of them were the Company's," Murdock said with an oily smile.

"I don't think all of them will have the Company's mark when we get them."

"You'll never get them. They belong to the Company now."

"What about the rest of our possibles, Mr. Murdock?" Melton asked.

"Gone, mostly I'd say."

"What do you mean, you'd say?"

"Blackfeet kept most of it. What little was left was traded to various trappers or other Indians."

"Horses?" Bellows asked.

"Blackfeet kept most of those, too."

"Where're the fort's horses?"

"I can't tell you that."

"Why not?"

"It would make my employers quite unhappy." Murdock shrugged, seemingly unconcerned.

"Mr. Murdock," Melton said evenly, seeing Squire coming with a dark glint in his eye, "I have more patience than Mr. Squire there but not much, especially at this time. My men and I have been through some very unforgiving times. We have been stolen of all our goods, we have walked for miles and weeks, starving. Hardships upon hardships. My patience, therefore, is near an end. Now, I am usually a peaceable fellow but I have been tortured by the Blackfeet and have learned some of their ways. I will be glad to give you an example of my new knowledge should you remain uncooperative. Now where are the horses?"

Murdock looked from one hard face to another. He did not like what he saw. "Couple miles mostly east and somewhat south."

"Want me to go get 'em, Nathaniel?" Ransom asked.

"Aye, lad. Take a few of the lads with ye. Don't kill them horse guards if ye don't have to. But don't hesitate if they be wantin' to protest too strongly."

Ransom nodded and turned, shouting at several men to join him. In moments, they were mounted and galloping out of the fort.

"Now, Mr. Murdock," Melton went on, "back to Nathaniel's original question. Where is Meisner?"

"I don't know."

"Ye must have some idea."

"Nope." A bit of smugness crept into his voice.

Melton suddenly slapped Murdock across the face so hard it almost knocked him out of the chair. It shocked everyone but Squire, who smiled a little.

"Does that aid your memory any, boy?" the Colonel asked.

Murdock shook his head to try to clear it. "With the Blackfeet," he finally said.

"Elk Horn's band?"

"Yep. At least that's what I think. But there is word that many bands'll come together."

"Mite early for the Sun Dance," Squire said.

"Yep. But I'm told they plan many a raid this summer."

After a minute or two of silence, Melton asked, "Why is the Company dealing with a man like Meisner? Or any of the other miscreants of the past couple of years? I have heard you have most of the Blackfeet trade sewn up."

"Most, yes. But not with some of the bands farther west and north. Like Elk Horn's. And Black Bull's." He smirked a little. "And 'tis all because of you, Squire." He was somewhat surprised that he got little reaction. "Seems those heathens are afraid of you, you bloody great ox."

"Reckon they might have reason to be," Squire said dryly.

"So what now, Nathaniel?" Melton asked.

He looked around, thinking. Then he said, "Slocum, what be your thinkin' on missin' out on raisin' more Blackfoot hair?"

"Well, now, ye know raisin' Blackfoot hair's about one of the most shinin' doin's for a man like me so I ain't sure ..." He stopped and stood there thinking, staring in question at Squire all the whole. Then a slow smile spread across his face. "Fetchin' out our plews back?"

"Aye."

Murdock burst out laughing. "You really are crazy, man. You'll never catch those boats."

"Mayhap, lad," Squire said tightly. "Abner, Li'l Jim, lock this shit pile and all his friends in one of the storerooms. Be making sure it be empty — no weapons."

As the two hurried off, Melton said, "We don't even know if there's another boat here, Nathaniel. And we don't know if any of our men can handle one. Murdock is right, we can never catch them."

"Ain't the river I be thinkin' of."

"By land?" Melton asked. "That's even crazier."

"Maybe," Peters threw in. "But we ride hard southeast, straight across Sioux and Pawnee land. River goes miles north, then east in a wide turn."

"That's dangerous country."

Squire snorted. "So be e'erything out here, Colonel. Ye be knowin' that. And it be our only chance. Write a letter to who'er ye be dealin' with in St. Louis. Be tellin' 'em what happened, that those plews be ours."

Melton looked at him for a few moments, then nodded and hurried to the house.

"Pick a couple of men ye trust completely, Slocum."

"I figure Abner, Hannah and even Li'l Jim, stinkin' critter that he is, are out of the question?" He winked at Li'l Jim.

"Aye, as be Marcel, Gideon, Billy."

"Damn, I would've picked any of those boys. I trust 'em without question," Peters said. When Squire nodded, he said, "Reckon I'll take Eli and Horace, if ye don't mind."

"They be good lads. Goin' downriver, them boats'll be makin' speed, even loaded as they be. But I reckon those boys'll stop at Fort Union for at least a day or two, likely a few. Ye push hard, ye just might make it to St. Louis before they do. Be givin' the paper to whoe'er the Colonel says to."

"No need to tell me that, ol' hoss."

"Aye. Take two or three extra horses per man. And a few more if ye be needin' for trade. And be takin' whate'er supplies ye need from the storerooms."

Calling for Eli Beale and Horace Dawes, Peters spun and hurried off to where Bellows had their group's horses. They got their own and a few others, then culled out several from the fort horses guarded by Cletus Ransom and some others just outside the fort. They loaded those with plenty of supplies.

About the time they finished, Melton came out of the factor's residence with an oiled paper packet. "There's four letters in there, Slocum, each addressed to one of my contacts. Good luck in your journey, Mr. Peters."

Peters nodded and was off.

Abner, Hannah, Li'l Jim, Ledoux and Hook gathered around Squire and Melton. "So what do we do about these fellows, Nathaniel?" Melton asked, waving vaguely at the storeroom where the fort employees were held. And the fort?"

"Burn it."

"Not with all the men inside?" Melton burst out, horrified.

"That be appealin', Colonel, but I reckon it be wrong." He paused a moment. "Marcel, take a couple men and start loadin' up supplies — powder, lead, food, whate'er else ye be thinkin' we can use. Leave out several kegs of powder."

Ledoux hurried off, calling for assistants.

"Abner, how many men we got locked up?" Squire asked.

"About a dozen. Plus them." Train pointed to the half-dozen or so tradesmen.

"Ain't fair mayhap but they will be join' the others. Gideon, you and Billy round up one musket for each of those men plus a full powder horn, but no lead balls, just a few bars of Galena."

"Anything else, Nathaniel?" Hook asked.

"One knife and one blanket each. Make sure each has some jerky and pemmican. Load e'erything on one horse."

"One?" Van Eck asked.

"Aye, lad."

The two hurried off.

Squire, Train, Melton, Hannah and Li'l Jim watched over the hubbub around the fort. A few minutes later, Hook and Van Eck came up with an overloaded horse. "All done," the former said.

"*Bon*. Take the horse south and be leavin' it with all the plunder somewhere. Don't go more'n two, three miles."

A bit baffled but accepting, the two young men nodded and trotted off on their task.

Minutes later, Ledoux walked up. "We 'ave everything we can take, mon ami. There still are *beaucoup* kegs of powder left."

"*Bon*. Be putting a couple or more in each buildin'."

"And a trail of it from each to each, eh?"

"Aye, lad."

While Ledoux was doing that, Hook and Van Eck rode back in and reported to Squire.

"Abner, you, Hannah, and Li'l Jim go get our prisoners and herd 'em out here."

CHAPTER 35

WHEN THE COMPANY men were standing before Squire, he said, "I be of a mind to make wolf bait out of the lot of ye. But *mes amis* be appealin' to my better nature to not be doin' so. There be some supplies and such a couple miles from here. Some of my lads will escort ye there. Then ye be on your own. Any of ye be givin' 'em trouble or tryin' to lag behind will be getting a lead pill in the brisket. Ye'd be wise to take what little be there and move on."

"You can't do such a thing, Squire," Murdock said.

"Oh, yes we can," Melton interjected. "And if you persist in your obnoxiousness, you will not even receive the small amount of supplies we have provided."

"Hell, we'll simply return here and wait for the next boat from Fort Union."

Squire and his men simply smiled.

"Gideon, you and Billy pick several lads and be marchin' these goat humpers to where ye left the plunder. We be pullin' out. Ye can be catchin' up to us. And mind what I told these lads: Anyone creates a fuss, ye're to shoot him down."

"Yes, sir," Hook said. Minutes later, he and four others were herding the Company men across the prairie. Before they were out of sight, the rest of Squire's group was pulling out. Only Squire, Ledoux and Melton stayed behind. Each held a burning twig.

"Well, Colonel, ye be the big chief of these here doin's. Ye go first."

Melton touched the burning twig to the line of black powder. It immediately began sizzling and crackling along on its destructive journey. To his right, Squire did the same with another line of powder and then Ledoux, to his right, did the same. The three mounted their horses, spun and galloped out. Just before reaching the trees, they stopped and turned.

Moments later, a series of thunderous, gratifying explosions ripped through the wood fort. Chunks of wood metal, fur and more flew high; fire began to lick at what was left; and smoke boiled into the sky.

"Waugh! That be most satisfyin'," Squire said.

"*Mais oui!*" Ledoux agreed.

"Colonel?" Squire asked.

"It feels rather strange for a businessman like me to celebrate the destruction of a business place. But, by God, this is a pleasurable sight to be sure."

————

"Village ain't far, Nathaniel," Train said. He, Van Eck, Hoke Williams and Simon Essex had been out looking for sign.

"Where be it?"

"Two miles or about, northwest. I got pretty close. They don't seem to be payin' much attention."

"They be in for a surprise," Squire growled.

"Reckon so. Village is backed by a river. Three rises make a semicircle around the rest with small passes between 'em. All three are topped by plenty of trees and brush. Ones of the east and south have pretty gentle slopes with some trees. Other one is mighty steep and mostly barren."

"How many be they?"

"Can't be sure, Nathaniel. Maybe forty lodges. Might be a few others farther back in the trees where I couldn't see 'em."

"Be near a hundred warriors or so. Hardly worth a worry." Squire grinned but to anyone but his friends, it would not he a pleasant sight. "Which ridge be the best for settin' a camp?"

"One on the east. Stream runs across one side. It's mighty small so we'll have to water the horses a few at a time but," he added with a vicious grin, "we won't be there long. Plenty of trees but they're spaced wider than on the south side. Easier to corral the horses but still protect 'em. A big clump of boulders is set back a bit. Good place for the women and young'uns to take cover.

"One on the south is pretty good, too; it is more direct overlookin' the camp but I think the one on the east is somewhat better."

Squire nodded.

"You do seem to have gotten quite close to them, son." Melton said.

Train grinned. "It's what I'm paid to do," he said with a laugh which was joined by the others.

"Have Mel, Sam and Vachon go out and bring in the others," Squire said.

"You did well, son," Melton said.

"'Course I did," Train said with a touch of arrogance as he turned his horse and trotted off.

A rather shocked Melton glanced at Squire. The giant mountain man, who grinned a little, said, "He be right, Colonel. It be time we both fully realized that he be among the best of us mountaineers now."

Eaton and Livers soon returned with Van Eck and Essex. Not long after, Vachon rode back to the caravan alone.

"Where be Williams?" Squire asked.

"I could not find 'im." He sounded a little distraught. "I follow 'is tracks but lost zem in ze rocks."

"Likely took by the Blackfeet."

"*Oui*," Vachon said sadly.

"I hope he be put under 'stead of caught up and brought back to the camp for those devils' amusement."

"*Oui*. Either way, *mon ami*, I 'ave even more reason to kill ze Blackfeets." With a grim look, he moved to the side of the travelers, off by himself.

"So, Nathaniel, to the south ridge we'll go and make our camp there." When Squire looked at him a little sharply, Melton chuckled. "It's what you were going to say anyway and I felt it my duty to exert a little of my authority."

Squire laughed and clapped Melton on the shoulder with a huge paw. "Ye be a shinin' chil', Colonel, and I be plumb proud to ride with ye."

Despite his age, his rank and all he had been through, Melton flushed in embarrassed pride. "Do we reach it tonight and make camp there?" he said after a few moments. "Or do we stay here or a little closer and wait till tomorrow to take our place there?"

Squire glanced up at the sky. The first hints of dusk were dimming the day's brightness. "Reckon we be getting there this e'ening. Abner says they be payin' no heed to anything. We'll be all right. It'll be a cold, dark camp, though. No fires. No need to be drawin' unwanted attention to us." There was eagerness for a battle in Squire's eyes. "Then we be payin' our respects to those scabrous, snake-humpin' sons of bitches."

Within an hour, they were climbing the ridge and the camp, such as it was, was being made. While it was, Squire strolled out to a spot where he could look over the Blackfoot encampment in the gathering darkness. Li'l Jim and Ledoux soon joined him. They watched dots of fire-light flare up.

"Zere are many 'orses, *mon ami*," Ledoux said.

"Don't be needin' horses."

"Just raising 'air on ze Blackfeets, eh?"

"*Oui.*"

"Ain't that Elk Horn's lodge down there near that little pool in the stream?" Li'l Jim asked.

"Aye, lad. That be his. And three lodges closer to us be Black Bull's," he added tightly.

"That mean's Light Eyes ..."

"Aye."

Li'l Jim knew better than to say anything else about the possibility — no, likelihood — that Squire's son would be in the village.

"'Ow we do zis in ze morning, *mon ami*?" Ledoux asked into the new silence.

"There be only one way for *L'on Farouche*," Squire said in grim tones.

"Straight ahead down those devils' throats," Li'l Jim said.

"Well said, lad." Squire turned and moved back into the trees. Li'l Jim and Ledoux lingered a few more moments, chatting quietly and then followed.

They headed back to the camp, such as it was. Before Squire could plunk himself down, three camp helpers — Augie Dunning, Cam Fitzgerald, and Lew Hurst — stepped forward. "We'd like to go with you tomorrow, Mr. Squire," Dunning said.

"Ye be certain? All of ye?"

The three nodded.

"Aye, then. Go fetch yourselves some weapons from the stores. Be ready come first light."

They raced off.

It was a somber though not worried camp, the men quiet and contemplating the next day's battle. Squire assigned a few men to guard duty. Before taking their stations, however, they spoke one by one to Melton, making their last will and testament. The Colonel wrote each down and had those who could write sign it; those who could not made their mark and were attested by others. Eventually, all the men in camp had done so, save one.

Melton found Squire sitting with his back to a tree, holding his infant son in his massive hands. It was a rather incongruous sight. Star Path sat next to him, smiling at the two males in her life. She was worried about what would occur the next day but she had confidence in her man and the others with him.

Melton squatted down in front of him. "Everyone has made out his will — except you, Nathaniel."

"E'en ye?"

"Yes."

"That be good."

"What about you, Nathaniel?"

"Don't be needin' one."

"Not likely you'll go under but there's always the chance."

"Aye, there be. Havin' a will won't be of no help if I do."

"But what of your possibles?"

Squire laughed. "What possibles? I don't have anything of value but my Hawken and *Noir Astre*."

"What about Star Path and," Melton pointed to the infant, "Mountain Bear?"

"Mayhap ye be right, Colonel. Give my rifle and *Noir Astre* to whoe'er ye think be best. Take Star Path and Mountain Bear back to her village."

"You don't want him educated in a white school?"

Squire shrugged. "That be up to Star Path." Then he grinned. "Ye be worryin' too much, Colonel. Ain't no Blackfoot can put this chil' under."

"As you wish, Nathaniel." Melton rose and started walking, shaking his head. Then he, too, smiled.

———

They lined up the next morning, most of them, as dawn was spreading its first pink rays across the little valley. Melton, Bellows, Ransom, Essex and Haines - plus the camp helpers - stayed behind. All the others, mounted, flanked Squire at the crest of the ridge. Hannah was to his right with Train just to her right. Li'l Jim was on Squire's left and Ledoux on his left.

Down below, the Blackfeet were beginning to go

about their daily business. Squire hesitated a bit yet, wanting more warriors out in the open where they could be fought instead of having to hunt them down amid the trees. But it would not do good to have too many of them prepared.

Then Hannah said, "It's time, Nathaniel."

"Aye, lass." He drew in a large lungful of air, then bellowed, "I be *L'on Farouche!*"

The words hung in the morning's still air for a few moments. Then Squire kicked *Noir Astre* into movement and went racing down the slope. The others, roaring war cries, were but a heartbeat behind.

Blackfoot shouts joined those of the mountain men as the latter charged into the village. The warriors grabbed weapons and prepared to face the attack as their women and children ran for safety in the trees. Arrows flew, gunfire ripped the air, and dust began to rise.

CHAPTER 36

THE SHARP CRACK of a gunshot was heard even over the din of battle. Out of the corner of his eye, Train saw Squire jerk a little as if hit. A heartbeat later, another shot rang out, and this time Train was sure the giant mountain man had been hit. One more and Squire sank to one knee. Blood ran from his mouth, staining the full, tawny beard. "Lord a'mighty," Train whispered, then froze for a moment. The shock of such a sight numbed him as if he had suddenly become encased in a block of ice.

He broke free of it when he sensed more than saw another Blackfoot charging at him. He swung his tomahawk with a maniacal burst of rage. The blade chopped nearly halfway through the warrior's midsection from the side, splitting him open and sending him flying several feet to his right.

Train spun to his left. Squire was still down on one knee but continuing to lash out at any Blackfoot that got near him. But Train could see he was weakening. Four warriors, seeing the giant mountain man wavering, sprinted toward him.

"No you don't, you scurrilous shit piles!" Train bellowed and raced toward them, aware that Ledoux, Li'l Jim and Hannah were racing that way, too. He flung himself at the Blackfeet, knocking them all sprawling. As he leaped up, Ledoux, Li'l Jim and Hannah converged on the sprawled warriors and swarmed over them. In moments, the warriors were dead and the three of Squire's people were turning toward the next wave of Blackfeet. Train swung to join them.

"Save him!" Hannah screamed at him.

Once again, Train was shocked for a heartbeat. He had never seen Hannah like this. Her face was a mask of rage and horror. He had seen her angry, furious even. And in pain and petrified in fright. But not this. This look told him that Hannah would take every bullet, every arrow, every tomahawk, war club or knife that the entire Blackfoot nation had if it would save Squire.

And he could do no less than whatever sacrifice it took on his part to do the same. Almost shivering with dread at the thought of the unthinkable, he turned to kneel at his friend and mentor's side. But as he did, he saw his friends, all with their rifles empty after the first assault and slung across their backs, take on another wave of Blackfeet.

"Best be gone, lad," Squire said, voice wavering. "This ol' chil' be done for. That be certain."

"No Blackfoot could kill you, Nathanial," Train muttered as he thought for a moment.

"Weren't no Blackfoot put these lead pills in me, lad. It be ..." He stopped, coughing up blood. "But I be goin' under for certain and I aim to take me a few more of these red devils with me."

"Shut that big, gapin' goddamn hole in your face,

dammit. I ain't lettin' your hair swing on some Blackfoot's lance. Can ya rise even a little?"

"Mayhap. Why?"

"Get you the hell out of here, dammit."

"Ye can't do that lad." His words were growing fainter.

"Ya once told me and Li'l Jim not to say such a thing to you. I ain't about to let you tell me I can't do something. Now pull yourself up some."

"What're ye ..."

"Just goddamn do it!" Train growled.

Squire's great beard and mustache split and he showed a blood-foamed smile. "Aye, lad," he whispered. With his fast-waning strength, he pushed to his feet, swaying.

Train slipped under him just as Squire began to fall, catching him across his broad shoulders. Train shoved himself straight, then shrugged a little settling Squire — all two hundred and eighty pounds of him — there. Train glanced over his shoulder. His friends — joined now by Jed Brand, Charley Worth and Gus Macgregor — had formed a semicircle around him and Squire. They were fighting with frenzied ferocity, the lot of them like whirling dervishes.

Train took a deep breath. And then he ran, heading for the ridge a hundred yards to his left, then began up it. With his adrenaline pulsing strong through him, his legs pumped strongly, his breathing hardly labored.

———

Like everyone, Vachon heard the rifle fire and saw Squire going down. "Merde!" He ducked a Blackfoot war club, knifed the warrior in the guts and then raced toward the group of Squire's people moving to protect him.

"Vachon!" Gideon Hook bellowed from some yards across the village.

Vachon stopped and glanced up the ridge where Hook was pointing. A faint cloud of gunsmoke still hung in the air. He glanced back but Hook was already racing up the hill on the left toward another puff of smoke.

As he began to run, Vachon saw Hannah ferociously battling two Blackfeet with a third heading her way. "*Sacre Bleu!*" he muttered. He barreled into Hannah and the two others, sending them all sprawling. He leapt up, grabbed a fallen warrior's war club and smashed the face of the third warrior.

Hannah had staggered up and slit the throat of one of the two she had been battling. Vachon kicked the other who was getting close to Hannah. The man sank to one knee. Vachon raced off, figuring Hannah could handle the last warrior.

"Thanks," she screamed as she did so, then turned and ran after Train.

"*Oui*, Mam'selle!" Vachon roared back.

Hannah looked around, torn between racing after Train as something of a protector or staying where she was in the midst of the battle with Li'l Jim and most of the others.

Li'l Jim saw her and yelled, "Go!"

She did, glad to see that Van Eck was following her example and joining her as an escort of Train.

Train was oblivious to it all. There was no thought. There was no up or down. There were no people. There was no pain, no weakness in his legs. There was no world around him. Just the drive that pushed him toward the top of the hill.

———

After sending Hannah on her way, Li'l Jim turned back to the battle. He dispatched another warrior, then saw a Blackfoot plunge a knife into Sam Livers. The mountain man went down and the Blackfoot loomed over him, ready to raise his hair.

"No you don't, you son of a bitch," he muttered as he raced the few feet to the men.

The Blackfoot looked up just in time to have his skull shattered by Li'l Jim's tomahawk.

Li'l Jim shoved the wavering body away and looked down. Livers grinned at him though the smile was thick with pain. "Well, ain't you some now, havin' some Black-foot try to carve your heart out and expectin'' me to save your hide."

"Figured you needed somethin' to do. You been sittin' 'round all morning'." He held out his hand and Li'l Jim helped him up. He stood there, weaving a little. Blood covered his shirt.

"You all right to move on by yourself, hoss?" Li'l Jim asked, a bit worried.

"Ain't sure."

But Li'l Jim couldn't wait. Another warrior was charging at them. He shoved Livers. "Go, hoss!"

Livers staggered away as Li'l Jim spun and ducked a war club aimed at his head. He swung his 'hawk but only managed to catch the warrior on the outside of one thigh. The Blackfoot jerked and the tomahawk flew out of Li'l

Jim's hand. The young mountain man snatched out his knife and plunged it into the warrior's innards.

As the Indian slumped against him, Li'l Jim saw another warrior over the man's shoulder. He shoved the dead man away and took a few steps toward the warrior, who was standing there watching him, and stopped. The warrior was huge, larger than any Blackfoot Li'l Jim had ever seen except ...

"Blue Mountain," he gasped.

"I am Light Eyes."

The two stood staring at each other for some moments. Finally, Nathaniel Squire's half-breed son said, "We not fight. Go." Then he slipped off into the trees.

Li'l Jim stood there another few moments, unsure that was had just happened was real. Then he shook his head and ran to join the fighting retreat, grabbing Livers along the way and helping him.

———

Atop the ridge, Melton appeared out of the trees. He took in the scene in a moment and his military training asserted itself. "Gideon! Vachon!" he bellowed to the two men racing up the hillside to where the gunshots were coming from. His voice rang loud and clear across the ridge. "Bring them back alive!"

He turned his head and yelled, "Clay! Simon! Get out there and cover them!"

A moment later, Clay Haines and Simon Essex charged down the hill, rifles in hand.

The two stopped as Train and the others hurried past. Each glanced at Train with awe. Then they stopped, knelt and fired.

Melton cupped his mouth with his hands and once more his voice boomed out: "Men! Pull back!"

Hannah and Van Eck stopped and spun. They, too, fired. Between them and the two others, they laid down a covering fire as the men below began slowly backing toward the foot of the ridge.

Up in the trees, watching over the horses, Cletus Ransom looked at Homer Bellows with pleading eyes. Bellows hesitated for just a second, then nodded. "Go, boy." As Ransom rushed off with his rifle to help those on the side of the hill, Bellows whispered to himself, "Be safe, boy." He angrily brushed away unbidden tears.

———

As he was reloading, Essex looked over to the hill on his right and saw Hook go down an eye blink before he heard a shot. "Dammit all," he muttered. He finished reloading and shoved up, starting to head toward Hook.

Hook saw him and waved him back, beginning his run up the hill again, cursing himself. A bullet had whizzed by his head though he did not slow. But just as another lead ball came his way, he stumbled over a rock and fell.

He looked off to his right, worried about Vachon and how he was faring. He figured that if he was being fired on, so was Vachon. But the French-Canadian was roaring up the hill, apparently unfazed.

Vachon was, indeed, unfazed. He simply wanted to get to the man who had put a lead ball or two in Nathaniel Squire. The giant mountain man and his companions had taken Vachon into the fold and made him one of them, saved his life even, right from the beginning. Now he felt he must pay them back and if he was to fall in the doing, so be it.

But he had no intention of failing, gunfire from above or arrows from below be damned.

Then he was among the trees. Despite his desire to gut the gunman and the enemy's resistance, Vachon heeded the Colonel's words and wrestled the burly, high-smelling man to the ground before hammering him into submission.

Far to his left, Hook was doing the same to another enemy rifleman.

Down below, Squire's men, led by Ledoux and Li'l Jim who was still helping Liver, began working their way back out of the village. Mel Eaton went down with an arrow in his chest. Gus Macgregor grabbed him by the scruff of his buckskin shirt and starting dragging him along. He figured Eaton was dead but he was not about to leave his friend's body to be torn apart by these savages.

The warriors, too, were retreating. More than two dozen of their fellow tribesmen lay scattered about the village and the fire from on the hill was deadly to anyone who lingered. Still, a few darted in, looking to take out one of the white men. Ledoux took a knife wound across his ribs before he chopped down the Blackfoot who had done it. Maurice Plante had a couple of ribs broken by a Blackfoot war club.

But then the village was empty, except for the bodies of the dead.

————

Train reached the top of the ridge and was so oblivious to the world that he would have kept running if Melton had not stopped him. With the Colonel's help, Train laid Squire on the ground. Then the world caught up with him. He sank to his hands and knees, limbs quivering from the exertion, his breathing strained and ragged. He was barely aware that men were filtering back into the camp.

Still shaking after several minutes, Train looked over at Melton. "How is he?"

"He's gone, son," the Colonel said, his voice drowning in sorrow.

"No," Train said, still gasping from his efforts. "No, dammit. It can't be."

Behind him, Hannah screamed, "No! No, no, no!" Her voice was an agonized wail. The death of only one other man would have elicited such a tormented howl from her. She tried to fling herself onto Squire's body but Melton and Marcel Ledoux grabbed her and kept her at bay.

From back a little amid the trees came a mournful, keening moan.

"Star Path," Hannah gasped. "Someone's got to help her ..."

"She's best left alone now, Hannah, you know zat," Ledoux said soothingly.

Before anyone could say anything else, Vachon strode in shoving his prisoner in front of him. Moments later, Hook came in from the other side with his prisoner. "Lookee here," he said, voice angry.

Vachon's eyes widened in surprise and anger. "'Oke?" he said, looking at his trapping partner. "*Qu'est-ce que vous avez fait* — What have you done?"

Williams shrugged. "I had a chance to kill me the big medicine mountain man."

"*Vous ête de la merde* — You are a piece of shit!" He was fuming.

"And you, I presume, are Jacob Meisner?" Vachon asked.

"Yah," he said proudly.

Melton surprised them all when he snarled, "Kill them!"

"There was a rumble of assent and Vachon offered, "*Avec plaisir.*"

As men moved in to fulfill the command, Hannah snarled, "No!"

Everyone turned to look at her in surprise and wonder.

"Oh, they will die. Be damned certain of that," she said in a voice that would have frozen the tail off the devil himself. "But just shootin' 'em or stabbin' 'em just ain't good enough. These bastards will suffer before they go under."

"They deserve it," Li'l Jim said firmly.

Assent was unanimous.

"Tie them to trees," Melton ordered. "And keep an eye on them. If they give any trouble, break a few bones." Melton surprised himself with his sudden disregard for civilized behavior. But these were different times and civility had no place here. "Some of you camp helpers, get fires going and food and coffee going. And a couple of you watch over the village just in case the Blackfeet gather up their courage again though it's not likely."

He looked around. The rest of the camp reflected his own gloom. And it was difficult to perceive that it was barely an hour after dawn. "How many did we lose?"

"Eaton, Crandall and Cummings," Van Eck said.

"Get a few men, Mr. Van Eck, and find somewhere to give them a decent burial."

"And Nathaniel?" Ledoux asked with a catch in his throat.

"No. He deserves better, of course. Let me think on it a while."

Ledoux nodded, an idea forming.

Van Eck and two men took the three bodies off.

———

Train was still too exhausted to really rise but he pushed himself up and over enough that he was sitting just a few feet from Squire's body. He stared unseeing, mind blank as Melton and Ledoux covered the corpse with his buffalo robe. Bellows and Ransom, who had silently come up, stood behind them, faces pale. Bellows's prominent Adam's apple bobbled as he fought the sobs from bursting out.

Across from Squire's body, Li'l Jim sat, face far more like stone than flesh. His eyes glittered with sorrow and hate.

The Colonel drifted off to see to the camp, spirits lower than a snake's belly. Numb, Bellows grabbed Ransom and the two stumbled back to the horses. Being with the animals was the only thing that offered them any solace.

The rest of the men sat or paced numbly, despondency settling over the camp like a thick, rancid fog. The women, for the most part, stayed back in the trees with their children, frightened and worried.

Star Path ventured out and plopped her solid body down, pulled the buffalo robe away from Squire's face and cradled his head. She rocked back and forth, moaning. Hannah plunked herself down next to her and stroked the Lakota woman's hair. The Indian did not cry but the young white woman did enough for both of them.

Finally, Hannah's sobbing, gasping tears ended. She wiped at her face, smearing the snot that had flowed freely. She wiped her hand on her buckskin shirt, kissed Star Path on the cheek, and stood. "It's time," she announced. She headed toward the two prisoners. The others followed.

They all stopped in front of Williams and Meisner. Each was tied to two trees, arms and legs stretched wide.

CHAPTER 37

"Who shall we start on?" Hannah asked in a frigid voice."

"Williams," Hook said. "Let that German bastard have a chance to cogitate on what's in store for him."

The others looked to Hannah, who nodded. She stepped forward and slapped Williams in the face.

"That all you got, missy?" he sneered.

She started to pull a knife but stopped when Vachon said, "*Excusez-moi*, mam'selle." She looked at him. "I think zis one, 'e belongs to me, eh?"

Hannah thought about it for a moment. She wanted to kill Williams more than anything. So did the others, she knew. He had killed Squire. But she realized that Meisner was the real villain and deserved the worst. Williams had betrayed his trapping partner so, she decided, he should be the one to take care of Williams. She nodded.

"*Merci*, mam'selle." He stepped up right in Williams's face. "Now, monsieur, it is not nice that you deceive Vachon. *Mais non*. I was always your *ami*. But you 'elp kill ze man who saved us, who took us in like we were 'is family, and you do zis, so you can maybe be a big man among de *Pied du noir*? Bah! *Vous est plus mauvais de la merde de chien* — you are worse than dog shit."

"Go to hell, you Frog bastard." He worked up what little spit he could in his dry mouth and shot it at Vachon. The spit landed in the French-Canadian's beard.

"Zat was not nice, monsieur. *Mais non.* You 'ave a bad mouth."

"Piss off. You ain't nothin' more'n the drippin's of a sick donkey's ass."

Vachon nodded almost thoughtfully. "I think ..."

"You can't think, you goddamn shit pile of a Frog."

"As I say, I think you say too much — too many bad things — with that mouth. Zat is not good and you deceive me all dese years with that wagging tongue of yours."

"That's right, you little rabbit humper."

"So, since you 'ave cause me and all dese odders so much trouble with *ta langue*, let us see 'ow you do wit'out one."

Williams's face tightened, unsure of what was coming.

"Monsieurs Jim and Ledoux, come, hold open zis man's mouth, nice and wide, eh."

Williams's eyes grew wide in fear and he clamped his teeth together. Ledoux grabbed his jaw and nose and started prying. Slowly, Williams's mouth opened, aided by Li'l Jim's punch to the man's stomach. Then the two held it open despite Williams's struggle.

Vachon reached out with his left hand and a powerful thumb and forefinger gripped Williams's tongue. His other hand came up with a knife and, in a heartbeat, Williams had only half a tongue in his mouth.

Vachon dropped the other half on the ground. "What 'ave you to say now, monsieur, eh?"

Grunts and screams poured out of Williams's mouth.

"Now, let me see what else zis chil' can do to pay you for your efforts to kill Monsieur Squire." He pretended to think a moment. Then nodded. "Ah, you fire bullets at 'im so maybe you like ze fire, eh." He looked over his shoulder. "*Mes amis*, some twigs and sticks to make ze fire, *s'il vous plais?*"

Wondering at the strange request, some of the men did as asked. Vachon piled the wood up on the ground between Williams's feet in a rough triangle up to the man's knees. Essex grabbed a burning branch from one of the fires and handed it to Vachon.

"*Merci.*" He knelt and shoved the branch into the base of the wood. In moments, it ignited and flames began reaching up toward Williams' crotch. He turned. "Now, monsieurs, and mam'selle, we go to pay our respects to Monsieur Meisner, *le grand tas de merde.*"

"Reckon Williams'll be occupied for a spell," Li'l Jim said tightly.

It was a grim group that crowded up to where Meisner was tied. They ignored the incoherent noises from Williams.

"You have heard of me, you pig-faced son of a toad?" Hannah asked, her face a marble mask of hate.

"Ah, de bitch dat fucks de warriors when she is not pretending to be a man. Ya."

Train went to hit him but Hannah stopped her man.

"No, that's someone else maybe. Perhaps your sister," she said harshly. "No, wait, that's you. Yes. You're the one who likes to lay with Injun warriors and pretend to be a man. Of course. You killed Mr. Squire..." her voice caught and she fought back a sob,"...because he wouldn't stick his pizzle in ..." She stopped when Meisner spit at her.

There was no stopping Train's fist from smashing Meisner's nose this time. Despite his continuing exhaustion, it was enough to flatten Meisner's nose and loosen a few teeth which the German spit out. Train was rearing back for another one when Li'l Jim stopped him.

Hannah wiped the spittle from her cheek. "Since you pretend to be a man, let's see what you got, eh." She pulled one of her knives, grabbed a handful of his buckskin trousers just below the belt and began cutting.

Meisner wriggled a bit.

"Best keep still, boy. Never can tell, a poor little defenseless woman might slip and ..."

Meisner stood stock still though he glared at her with hate-filled eyes. Hannah offered him an evil smile and returned to sawing away the front of his trousers. Before long, his manhood was exposed.

"Ah, dot is better, *fraulein*. A little air for de big fellow."

"It gets any bigger and we might just be able to see it," Hook said. There was no chuckling as there usually be at such a comment.

"*Klicken Sie auf die hölle sie schwarz bastard.*"

"What in hell's that mean?" Hook demanded.

"I don't know, son," Melton said quietly, "but I can assure you it's not complimentary."

"You seem brave now, you wretched maggot," Hannah said in a cold voice. "Let's see how ya do bein' carved up." She sliced open his shirt and shoved the sections of it apart, exposing Meisner's torso. "I think I'll start here." She jabbed the knife an inch deep, eliciting a small hiss of surprise more than pain fro Meisner.

"Reckon my judgment's a bit off," Hannah said, no apology evident on her voice. "Let's see if this is better." She dug the knife in a tiny bit, just enough to get through the epidermis. Then she began slicing downward. Li'l Jim stepped up and started doing the same on the other side of Meisner's chest. Meisner kept his calm, letting out only another hiss now and again. When they reached a spot just above the hip, Li'l Jim started carving across the top of the chest, Hannah across the lower stomach.

Meisner sucked in a couple of breaths, then smirked a little. "Dot is de best dat you can do? I haf had worse done to me by *mein kinder* tickling me."

When all the cuts were connected, Li'l Jim pried away a corner of the skin at the top, then tugged a little gently — for him — pulling the skin a little free, then a bit more.

Li'l Jim grabbed the piece of loose skin and ripped it down and away.

Meisner screamed as all the muscles and veins in his torso were suddenly exposed to the air.

Several men scooped up handfuls of dirt and, coming closer, patted it on the exposed flesh. Meisner screamed again.

"Seems zis fellow, 'e is not so tough as he think, eh," Vachon said. "'E scream like a little girl." When Hannah cast a glance at him. he smiled. "I said little girl, mam'selle. not a woman like you, the one ze Lakota call *Ohitekah Winyan* — Fierce Woman." He looked over his shoulder. "*Pardonez-moi.* It seems Monsieur Williams 'e is not warm enough."

"Don't worry, hoss," Van Eck said. "I'll be happy to stoke his fire for ya."

"*Merci, mon ami.*"

Soon the fire was burning a little higher and Williams was beginning to dance as much as he could to try to keep the flames from his genitals.

As the others started peeling the skin inch by inch off Meisner's arms, he was no longer so confident. He screeched and wept. And before long, Williams's shrieks were added to the din.

Finally, Melton shouted, "Enough!"

Everyone turned toward him. Hannah's glittering green eyes were feral; Abner's and Li'l Jim's faces were stony.

"Torturing these despicable wretches any longer will not bring our Nathaniel back." His voice quavered at the last. "It's time we saw to our friend."

"What'll we do with these two?" Train asked, barely able to contain his grief-fueled anger, chucking his thumb over his shoulder.

"Just kill them and be done with it.

"Zat will not do, Colonel," Ledoux said gruffly.

"You have a suggestion, Marcel?"

"Leave zem right where zey are."

There was a rumbling of agreement.

"So it will be." Melton paused, wiping a hand across his face. He was bone weary and worn down by grief. "Now I must think. Try to come up with a good place to ... to lay our great friend to rest." He almost staggered but Rising Sun hurried up to him.

"I know where, Colonel," Ledoux said. "Ovair near ze South Fork of Deep Creek." When everyone looked at him blankly, he said, "It is where 'e buried Singing Grass."

"His Nez Perce wife?"

"Oui. It is not far."

"What'll Star Path say?" Hannah asked, worry momentarily overcoming her loss.

"I 'ave talk with 'er. She says it is all right wit' 'er. But on one — 'ow do you say? — condition."

"And what is that?" Melton asked.

Ledoux turned to look at Abner, Hannah and Li'l Jim. "She say she agree only if you t'ree will take 'er dere when she die so she can be buried with bot' of zem."

"All three of us'd travel to hell's council fire and back if need be," Train said. Li'l Jim and Hannah nodded.

"*Bon.*"

———

Train slid down the steep canyon slope to the cave where Singing Grass was buried. The front of her natural mausoleum was blocked by boulders. The big young man studied things for a bit. Then he nodded. "Send down a couple kegs of powder," he shouted.

In moments, two of the half-dozen kegs of powder they had left of those taken from the fort were being lowered to him on ropes. He placed one as close to the cave mouth as the boulder would allow, laying it on its side. He cracked it open and poured out some of the explosive, making a small pile that reached the hole. He cracked open the second one and poured out a thin trail to a spot behind some other boulders, then went and placed that keg a couple feet from the other with a stretch of powder connecting the two kegs. He went behind his protective wall of rock, pulled out his flint and steel and struck one against the other. It took several strikes but the powder finally ignited and Train hunkered down.

The sizzling line of gunpowder raced along.

Suddenly, there was a blast that shook the canyon. Chunks of rocky shrapnel flew about, shooting out from the thick cloud of bluish smoke and raining down on the canyon floor. Train was hit by a few pieces but they did little harm.

Then there was silence. Train rose and moved forward. The cave was open enough to be able to inter Squire. Train gritted his teeth against the grief for a moment, then yelled up. "It's time."

Squire had been wrapped in a couple of buffalo robes. Ledoux and Hook had tied two ropes around the corpse and they now began lowering it. Hannah and Li'l Jim, each held with a rope, were also lowered, helping to guide Squire's body.

The three — with Train doing most of the work — managed to get Squire's body in the cave. Then all three sat there, trying not to cry as they said their farewells to the giant who had become so special to them. Then they went outside, grabbed ropes and called to the men above to pull them up.

"You said your goodbyes?" Melton asked quietly. When the trio nodded, the Colonel added, "Then it's time to complete the burial."

"Wait," Train said. "Nathaniel has his medicine bundle and his possible bag and 'hawk and knife but he needs his rifle and a horse to ride in the afterlife. I'll get *Noir Astre*."

"No!' Ledoux said sharply. Everyone looked at him. "Yes, 'e needs *un cheval* so we give 'im a horse but *Noir Astre? Mais non!*"

"But he needs *his* horse," Train protested.

"Another 'orse will do. *L'on farouche*, 'e will understand. We will give 'im ze Colonel's 'orse. It is a big animal, good for *L'on Farouche* in ze Spirit World."

Melton was surprised but nodded.

"But ..."

"Monsieur Train, *Noir Astre* is a special animal and 'e 'as yet another role to play." He stared at Train.

Train shook his head, not quite understanding but somehow knowing not to argue.

"And his Hawken?" Li'l Jim asked. "He'll need that for certain."

"No. That, too, is special. You will see."

Before long, Melton's horse had been killed and lowered into the canyon with one of the corps' spare rifles. It was not in the cave, not even all that close, but the men figured Squire would find it when he reached the other side. Then, with muscle and black powder, the caved was closed up once more.

It was a somber camp that night, with quiet talking among some of the men. And in the morning, still grieving, they mounted up, knowing now what would be done.

"*Allons-y,*" Ledoux said.

A CRACK of thunder bounced from cliff to cliff and a brilliant shard of lightning split the sky, bathing the Blackfoot village in an eerie blazing white.

The villagers thought little of it. Rain would come but they had snug lodges, plenty of wood for warming fires. The giant mountain man was dead and the other white men had been chased off so they had no reason to move such a comfortable camp.

More thunder came, this time rumbling low and menacingly, sounding like a stampeding herd of buffalo. Quiet fell for a moment, then a voice rang out over the village.

"I be *L'on Farouche!*"

It was followed by another shudderingly sharp crack of thunder and blaze of lightning.

The village came to a halt. Then someone pointed toward the ridge. There, sitting on a massive black horse, was a giant of a man, a large rifle resting on his thigh, barrel skyward.

As a sharp ear-splitting bang of thunder tore through

the air, the horse began slowly making its was down the slope.

"I be *L'on Farouche!*" the man roared again.

The Blackfeet, their spirit and medicine broken, fled in terror.

The giant man on the massive horse stopped amid the empty village.

Failing to hold back the tears, Abner Train whispered, "I be *L'on Farouche.*"

John Legg has published more than 55 novels, all on Old West themes. BLOOD OF THE SCAL-PHUNTER, is his latest novel in the field of his main interest — the Rocky Mountain Fur Trade. He first wrote of the fur trade in CHEYENNE LANCE, his initial work.

CHEYENNE LANCE and MEDICINE WAGON were published while Legg was acquiring a B.A. in Communications and an M.S. in Journalism. Legg has continued his journalism career, and is a copy editor with The New York Times News Service.

Since his first two books, Legg has, under his own name, entertained the Western audience with many more tales of man's fight for independence on the Western frontier. In addition, he has had published several histor-ical novels set in the Old West. Among those are WAR AT BENT'S FORT and BLOOD AT FORT BRIDGER.

In addition, Legg has, under pseudonyms, contributed to the RAMSEYS, a series that was published by Berkley, and was the sole author of the eight books in the SADDLE TRAMP series for HarperPaperbacks. He also was the sole author of WILDGUN, an eight-book adult Western series from Berkley/Jove. He also has published numerous articles and a nonfiction book —

SHININ' TRAILS: A POSSIBLES BAG OF FUR TRADE HISTORY — on the subject,

He is a member of Western Fictioneers.

In addition, he operates JL TextWorks, an editing/critiquing service.